IN THE DARK

CHELSEA CURTO

For the Halloween lovers.

AUTHOR'S NOTE

Three years ago, someone in the Universal Orlando pass holder Facebook page wrote a post thanking a specific Michael Myers for guiding them back to the line in a haunted house at Halloween Horror Nights. As someone who has been going to HHN for years, my first thought was: what an incredible meet cute?!

The idea for a romance book featuring a haunted house meet cute never left my mind, so here we are: with an unhinged, absolutely wild, low-plot, high-fun story that's so far out of my usual genre, I giggled and blushed while writing it.

If you're new here, I usually write sports romances. A dark(ish) romance is very different for me, but at its core, In The Dark is reminiscent of all my other books. There's a man who is obsessed with his woman. There's a strong, fiery female main character. There is banter. Spice and lots of laughs.

That being said, I know this book won't be for every reader who has picked up one of my stories before, and that's okay. As an author, I want to write books that excite me. I want to push myself, to not confine myself to a single box in the literary world, and this definitely pushed me.

It's silly and funny and far from the next great American novel, but *I* love it, and that's what is most important.

Please read the content warnings with care. This book contains very graphic content, and I want to make sure you're protecting yourself before you dive into Max and Hunter's world. My DMs on Instagram are always open if you want to chat more, and I hope you enjoy!

Xoxo,
Chels

CONTENT WARNINGS

In The Dark is a romance that features a happily ever after, but it's important to me to share a few content warnings readers might want to be aware of.

-explicit language
-explicit sexual content (including a scene when the FMC is consensually shared by two men)
-mention of murder
-on page murder
-on page torture (not to either of the MCs, but performed by the MMC)
-stalking
-voyeurism
-on page roofie scene
-on page attempted sexual assault (not done by the MMC)
-mention of a parent's death
-mention of rape (not detailed, no descriptions)
-CNC
-blood
-knife play

-obsession by the MMC

As always, take care of yourselves and protect your heart. If you have any questions about any of the things listed above, please know my DMs are always open (@authorchelseacurto on IG).

ONE

MAX

"I CAN'T BELIEVE I agreed to be dragged through a haunted house." I groan and pull my blonde hair into a high ponytail. "I hate being scared. I hate being in confined spaces. I hate the dark. This is a thing of nightmares. How did agreeing to watch your show turn into sacrificing myself to men in masks? That wasn't part of the plan."

"Plans change, and men in masks are fun." Skyler looks at me in the bathroom mirror, her mascara brush poised halfway to her eye. "I saw you watching those videos the other night."

"Internet thirst traps are not the same as people purposely trying to scare the shit out of you. Did you *have* to work at the scary event? You could've picked the holiday show and been a festive little candy cane," I say, bringing up Fright Nights, the two-month long Halloween event at Orlando's premiere theme park, Adventure Oasis.

The whole place transforms from late August until the end of October, the family-friendly roller coasters and character meet and greets you'd find during the day turning into ten haunted houses and scare zones full of horror movie characters brought to life as soon as nighttime creeps around.

Fright Nights has won international awards for its scare value and entertainment production. People flock from all over the world to experience the jaw-dropping fear the event boasts about, and come October, every night is sold out. Wait times for haunted houses can be as long as three hours, and I don't understand the appeal. It has a cult following with merchandise, message boards where speculation starts in late March about what the haunted houses might be, and souvenir cups people pay twenty dollars for.

I've lived in Florida my entire life and have successfully avoided ever going, but with my best friend performing in the event's stunt show with acrobatics, aerialists, and enough pyrotechnics to burn down a city, I can't evade it much longer.

"I'm not one to pull the guilty conscience card, but I do remember going to your first grader's holiday concert last December. My ears almost bled from their lovely rendition of *Jingle Bells* performed on recorders. A haunted house can't be much worse." Skyler caps her tube of makeup and faces me. "It'll be easy. Four minutes of being scared, then you'll be in the VIP section for my show. There won't be any surprises. I'll point out every actor so you know what's coming. That's all they are, you know. Performers just like me."

"Except the knife they're holding looks real and they're yelling in your ear."

"Children go. There was a literal ten-year-old sitting in the front row at the show last night. He had the biggest grin on his face."

"Probably because your costume is gorgeous lingerie that shows off your hot body. I bet he was in heaven. Oh my god." I cover my mouth. "Do you think any of my students will be there? Forget the haunted house. Running into one of my kids outside of school is my biggest fear."

"Chances one of your first grade students are out past ten on a school night?" She laughs. "Pretty slim."

"What about their parents? I've had conferences with those people where I talk about academic performance and social behavior. They think I'm a professional who has my shit together. Would they judge me if they saw me double fisting alcoholic beverages so I can make it through the park without crying?"

"If they did, they suck. Teachers are humans too, Max, and you're allowed to do adult human things."

I sigh. There's no way I'm going to win this argument, and a promise is a promise. With twenty-two years of friendship between us, she's stood by my side more times than I can count. Through breakups, hard days of teaching when I wanted to quit, and the general exhaustion required to simply fucking *exist* these days, Skyler has been there. It might take some liquid courage to get through the night, but I know I can be there for her too.

"The holiday concert was terrible, wasn't it?" I grin. "One house, one show, then I'm leaving."

She squeals. "This is going to be so much fun. The show is *so* good this year, Max. I twirl around on silks hanging in the air!"

"My little daredevil." I pinch her cheeks and head for my closet. "What should I wear? Jeans? A skirt?"

"Definitely not jeans given it's still a thousand degrees outside, and there are tens of thousands of people walking around. Goddamn Florida and it's no fall weather. Oh! What about your black leather skirt and the orange crop top that makes your boobs look good? Very on brand with the Halloween vibes and super cute."

"Am I looking for a boyfriend in a haunted house?" I laugh and find the outfit she suggested. "Speaking of, which house are we going to do? I'm vetoing anything with clowns. I *hate* clowns."

"The holiday house has an eight-foot clown that pops out at the exit when you think you're in the clear. That would probably traumatize you for life."

"I can barely watch the previews for a scary movie and you want me to walk by a murderous clown? Absolutely not."

"Okay, so not that one." Skyler taps her cheek. "What about a house dedicated to the monsters from classic horror films? Vampires are hot."

"That sounds like there are going to be werewolves running around." I switch my T-shirt out with the crop top and pull it over my head. "What other houses are there?"

"The Halloween one is popular."

"Haven't they made eighteen versions of that movie? Are there any original stories left?"

"There have only been thirteen and a half remakes. What do you think about this color?" Skyler puckers her lips, showing off the fire engine red painted on her mouth. "Too much?"

"It's never too much." I smile her way. "You look so hot, Sky. How do you not sweat all your makeup off?"

"There is *a lot* of sweat." She checks her teeth in the mirror, happy with her reflection. "We have thirty minutes between shows to put on fresh deodorant, fix our hair, and get back out there. It's hectic and busy and so physically draining, but I love it so much, Max. You know how happy dancing makes me."

"I'm so proud of you, Sky. And I'm so sorry I haven't been to any of your shows this Halloween season." Guilt presses heavy on my chest, and I sigh again. "If I can handle tonight, I'll come back for round two."

"Really?" She wraps me in a tight hug. Some of the glitter she's wearing gets on my arm, but I don't mind. "You're the best friend ever."

"Don't get ahead of yourself. I might break your hand when we walk through the house. The second someone pops out from behind a wall, I'm going to lose my mind. Will I get arrested if I punch them in the face?"

"And banned from the park."

"So, I'd be escorted out? That might be worth it. I could handle a night in jail if it means not having to deal with mummies and zombies."

"Come on." She drags me out of my room and toward the kitchen. "Let's take a shot. That will help you relax."

"Like I'm going to turn that down." I lean my elbows on the counter and blush. "I might've browsed some Fright Nights pictures so I could know what I'm working with, and it got me wondering."

"Oh? About what?"

"You have to tell me the truth. What do the guys in masks look like underneath their costumes? Do you see them backstage?"

"A lot of them are pretty cute." Skyler grins and pulls a handle of vodka down from our liquor cabinet, pouring us two shots. We knock the glasses together, throw them back, and I grimace at the burn. "Wait. Is that what you're into?"

"I guess? Maybe? But it's not only scary masks. It's motorcycle helmets. Goalie masks. Bandanas pulled up over someone's mouth. I think it's the unknown that I like. It's a mystery who you're talking to, and there's something so hot about that."

"That whole 'if I find you, I get to have you' game with someone you don't know would be so fun."

"Yeah. It would be." My cheeks heat. I grab the vodka and pour myself another drink, grateful I'm not driving tonight. "Confession time: I've always wanted to try something like that, but I've never asked for it. I've never known *how* to ask for it. Brian was so boring in bed. I faked almost all of my orgasms with him."

"Of course he was boring. His name is *Brian*," Skyler says, mentioning the ex I broke up with two months ago after he cheated on me. We dissolve into a fit of giggles. "He probably liked to leave the lights on when you had sex, didn't he?"

"I plead the fifth." I smile and toss back the second drink. It goes down smoother this time, and I dab the corner of my mouth with a paper towel. "Since we broke up, I've been reading a ton of romance books. I'm exploring things I might like in the bedroom so I can share those desires with the next guy that comes along, and I'm learning a lot about myself. Like, there's something so sexy about surrendering your power to a partner you trust. They'd be rough with you and play out your fantasies, but after, they'd take care of you. A devil and an angel, you know?"

"Oh my *god*. My little Max isn't so innocent, is she?"

"Hush." I swat at her arm, smiling again. "I have no clue how I'd meet someone like that. Is there an app?"

"What about after a PTA meeting at school?"

"Please. I doubt Tommy Dallworth's dad would be interested in something other than the stock market. When is the right time to tell someone your bedroom preferences? After the third date? The fifth? A year down the road when you say, 'hey, honey? Could you tie me up and gag me while you fuck me? And after, could you chase me? Don't forget to start the dishwasher.' Is that something I should put in my Tinder bio? *Learning my kinks. I'm also attracted to men who don't show their face?*"

"You're not going anywhere near Tinder. Those finance bros talk a big talk, but none of them deliver. It's like they read the books that are popular right now so they can pretend to know what they're doing. They don't. Trust me." Skyler huffs, a frustrating story behind the exhale. "They say they'll give you what you want, but when you ask them to smack your ass, suddenly they don't want to do it anymore."

"Weren't you seeing some guy pretty regularly?" I pour another round of shots for us and slide the glass her way. "It was a friends with benefits arrangement, right?"

"He went and got a girlfriend."

"Damn him for being someone who likes commitment. Monogamy is making you sexually frustrated, isn't it?"

"You have no idea." She downs the drink and fans her face. "No more. I need to have a clear head for the show. I'm working with that asshole, Dominic, tonight. With our history, he'll trip me and make it look like an accident."

"Sounds like a love story waiting to happen."

"More like a homicide. If I can get through the next month leading up to Halloween without murdering him, I'll be proud of myself."

"Let's try to keep the violence to a minimum." I put the cap on the handle of vodka and take a deep breath. "I'm ready. Take me to hell, Skyler Buchanan."

TWO
HUNTER

"I'M GETTING TOO old for this shit." I look down at the navy-blue jumpsuit in my hands. My knees already hurt, and the night hasn't started yet. "I can't hear out of my left ear."

"Definitely can't be all the motorcycle riding you do without hearing protection." Leo Reynolds, my roommate and best friend of over twenty years, tosses a grin my way. "I can't believe this is your last year putting on a costume and scaring the piss out of drunk idiots."

"I can. My entire body aches. Retiring from entertainment sounds like a dream."

"Come on, man. Admit it. You're going to miss being the signature face of Fright Nights, aren't you? The guy everyone tries to find while they're in the house and the one in all the promo commercials. My little celebrity."

"Stop kissing my ass, Leo." I laugh. "I still don't understand how people can tell it's me. A dozen of us dress the same way. The lighting is shitty. You can't even see my face."

"The tattoos are pretty obvious, dude. You have a fucking *dragon* on your hand."

"Might need to start covering it up." I step into the jumpsuit and pull it over my undershirt. "If I hear one more high-pitched scream, I'm going to lose it."

"Wow. You're a grouchy fuck tonight. That's unusual."

"Sorry. I'm exhausted."

"You need to get laid."

"I'm not sure how I'm supposed to do that."

"Don't tell me you need a lesson on the birds and the bees." Leo clears his throat. "Hunter Wilder. When a man loves a woman—"

"Shut up." I throw a pair of socks at him. "I know how biology works, and I've never had any complaints in the past about my knowledge of female anatomy."

"Now you're just showing off."

"What I meant was I work until three in the morning. I sleep until two in the afternoon. My nights are spent sweating my ass off in ninety-degree weather with one hundred percent humidity. Doesn't leave a lot of free time for fucking."

"In a few weeks, you can fuck whoever you want, whenever you want," he says. "And who knows? Maybe tonight will be the best night of your life. You'll meet someone, bring them home, and live happily ever after."

"You're not allowed to watch any more rom-coms. I'm banning Hallmark from our television." I sort through the prop box against the wall, finding my mask and favorite fake knife. I spin the rubber weapon in my hand and tuck it in my pocket. "This isn't nearly as good as the real thing."

"Pretty sure giving us actual weapons is a lawsuit waiting to happen." Leo levels me with a look. "You haven't hacked up anyone in a while, have you? Do you miss the rush of death?"

"It's only been a few months since I've engaged in my extracurricular hobbies, but I have a job scheduled in two weeks." I roll my shoulders and stretch my neck. Popping a Tylenol before my shift tonight was a necessity, and I'm wishing I brought the bottle. I should start doing something atrocious like Pilates to make myself more limber. "And don't say *hacked up*. That makes it sound like I run around chopping off heads for fun. It's more sophisticated than that. I get rid of people who have no place in society. People who hurt others and take advantage of those weaker than them. There's a difference."

"Right." Leo nods like he understands, and maybe he does. He's seen all the messy shit I've been involved in and hasn't said a word about any of it. He's never judged me either, which makes him a goddamn saint. "You *do* have fun when you do it, don't you?"

"Yeah." I smirk. "Best adrenaline rush in the world."

"Guess Elle Woods was wrong about happy people killing other people."

"She wasn't wrong about the endorphins, though."

"Fuck. I'm a sucker for a smart woman. And all that pink? Sign me up." Leo pulls on his own jumpsuit and fixes the sleeves. "What position do you want to start with in the house tonight?"

"I'll take the third room. You got the back?"

"Yup. Switch after the third break?"

"Sounds good to me."

He bumps my fist with his and waves. "See you out there, cutie pie."

I file out of the air-conditioned breakroom trailer and step into the sticky early evening air. I make my way over to the house supervisor on duty, laughing when I see another friend waiting for me.

"Janey. Is it too late to call in sick?" I ask.

"Not a chance. We're already short-staffed for a Thursday. I'm not letting you out of my sight until you're in position," she says. "Even then I might attach you to the wall so you don't go anywhere."

"Kinky. I didn't think I was your type."

"You wish you were my type."

"I wish for a lot of things, J." I toss her a lopsided grin and slide my mask in place. "But, fine. I'll stay put only because I love you and you knew me back when I had a terrible haircut. I can't have you showing evidence of my early twenties to anyone."

"Seems like yesterday we were working in attractions and getting paid minimum wage. Look at us now: scare actor of the year for the last three years and me, the lucky asshole who gets to deal with you five nights a week." She pinches my cheek and we walk toward the soundstage where the haunted house is set up. "It's going to be mayhem tonight. The event is sold out."

"Doesn't surprise me. First day of October. The fall girlies are drinking their pumpkin spice lattes. Halloween is creeping up. Are you and Mila taking Bailey trick-or-treating?"

"We are." Janey smiles at the mention of her wife and daughter. "I won't be here that night, so you better be on your best behavior. No fighting allowed."

"Hey. That douchebag swung at me first," I say, bringing up the guest who decided to deck me in the face last week.

I did my job, popping out from behind a corner like I'm paid to do, and he threw a punch at me. My retaliation was self-defense.

I also really fucking hated his polo and khakis, so it might've been a *little* personal.

"I know he did, and so do the police. He's banned from the park for life."

My heart warms in my chest. Janey always takes care of me, and she has for years; escorting away a group of girls who started to grope me when I tried to exit the haunted house for a break. Keeping idiots out of the line so they don't try to fight the actors. Feeding me after my mom died so I didn't wither away.

Intervening when my nose gushed blood last week was one of her finer moments. I wouldn't still be working here if it wasn't for her.

"I'll be good when you're gone, and I'm glad you get the night off. You don't want to miss out on those memories with Bailey," I say.

"I can't believe she's seven. It makes me feel ancient."

"Because we are ancient." I smile as she holds the door to the soundstage open for me. The people waiting in line erupt in cheers when they spot me, and I give them all a wave. "My knees cracked when I got out of bed this morning, and I had to stretch for twenty minutes before I ate lunch."

"You're taking care of yourself, right?"

"C'mon, J. What's the phrase? God gives his toughest battles to his strongest soldiers? I'm fucking Hercules."

"And I'm suffering from religious trauma." She clasps my shoulder. "Time to get in there. They're all here for you, Hunt."

"No pressure or anything." I take off the robe wrapped around my body to hide my costume and hand it her way. "See you on break."

"Be good," Janey warns.

"Where's the fun in that?"

"DUDE. THAT FIRST SHIFT WAS WILD." Leo yanks off his mask, throwing it on the couch in the breakroom. He downs half a bottle of water and wipes his mouth. "Enthusiastic guests make this job so fun."

"It's a good crowd tonight." I run my hand through my dark hair, dragging my fingers across my scalp. The strands are wet with sweat, and I wipe my palm on my jumpsuit. "Seems like we have a lot of first timers."

"I love the virgins."

"I've lived with you for years, Leo. I unfortunately know everything you like."

"Because you're a lucky bastard." He pops a chip in his mouth, taking full advantage of our forty-five minutes away from the crowd. I'm wondering if I can sneak a quick nap in. "Life is good, isn't it? The weather is cooler than it was back in August. It gets darker earlier. It *feels* scary, you know?"

"I'm only mildly uncomfortable in my costume, not bordering on a heat stroke." I yawn and take a seat on one of the long couches, stretching out my legs with a groan. At six four, I barely fit, but it's better than standing. "Want to switch positions after our next break? I'm bored."

"*Please*. The cops at the exit won't shut the fuck up. They're obnoxious as shit, so good luck. They told me I got too close to someone but didn't do anything when the dude in the ugly ass boat shoes kicked me in the shins."

"Fuckers," I grumble, knowing it's a battle every year with the security team they put outside the house. They like to ignore us when an actor is being harassed but have no problem calling our supervisors when they think we're the ones being unruly. "I'll have some fun with them later. I love pissing dickbags off."

"This is why we work so well together." He throws a bottle of water my way. I catch it against my chest and yawn again. "Some of the guys are going out after we finish for the night. Want to join?"

"At three in the morning? Fuck, no. It's a struggle to keep my eyes open right now. I'm also thirty-five and well aware nothing good happens after two a.m."

"Plenty of good things happen after two a.m. I'll prove it to you. I bet I'll come home with an excellent story, or I'll do the dishes for a month."

"That sounds like a bargain I can't pass up." I chug half the water and drop my head back. "Don't expect me to bail your ass out of jail."

"I'm a law-abiding citizen unlike other people in this room." Leo ducks when I lob the water back his way, letting out a wail when it nicks his cheek. "Don't mark up my pretty face."

"Humble as always, Reynolds," I say, closing my eyes and putting a pillow over my face. It smells like Doritos, and I try not to gag. "Leave me alone. I need my beauty sleep."

"I'll wake you up in a few, old man. Dream of me," he says, and I hold up a middle finger to flip him off.

THREE

MAX

"ARE YOU READY?" Skyler scans her employee ID at the Adventure Oasis turnstiles, getting us into Fright Nights for free. She reaches for my hand and pulls me close. "You made it out of the car. That's step one."

"Of course I'm not ready." I let her lead me down the main stretch of sidewalk that brings us deeper into the theme park while I try to squash down my panic. "Nightmares, remember?"

I used to come to the park as a kid, but I've never seen it like this: decked out in Halloween decorations with unsettling fog that billows in the wind. An ominous sign welcoming you to the event that's covered in spiderwebs. Coffins lining the street, shrieks of fear piercing the night air.

The sound of a chainsaw roaring to life adds to the ambience, and my body buzzes with anticipation and dread. Groups of friends huddle together as they run past us. A pair of girls scream and jump out of the way from a zombie that appears out of nowhere.

We're barely in the park, and my palms are already

sweating. I'm twitching, trying to take a deep breath but failing miserably, and I know I'm so fucking screwed.

"The house we're doing is near the back. We have one scare zone to get through, then we'll be there. I'm pretty sure a guy I slept with last year is one of the managers tonight, so he might let us skip the line." Skyler keeps our fingers intertwined, guiding me past a makeshift graveyard filled with tombstones and skeletons. "Do you want a pro tip from someone who's done every house every year since Fright Nights started?"

"I can't believe you do this *willingly*."

"The actors are more likely to go after you if they see that you're terrified. It's like a game for them."

"Lovely." I move around a fake spider that's four feet wide. It looks so realistic, I swear it moves in my direction. "They're going to have a field day with me."

Skyler laughs and turns us down a path to the right. "I've started to find the places where I think the actors will be hiding in the house: behind corners. Behind a mirror. Definitely behind anything that looks like a curtain. When you learn where they are, there's less of a surprise."

"What if I keep my eyes closed?"

"Then you won't know they're right next to you until they whisper in your ear."

"*Fuck*. I'm going to have to sleep with the lights on for days. And I'm probably going to buy an ax to keep next to my bed." The shots we took before we left the house are working their way into my bloodstream. I'm warm. Teetering toward tipsy, and I hope the alcohol offers me bravery I doubt I'll find anywhere else. "Okay. I'm not saying I'm enjoying myself, but this place looks so different with all the decorations up. I can't believe how much detail there is."

"They spend months getting everything ready. If you

go backstage in May and June, you'll see props and designs being put into place."

"That early?"

"Oh, yeah. Every single inch of the haunted house has a purpose. Some of them have secret buttons you can hit that trigger special effects. The production teams think of everything."

We reach a haunted house. The words *TERROR BROUGHT TO LIFE* are written on a metal sign with a hundred different warnings listed under it. Sensitivity to fog, to loud noises. Fear of enclosed spaces and the dark. Intense special effects and sudden movements.

For someone who hates all of the things mentioned, I'm sure I'm going to have a *wonderful* time.

A crowd congregates around the entrance, and Skyler waves to a guy talking into a walkie-talkie.

"Who's that?" I ask. "He's cute."

"Dustin." She smiles and tugs me in his direction, keeping our palms pressed together. "Hi," she exclaims when we get close, finally pulling away from me so she can give him a hug.

"Skyler." He grins and embraces her. His hands linger on her waist for a second too long, and when he pulls away, his cheeks are pink. "What are you doing here? I thought you were in the show."

"We don't start until nine," she says. "I'm here early so I could bring my best friend to her first Fright Nights before I go on."

"First-timer?" Dustin looks over at me. "What do you think so far?"

"I mean." I wave my hand in the direction of the wait time boasting a ninety-minute queue. "Clearly people love it. I'm glad they're having fun, but I'm not one of them."

Dustin laughs and glances back at Skyler. "Janey, my

co-manager, is dealing with a fight that broke out toward the exit. Normally I'd offer to walk you through the house, but I need to make sure we don't have any more issues before she gets back. The night is young, and drunk idiots always bring the mood down."

"So, I shouldn't punch the person who lunges at me?" I ask, and he shakes his head.

"Please don't. I hate paperwork. Head up the VIP line to the soundstage and tell them I sent you. They'll slip you in so you don't have to wait."

"You're the best." Skyler hugs him again then gives his chest a gentle shove. "Text me sometime. I don't want Fright Nights to be the only time I know you're alive."

"I'll see what you're up to this weekend." He hooks his thumb over his shoulder. "Entrance is that way. Have fun."

"No paperwork," I repeat, giving him a salute as we head up the line. "What the hell, Sky? He's so nice."

"He is, isn't he?" Skyler links our arms together and practically skips toward the large white building ahead of us. I don't know the last time I saw her smile this much. "He's not the type of guy I typically go for, but he's *great* in bed."

"Really?" I glance behind us, laughing when I spot Dustin watching us walk away. "I'm surprised."

"So was I when he tied my hands to the headboard and ate me out until I came three times," she says, not fazed when the attendant in front of us overhears her declaration. "Hi! Dustin sent us this way."

"Perfect." The attendant stops the flow of the regular line, ignoring the eye roll and protest from a guy holding two beer cans, and gestures us forward. "Y'all can go on in. They just did a shift change, so the actors are ready to go. You'll be the first ones with the new crew."

"Great," I mumble, almost refusing to move when Skyler tugs me behind her. "Are we really doing this?"

"Yeah, babe. We're really doing this. Hold onto me, okay? I promise we'll be out of here in no time."

I step close to her, hooking a finger in the belt loop of her jean shorts so we don't get separated. It's so dark, it's almost impossible to see where we're going, but I can make out a house at the end of a long hallway. There's a porch with a rocking chair on it. A mailbox and fake grass. Old-time music plays, giving me a false sense of security. I don't let myself relax, following Skyler as we make our way inside.

I'm squeezing her hand so tight, I'm afraid I'm going to break her fingers. I keep my eyes downcast, studying the floor instead of what's ahead of us. Out of my peripheral vision, a figure pops up behind a window, and I don't let myself look at it straight on.

Out of sight, out of mind, and I'm not going to let these fuckers get the best of me.

I heave a sigh of relief when Skyler maneuvers us down the first straightaway.

"Okay," I breathe out. "This is easy. A stroll through the park."

"I told you—" She yelps and laughs, pulling away from me slightly at the flash of a light. There's a scream and the loud clatter of something falling to the ground up ahead. "Damn. That one was good. I didn't even see him."

"I see nothing, and it's better this way."

"We're just walking through a house. Pretend it's *our* house, and we're going from the kitchen to the living room for movie night."

"It's a house full of deranged people holding knives." I step over a puddle that looks like it could be blood and grimace. "Normal behavior."

"Fake knives," she corrects. "They—"

A loud sound makes my ears ring. A figure with a mask and a weapon raised above his head appears inches away from me, and I lose it.

Fuck this.

I scream, hurtling toward what looks like a path leading to the exit. I make a left and then a sharp right, not letting myself stop moving until I'm someplace quieter. *Brighter*, and out of the way of danger. Putting a hand on the wall, I look for Skyler, and that's when I realize none of my surroundings are familiar.

A water bottle leans against a door marked *EMER-GENCY EXIT ONLY.* A flashlight and neatly folded robe sit on a small table, and it's very obvious I'm nowhere close to where I should be.

I've somehow stumbled into a back of house area, completely lost and totally alone.

"Fuck," I whisper. I whirl around, trying to figure out which way I should go, but I'm disoriented. I'm clueless about where I am in proximity to where I was before, and I wring my hands together. "*Fuck.*"

"What the hell are you doing back here?" a deep voice asks from behind me, and I freeze.

Everything moves in slow motion as I turn, staring right into the eyes of a man wearing a mask that covers most of his face. He's tall, easily over six feet and towering above me, with broad shoulders that tell me he works out. There's a tattoo of a dragon on the back of his hand. Dark hair sneaks out from behind the mask, and when he turns his head to the side, I notice a smaller tattoo on his neck, right near his collar.

I swallow, throat dry and voice gone. I shuffle back, moving until my shoulders collide with a wall behind me. I tilt my chin to look up at him, and when I do, I notice his long fingers curled around a knife.

Fake knife, I try to tell myself.

None of this is real.

He's just a man. Someone you'd see at the grocery store.

"This area is off-limits to park guests," he continues, his tone like gravel as he steps toward me.

"I'm lost." I try to control my racing heart. My eyes shift to the knife he's holding. The twist of a warm, unexplained sensation settles in my stomach when he tosses the prop in the air and catches it with ease. He tucks it in his pocket, and I squeeze my thighs together. "I've never been here and—"

"Are you okay?"

"Do I *look* okay?"

"Silly question." His laugh is soft, humored. His voice shifts to sweet and steady. Something I can trust. "I'll get you back to where you need to be."

I don't have the chance to argue with him about being a proud independent woman who doesn't need help because he's lifting his mask, revealing an alarmingly gorgeous man with brown eyes and a thin gold necklace resting against his throat. His gaze meets mine and I almost whimper, attraction pulsing through me when he tosses me the hint of a smirk.

"Turn around," he says, and I move without thinking. My body doesn't belong to me anymore. I pivot in place while he stands behind me. He rests a hand on my hip, his palm heavy and warm on the sliver of exposed skin sneaking out from under my shirt, and I stop breathing altogether. "Why are you so jumpy?"

"Because this is my idea of hell, and I'm being manhandled by a person I don't know who has a knife in his pocket."

"There's probably a joke in there about being happy to see you." My elbow inadvertently—or maybe purposely—lands in his stomach, and he laughs again, the exhale warm on my neck. "Not in a joking mood. Got it. Serious business only. The knife isn't real, which means it's not nearly as fun." His voice turns to velvety smooth and rich, and it takes everything in me to not squirm in his hold. "You've never done Fright Nights?"

"No." I turn my chin to look up at him, caught off guard when I find him looking down at me. Full attention, flecks of green around his pupils. Devastatingly beautiful in such a mysterious way. He blinks, and I want to know his name. I want to know what other tattoos he has, and if he'd let me touch them. "I've lived in Florida my whole life, and I've successfully avoided this hellhole. I won't be back."

"That's a shame." A new smile pulls at his mouth, and his thumb drags along the waistband of my skirt. My nipples get hard, and I wonder if he can tell I'm blushing. "I was hoping I'd see you again."

"Sorry to burst your bubble, Michael, but I'm a one and done girl." As fearful as I am, intuition tells me this man is safe, so I lean back half an inch. My back connects with his chest—taut, hard muscles are hiding under his navy-blue jumpsuit. He lets out a low hum, and it's embarrassing how easily the sound turns me on. "This is where our story ends."

"Too bad. We would've had something fun to tell the kids." Fingers brush against my bare skin again, and another shiver racks my body. I've never been drawn to someone like I'm drawn to him, and I'm dizzy. Faint from the heat and the alcohol. "My name is Hunter, by the way. And you are?"

"Maxine, but everyone calls me Max."

"It's been a pleasure, Maxine. If you ever feel like getting lost in my line again, you know where I am."

"Thanks, but—" I lick my lips. His eyes bounce to my mouth and hold there. "The exit would be great."

"With pleasure," he muses, and it's obvious this man gets whatever and whoever he wants. He breathes, and women throw themselves at him. Someone so far out of my league, I'm surprised he hasn't left me to fend for myself. "I'll miss you greatly. This has been the highlight of my night."

"It's been the worst part of mine," I say, and his laugh is a caress. Liquid heat I want to feel everywhere on my body.

"Really?" Hunter leads me to a place that looks vaguely familiar. The screams are getting louder and the lighting is turning dark again. "I'm flattered."

"How do I get out of here?"

"Straight ahead. There's an attendant who will show you an emergency exit that will lead you where you need to go."

"Great. Thanks." I spin in his hold, stepping back to put distance between us. Looking at him again was a mistake. "Hope you don't have to rescue anyone else tonight."

"Happy to help." He reaches out, tucking a small piece of hair behind my ear. His thumb grazes down the line of my cheek, and my eyes flutter closed for the heartbeat of a second. "Good luck out there. If you get bored, I'm here the rest of the night."

With a gentle push, Hunter moves me away from the back of house area. I ignore the excitement that rushes through me when he slides his mask back over his face and offers me a wink, and I rejoin the line of haunted house goers. I spot the attendant he mentioned, hustling her way and asking to be guided to the exit.

The fresh air is cool on my sweaty skin the second I step outside. I take a deep breath, the last ten minutes racing through my head and feeling like a story I've made up.

"Max!" Skyler runs up to me, wrapping me in a tight hug. "What happened? One second, you were behind me. Next, I couldn't see you!"

"I made a wrong turn." I hug her and sigh. "It took me a minute to find the right path."

"You were probably terrified. I'm so sorry we got separated. That's totally my fault." She pulls away and runs her hands up and down my arms. "Are you okay?"

"Yeah." I blink and check over my shoulder, finding nothing but security guards and park guests leaving the house in fits of enthusiasm and high fives. I smile, a blush creeping up my neck. *The knife. His mask. His big, strong hands.* "I conquered my fears. It wasn't bad at all."

FOUR

HUNTER

MAXINE, *Maxine, Maxine.*

I haven't stopped thinking about the blonde all night. I blink and she's there with her leather skirt and tight orange shirt. It pushed her tits together and made her skin look soft and tan, and I swear I can smell her perfume on my jumpsuit.

I might never wash this thing again.

"Dude." Leo snaps in my face and I turn my chin, forgetting where I was for a minute. "What the hell? I've been talking to you, but you're staring off into space. I'm too sensitive to be ignored."

"Sorry." I give him a grin and scrub a hand over my jaw. "Distracted."

I don't know the last time a woman had such a hold on me like this. One interaction, and I'm wanting to find out her last name. I'm imagining what she'd look like spread out with my head between her legs and if she sleeps with socks on.

I wonder if she made it home okay. If she's curled up in bed thinking about me the way I'm thinking about her.

What a little heartbreaker.

"Shit. Did the cops give you an attitude at the exit too? I swear to god if they try and fuck with us again, I'm going to—"

"They suck, but I can deal with them. It's something else."

Leo drops in the seat at the table across from me, worry on his face. "What's wrong?"

"I had a situation with a guest earlier."

"Another drunk frat dude? I hope you put him in his place."

"No." My grin stretches wider, trying to remember everything about her. "A woman."

"You're going to have to elaborate right fucking now, Hunter, because we only have fifteen minutes before I have to go scare the shit out of our last group of guests. If you leave me on a cliffhanger and make me wait to hear more, I'm going to strangle you."

"Sure you are." I laugh and flex my arm, my biceps nearly twice the size of his. "I'd like to see you try."

"I'm puny but mighty."

"Does that apply to your dick too?"

"Fuck you." Leo kicks me under the table. "Tell me, or we're no longer friends."

"You're not dramatic at all." I stretch out my legs, wincing at the twinge of pain in my knee. "I was in the second part of the house. The window scene, you know? I was about to pop back out on my cue, but a woman got lost. She made a wrong turn in the bedroom and—"

"I told the set guys that corner was confusing."

"Clearly, because she ended up backstage, terrified. She thought I was going to hurt her. I had to lead her back to the line, but I wish I hadn't. She was hot. Now I'm dreaming about her."

"Am I not a psychic or what? I fucking *told* you tonight would be the best night of your life. And, look! You met someone! I'm so goddamn good."

"Nothing is going to come from it. Thousands of people went through the line. I have no way—" I sit up. "Wait a minute. Do you still have that friend in park security?"

"Brennan? Yeah, we're cool. Why?"

"I wonder if he could pull the tapes from the entrance gates and parking garage. I could find her license plate and figure out where she lives. What her last name is and where she works. I could *happen* to drop by."

"Slow down there, creeper. Women don't want to be stalked. They want to be pursued. There's a difference," he says.

"Yeah? And what difference is that?"

"Hiding in the shadows seems like a big one. Showing up at their place of work unannounced is also a huge red flag."

"I'm not hiding in the shadows. I'm using my resources. Taking her on a long, romantic walk, except she doesn't know I'm there."

"That is literally stalking."

"Potato, poh-tah-toe. I'm not kidding when I say there was something special about this girl."

"Special like her tits?" he asks, and I roll my eyes.

"I mean, yeah, her chest was nice, but it was more than that. It was like I was drawn to her, man. I didn't want her to leave. I wanted to keep making conversation, and for as scared as she was…" I laugh. "I'm probably reading too much into it. It seemed like she lingered. And I liked it."

"I need specifics on the lingering. Did she ask you questions? Did she touch you? Did you touch her? You have *got* to get better at storytelling, Hunt."

"You are so nosy."

"You started it!"

"There wasn't any touching except for the arm I put around her waist. And then she like, melted into me?"

"Now we're getting somewhere." Leo rubs his hands together. "If I'm not the best man at the wedding, I will riot."

"I was thinking more like fucking her in my bed, but if you want to watch, I'll leave the door open."

"Kinky." He grins. "It's been a while since we shared someone."

"There's no sharing." My tone drops to lethal. Possessive. I'm daydreaming about her long legs and her wide, blue eyes. "She's mine."

"Easy, killer. I'm not stealing her from you. You don't even know her name."

"It's Maxine. Max for short." I groan, wishing I had been more proactive when she was around. I keep my phone on me in the house. It would've been easy to get her number to meet up when I got off work, but I was too caught up in how goddamn beautiful she was. Rendered useless by how soft her skin was and the hitch in her voice. "And I'm going to track her down."

"If anyone can, it's you." He stands and stretches. "Let me call Brennan and report back."

"If I like his answer, I will let you watch," I say, and he lights up.

"I've always been motivated by incentives." With a salute, he flings open the breakroom door and presses his phone to his ear. "Brennan? Hey, man. It's Leo over in entertainment. Listen. I need a favor."

He gives me a wink and disappears outside, continuing a conversation I can't hear. I sigh and move to the couch, staring at the fluorescent lights above me and wishing my mom was around so I could ask for her advice.

She used to talk me through all my relationship issues. She loved to tell me to get my head out of my ass and taught me how to treat a woman right.

Fuck.

She should be here.

I should've done more so she would be here.

I rub a hand over my chest then curl my fingers into a fist, anger flowing through me like it always does when I think about my past. I take a deep breath, practicing the exercises my therapist gave me to do when the grief sneaks up on me without warning. The meditation is interrupted by Leo standing over me, waving his phone in front of my face.

"Brennan said he'd get back to me, so—whoa. What's wrong?" Leo nudges my knees out of the way so he can sit down. "You look pale."

"Nothing. Just—"

"Your mom," he finishes for me. He lifts my legs and puts them in his lap. I don't bother protesting. "Coming up on ten years. I know."

"You're a good friend, Leo."

"I'm the best fucking friend." He pats my shins and leans back. "What triggered it tonight?"

"Who knows? It's always random."

"What are we going to do this year?"

"Flowers, probably. Maybe I'll make a cake. You know how much she loved to bake. I might be shit at it, but it would be a good way to honor her."

"I put on the freshman fifteen in high school because of her cupcakes and pies."

"She loved having you as a sous chef. The best cleanup crew," I say, laughing while I reminisce. "It's stupid. I wish

I could text her and tell her about this girl. I wish she would call me out and tell me how to do things correctly. *Woo her*, she would say."

"She'd also tell you to get a haircut." Leo reaches over and messes up my hair. "Way too long, Hunt."

"More for a woman to grab onto and hold."

"Doesn't fall under wooing, dude."

"You're right." I smile. "I'm okay. This time of year is always weird. Halloween used to be my favorite holiday, and now…" I trail off. "It's complicated."

"She'd be so proud of you. Getting out of your shitty situation with your dad. Putting him in his place."

"Six feet under."

"Should be more like twenty." Leo scoffs. "I'm sure your Mom is looking down on us and smiling from ear to ear."

As if on cue, the light above us flickers. The air conditioning kicks on, and I grin.

"There's Mom. She always had a flair for theatrics. You two have that in common." I pat his shoulder. "Thanks for checking in. I'm going to get a haircut in the morning and take some flowers to her grave. Want to come with me?"

"Of course I do." He wipes under his eye and flips me off. "Enough with this sad shit. Tell me more about this girl of yours."

"She's not mine. Yet," I add with a grin. "When we hear back from Brennan, we'll put the plan into motion."

"And by motion you mean—"

"Look into cameras I can install in her bedroom so I can make sure she's sleeping well? Maybe."

"Fuck." Leo sighs and shakes his head. The alarm on his phone chimes, letting us know we need to get ready to head back to the house. "I hope when they make the

Netflix show about you, they pick someone really fucking handsome to play me. I'm thinking… what's that guy from that show with the girl who likes both brothers? The older one. He's good-looking."

"You have red hair, Leo. The two of you look nothing alike."

"Where there's a will, there's a way." He eases my legs off of his lap and pops to his feet. He holds out his hand and I take it, standing too. "Ready?"

"If I have to be." I yawn, wishing I could spend the rest of the night thinking about my haunted house girl. "Let's do this."

I'm going to track you down, Maxine.

And when I do, I'm going to make you mine.

FIVE

MAX

"WHAT ARE YOU DOING TONIGHT?" Skyler puts the finishing touches on her makeup and pulls away from the living room mirror where she's been getting ready. "I'm so sorry if your shitty experience at Fright Nights on Thursday ruined the rest of your weekend. I feel so bad."

"It's not your fault I got turned around." I smile at her from the couch, cozy under two blankets despite the temperature hovering around eighty degrees outside. "And my night is going to be lovely because no haunted houses are involved. I'm keeping it low-key: a movie. Popcorn. Maybe a face mask. It's going to be lovely."

"Will you be okay here alone? I can call out. I have plenty of PTO."

"I promise I'm fine. If I get scared, I'll start throwing books at whatever creepy things are lurking in the bathroom. I'm sure the ghosts are nice."

"Since you're not totally traumatized, maybe I can convince you to come back for a second round of Fright Nights?"

"We'll talk when you get home." I bring my legs to my chest, resting my chin on my knees. I smile her way, so proud of my best friend. "You were fantastic in the show, Sky. The way you held yourself up on those silks was unreal. The arena was electric when you came on the stage."

"Thanks, babe. It's amazing how much fun you can have when you're living out your dreams. Doing events like this? Feeling the crowd's energy and their excitement? The joy I get going to work? People shit on theme park workers, but this is my calling." Skyler grabs her purse off the hook by the front door and fluffs her hair. "We're going to have to wait and talk about round two over coffee and pancakes tomorrow morning." Her face lights up with a grin. "I'm going to Dustin's tonight."

"Oh *Dustin*, huh? Behave yourself."

"I've never behaved myself before, and I'm not starting now."

She blows me a kiss and disappears out the front door. When I hear her car backing up, I dig my phone out from where I've wedged it between the couch cushions. I pull up the Adventure Oasis social media page I've been scrolling, embarrassed to admit internet sleuthing has taken over my life the last seventy-two hours. It's bordering on concerning behavior, and I can't believe I'm letting a man occupy so much of my time.

Putting on my best detective hat and doing a deep dive into figuring out who the hell the hot scare actor—Hunter—is has yielded zero results. I've searched Adventure Oasis's tagged photos, Fright Nights pictures, and the accounts they follow. I've scoured comment sections, and while there's been a mention of *the guy with a dragon tattooed on his hand*, there's nothing with a full name or social media handle attached to it.

No matter how much sleuthing I do, I doubt Hunter remembers me.

In a room of a thousand people, I blend in rather than stand out. I always have, at five eight with pale skin that burns when I'm in the sun for too long. Blonde hair that frizzes in the Florida humidity and thighs that brush against each other after years of playing high school and collegiate soccer. No special features, nothing unique, and when Brian used to call me *cute, but not hot*, I believed him.

I was hoping I'd see you again.

Hunter's voice echoes in my ears, and my body suddenly feels like it's on fire.

How many times has he used that line on a woman walking through his haunted house? Once a night? More? Is he a playboy? Someone who is secretly shy and hates the attention he gets?

I jump to my feet, desperate to know the answer. I march to my bedroom and pull a jean skirt and black halter top from my closet. The makeup I put on is enough to hide the bags under my eyes after a long week of teaching, and I grab my keys before I have time to talk myself out of my act of spontaneity.

So many of my friends have had one night stands. They've met a guy at the bar and hooked up with him in the bathroom to have a little fun, and for someone who has done nothing but dedicate her life to teaching, long-term relationships, and playing by the rules, I want to have a little fun too.

Seeing if I can track down Hunter a second time feels like a prize from a game I don't know I'm playing, but one I want win. The drive to Adventure Oasis is fifteen minutes up the road, the traffic light for a Saturday night. After a quick detour to the admissions window to buy a ticket I didn't budget for, I enter the park, my heart pounding with every step.

This is crazy.

Absolutely insane.

Did I really spend money to visit a guy who was *nice* to me?

Do I really think this man is going to *remember me*?

Or is it because last night I had a dream about the knife in his pocket, the ways he could use it if it were real, and what it would feel like pressed against my throat?

God.

I wonder if the that stems from my parent's divorce when I was ten, some deep-rooted daddy issues the reason for my fascination.

A therapist would have a field day with me.

I roll my shoulders back and keep my head lifted high through the scare zones, undeterred by the fake insects and actors walking around with machetes. I give myself a pat on the back for being a badass when I reach the house, spotting Dustin at the front of the line.

He must recognize me, because he waves, gestures me over with a wide grin, and takes out the earpiece he's wearing.

"Max, right?" he asks.

"Hi. That's me. Skyler's friend," I say.

"Is she with you?"

"No. She's getting ready for the show." I smile. "I hope you two have fun tonight."

"Thanks. She's, uh, a nice girl." Dustin blushes and rubs the back of his neck. "Do you want to go through the house again?"

"Is that okay? I'm learning to conquer my fears, and the other night wasn't totally terrible. I figured I'd give it another go."

"Use my name up at the top, and they'll get you in." He looks at me, grinning. "Conquering your fears, huh? I would've thought something inside caught your eye."

"Nope. Nothing at all." I smooth my palms over my skirt to give my hands something to do. Excitement dances up my spine. "Just embracing the Halloween season."

"I see. Make sure to say hi to Michael for me." Dustin winks and unhooks the chain that blocks the VIP line. "Word is he's been asking about the blonde girl he met the other night, but I think it's more fun to make him figure it out on his own."

My heart almost falls out of my chest.

He talked about me?

I have to stop myself from skipping on the walk up to the house, feeling like a teenage girl with a crush. Adrenaline courses through me, and I'm practically giddy when the attendant shuffles me into line behind a family of four.

Attempting the haunted house is more terrifying without Skyler to guide me, but as I step inside the dark soundstage, I try the technique she taught me the other night. I assess my surroundings, always one step ahead. I find the actors hiding behind a curtain before they can scare me, and it works like a charm. I'm having fun, and one guy even offers me a wave that makes me laugh.

I approach the corner where my misstep occurred the other night with a swarm of emotions. The group that entered the house after me is still in the previous room shrieking their heads off, and I slow down. I take my time searching for any sign of him, my masked man.

A light flashes.

A prerecorded voiceover track rolls.

What would be Hunter's cue to pop out and scare guests comes and goes, and no one in a costume appears.

I'm in here alone with a stuffed dead body and fake blood, defeated and feeling ridiculous as hell.

I start for the next room, following the path and making a point not to stray from the marked route. I turn a corner, and a hand wraps around my wrist. I gasp, surprised by the rough tug on my arm and the palm over my mouth that prevents me from screaming.

I dig my feet into the ground, trying to dodge my attacker. He's stronger, deliberate with his movements, but the softness of his touch catches me off guard. His thumb grazes over the pulse point on the inside of my wrist. A reassuring *"you're okay"* mumbled in my ear and a hand on my waist.

I don't know where we're going, but when we reach our destination, I blink. My vision adjusts to the different lighting, a man coming into focus, and I recognize the eyes staring back at me immediately.

Hunter.

"Maxine," he says, my name a rumbly exhale. He pulls his hand away from my mouth, dropping his arm to his side. "You came back for me."

"What is *wrong* with you?" I twist out of his hold and put my palms on his chest, giving him a shove. "You can't go around accosting women and touching them without permission just because you have a pretty face."

"You think I'm pretty?" He lifts the mask over his head, and… *damn him.* He's just as attractive as he was Thursday night. Sharp features, the hint of a five o'clock shadow on his jaw. A smile that's a mix between curious and cunning and a small white scar above his right eyebrow. "I knew you were a sweetheart."

"Someone's vain." I cross my arms over my chest, glaring at him. The bastard keeps grinning. "This place scares the shit out of me, and you think grabbing me without warning is going to make it more enjoyable?"

"You tell me. Are you having more fun now than you were three minutes ago?"

"Irrelevant."

"Someone's feisty. I've always liked that in a woman." Hunter leans against the wall, casual and relaxed as he watches me. "I missed you, Maxine. Did you miss me?"

I dip my chin. I'm not sure how to tell him I've looked at every social media channel available in hopes I'd see him again.

"Yes," I breathe out, admitting the truth. There's no point in playing coy. "I came here tonight looking for you."

"I'm glad you found me and not one of my coworkers."

"I think you mean you're glad you're the one who harassed me and not someone else."

"That's right." He laughs, easy and light, but he stops abruptly. "I'm sorry. Consent is important to me. I shouldn't have touched you like that."

"Oh." I shift on my feet. The seriousness in his tone is stark, and I shiver. "It's okay. I forgive you. I don't... I'm not mad."

"Why did you come back to see me, Maxine?"

"Max. You can call me Max."

"Max," Hunter repeats, stepping toward me. I walk backward until my shoulders hit a solid wall. His eyes bounce to my mouth when I let out a startled noise. "You don't know anything about me. I could be dangerous, and you look like a girl who doesn't bend the rules."

"What if I want to bend the rules?" I lift my chin, distracted by the knife he's holding. He runs his finger along the blade, down then up, and I imagine what it would feel like against my body. "What if I want to be bad?"

"That's the wrong thing to say to a guy like me." He leans forward, a hand on the wall next to my head. He's caging me in, body almost flush against mine. "I have a habit of getting attached to things. If you keep talking to me like that, I might fall in love with you."

"I don't want love. I just…" I trail off, not sure *what* I want.

To let loose for once in my life?

Sex?

Someone to help me live out the desires I've kept hidden away?

I'm a relationship woman, the person who needs an emotional connection before I can be intimate with a man.

Not with him, apparently.

He makes me want to step outside my comfort zone. To try the things I've been so afraid to admit I might enjoy, and the notion is intoxicating.

"Just?" Hunter traces the knife along the line of my throat. My breathing jolts. My brain recognizes it's still rubber, still not a threat, but the explicitness of being here, of finding him and letting him touch me like this sends a wave of pleasure through me. "Just what, Maxine?"

"Fun," I whisper, my mind making the decision for me. "I want to have fun."

"Do you want me to touch you?"

"Yes."

"Do you want me to touch you right now? Or would you rather we wait until I'm finished with my shift so I can take you to my bed?"

"I'm not sure." My pulse races, and my nipples are hard. "Could you—is it even possible to touch me here? There's only a—"

Hunter lowers his head and blows a hot puff of air against the crook of my neck. I gasp and reach out to grip his shoulder, confused when he laughs.

"You think I need a bed to make you come, Maxine?" He kisses my collarbone, one hand still planted firmly on the wall, and my eyes flutter closed. "Three fingers in your cunt and a few minutes are all it would take for you to scream my name. And since I'm a gentleman, I'd leave your underwear on. There wouldn't be a hair out of place. You'd walk out of here without anyone knowing you just had the best orgasm of your life, because you're a good girl, aren't you?" He rocks his hips forward, and I feel the brush of his hard cock against the inside of my thigh. "But maybe tonight you'd like to be my little slut."

Holy hell.

My brain is going to short circuit.

I've never had a man talk to me during sex. I'm used to silence, a quiet thrust and the occasional moan. I've been afraid to be too loud, too enthusiastic, but a soft groan slips out of me at the hot swipe of his tongue on my neck.

"Yes." My voice shakes. "I want that."

"Where do you want me to touch you? Here?"

His fingers dance along the curve of my jaw, a slow tease down to my throat. He gives it a light squeeze, the hint of pressure. It's nowhere near the point of causing pain, just enough for me to know he's there.

And *hell* do I want him there.

I nod, and Hunter smiles.

"How about—" His touch moves. He brushes his fingers over my chest, a low hum rattling out of him when he feels my hard nipples through my shirt. "I bet there too, huh?"

"Yeah," I say, managing to find my voice. My eyes open, and I catch him staring at me. "That's—I—"

"Doing okay?" he asks, twisting my nipple. A cry escapes me, and I hold his arm to keep myself from losing my balance. "Shh, baby. You can't let anyone hear you. I don't want to get in trouble. Can you be good for me?"

"I'll try. I'm sorry." I might be panting, but I can't help it. I'm worked up from the way he's cupping my breast. From the way he's lowering his neck and closing his mouth around my nipple, wetting my thin tank top until it's suctioned to my chest. "*God.*"

"You learned my favorite pet name so quickly. We're a match made in heaven." Another twist, and I have to bite my tongue to keep from moaning. "But you didn't answer my question."

"W-what question?"

"Are you doing okay?"

"Is it not obvious?"

"I need to hear it, angel. You have to tell me. Use your words."

"Okay," I almost cry out, reduced to one-word answers.

I know I've been horny lately, getting myself off to the books I'm reading while I daydream that I'm the one in a dark romance being chased, but this kind of contact shouldn't send me spiraling.

I'm close to begging Hunter to drag me somewhere else and have his way with me. To spin me around and fuck me against the wall, not caring who could see.

Who *am* I?

"We can do better than okay." In the most painstaking glide of his fingers, Hunter moves away from my chest. His touch teases down my body to my stomach, a thumb running along the waistband of my skirt. "Did you wear this on purpose, Maxine? Hoping you'd run into me?"

"No," I say, but it's a lie and he knows it. "I like it because it makes me feel good."

"Can you do a spin so I can see how sexy you look?" Hunter drops his hand and takes a step back. His eyes roam down my body, heat behind his gaze. "Please?"

I blush. The instructions are sexier than what he was doing to me a few seconds ago, a secret show only for him. I move away from the wall and stand up straight, fixing my shirt and my hair. I turn, shuffling my feet in a circle until my back is to him.

Part of me wants to be self-conscious. I wonder if I look stupid, if I'm doing this right, but I hear the hitch in his breathing. I can hear him fighting off a low groan that tells me he's enjoying this as much as I am. A jolt of electricity races through me, and I make my movements more purposeful.

My hips sway. I drop my head back, hair brushing against my shoulders. I lift my arms above me, relishing in the moment. I'm not Max Walters, first grade teacher who drinks a cup of tea before bed.

No.

Tonight, I'm Max Walters, the bad bitch who's going to have a long overdue orgasm.

"Stop right there." Hunter's voice is hoarser than before. "And put your hands on the wall."

Nothing about it is controlling. There's a choice buried in there, an out if I want it, but I don't. I want to do whatever he says, so I push my hips back.

"Like this?" I ask.

"Spread your legs."

My body moves on his command. I lean forward and step my feet apart. Bending from my waist, I prop my arms on the wall, the cool air of the house licking up the back of my thighs as my skirt rides up. The curve of my ass is showing, and I wonder how much of me he can see.

"Wow." Hunter's boots thump across the floor. He crowds my space, a hand in my hair as he wraps the strands around his wrist and gives a tug. "Such a beautiful slut for me."

I can't help the moan that escapes me. It's so filthy, and I want him in a way I've never wanted anyone else.

"What else should I do?" I ask.

"What else do you want to do?" he asks, and the consideration is not lost on me.

"You're in charge." I look at him over my shoulder, his pupils wide and jaw slightly unhinged. Restraint etched on his face. "You tell me."

"I'm not sure you want me to be in charge, angel." He positions himself until he's directly behind me, chest pressed against my back. I can smell his cologne: cedar, the hint of spice. I can see another tattoo hidden under the rolled sleeve of his jumpsuit. "When I play with things I like, I make sure to have my way with them."

"Does that mean you like me?"

"Oh, Maxine." He tucks a piece of hair behind my ear, mouth right at the pulse point on my neck. "That's one way to put it."

SIX
HUNTER

I SHOULD BUY A LOTTO TICKET.

I manifested Maxine showing up tonight, and here she is. Warm and soft against me. Legs spread and breathing hard, her skirt hitched halfway up her thighs. She came back because she wanted to see me, and *fucking hell* did I want to see her.

I fucked my fist to the thought of her last night. I imagined those big blue eyes that widened when she saw me for the first time. I remembered her tight shirt and her big tits, and I wondered what she would look like with my cum on her chest. How pretty she would be on her knees while she sucked my cock.

There's a good chance I'm obsessed with her already.

I brush her hair away from the back of her neck and press a kiss there. She melts into me, her limbs relaxing, and it's my turn to let out a staggered breath. It's been too long since I've been with a woman, and this one is having an obvious effect on me.

There have been friends with benefits over the years

and people with mutual interests who have caught my attention for a night or two, but there's something exciting about a girl who doesn't know exactly what she wants. Who's nervous and excited at the same time, and I can't wait to see how far I can push her.

"Can I touch you again?" I whisper in her ear.

A not-so-wild guess would tell me going into haunted houses and letting men have their way with her isn't something she does frequently, if at all. She's too sweet, too much of a rule follower. Someone who is running on pure adrenaline and lust, not coherent decision making, and I need to make sure she's still onboard with all of this.

My own sexual limits are practically nonexistent. I'll try anything once and enjoy unconventional things others don't. Do I like the murky waters of roleplay, discussed abduction, and a woman trying to fight me off? Fuck yeah, I do, but consent is a non-negotiable for me. If she doesn't give me explicit permission, I'm not going to put a hand on her. I'll walk away, hard dick and all, and still chalk this up as one of the best nights of my life.

There's a long pause, and I stand there patiently. I have thirty minutes before my replacement comes in and bumps me to my break, and I'll wait as long as it takes. Maxine's shoulders sag. She drops her head into the crook of my neck and lets out a stuttering sigh.

"Y-yes," she finally says.

I suppress a groan at her answer and again when she wiggles her hips, ass brushing over the outline of my throbbing cock.

"Yes, what, Maxine?" I give her hair another tug, tilting her chin back until our eyes meet. "I need to hear you say exactly what you want from me."

"I want you to touch me." It comes out as a rush of

words, and I grin. "Anywhere you want. Please. I-I… I need you, Hunter."

Fuck me.

I kiss the spot above her shoulder and run my tongue along her skin. "If I do something you don't like, you need to tell me. Can you do that?"

"I promise."

"Such a good girl." I take a step back and push the hem of her skirt all the way to her waist. A lacy black thong greets me, and I drag my hands up, looping an arm around her waist. My fingers brush against the front of her underwear, and it's impossible not to groan when I find a damp spot between her legs. *Wet.* Already so fucking wet. "All of this is for me?"

"I can't explain it." She wiggles her hips again, and I hope she can feel how hard I am. I'm close to yanking down the zipper of my jumpsuit and fucking her right here, right now. Against the wall. On the floor with my hand behind her head so she doesn't get hurt. "I've never been like this with a guy before. It takes *work*. A lot of— you… I—" She stops for a breath and gasps when I yank her underwear to the side and drag my knuckles along her soaked entrance. "You make me want things I've never wanted before, and I don't even *know* you."

"What do you want to know?" I rub a slow, teasing circle over her clit and hum when she moans. "My last name? My favorite food? My credit card number so you can buy yourself whatever you want? I can give you the world if you let me, Maxine." I push a finger inside her, finding her cunt wet and tight. She squeezes around me, and I'm going to dream about her pussy for days. "But if not, the least I'm going to give you is the best orgasm of your life."

"That sounds like a line." Her words falter when I

press her chest into the wall and yank her hips back, bending her at her waist. She rests her head on her fore-arm, long hair curtaining her face from view. "Something I've heard from men before. Guess what? It's never true."

"You mean boys." I add a second finger, curling them inside her while she bucks against me. "Men would make it happen. They'd know that you probably like it when—" I use the palm of my other hand, pressing it against her clit. Her moan is heady and low. "When I touch you right there."

"Hunter." Maxine's hand flies out, palm flat against the wall to hold herself up. She lowers onto my fingers, then brings her ass back up, fucking herself. I wish I hadn't left my phone so far away. I want to record this. I want to play it on a loop and slow it down so I can watch how she drenches my hand. I wonder if I could make her squirt. "Please."

I'm going to like it when she begs.

"Do you want to come?" I move the hand touching her clit to her stomach, pulling her flush against me. I hold her in place, a third finger sliding in her easily. "*Fuck*. It's like your cunt was made for me."

"*Yes*, I want to come. Why else would I—it's been too —" Maxine pauses for a ragged breath. "*Hunter*."

"If I had more time, I'd fuck you with the handle of this knife." I release her and bring the prop to her throat, gleeful when she tightens around me. "When you were dripping down the blade, I'd make you suck it clean. Then I'd fuck you against this wall so hard, you'd have bruises."

"I almost didn't come back to see you." She's panting. Writhing against me and making my cock so hard, it hurts. If I'm not careful, she's going to make me come in my pants, and that would be fun to explain to Leo. "I'm so glad I did."

"Needy slut who knows what she wants." I drop the knife on the ground and grip her throat. It's not as rough as I would normally be, but she still whimpers. She whispers my name, and I wonder if she's ever tried any breath play. "And what you want is me. I want you too, but what I really want is for you to come on my hand. Give me something to taste for the rest of my shift, baby."

Maxine whimpers again, and I can tell she's about to fall apart. Sweat rolls down her cheek, and she reaches behind her to hold my neck. I let her claw at my hair, hoping she's leaving little marks behind. I roll my hips, pressing into her ass, and she gasps.

"You're so big," she breathes out.

"We'd have to warm you up before you took my cock. I wouldn't want to hurt you."

"God." She laughs. "Where have men like you been all my life? Thoughtful. Hot. An expert on the female body. Are you even real?"

"I've been right here, waiting for you." I nip at her neck and suck on her skin. "What's your orgasm record in a night? Five? Six?"

"Record? It's always been one and done. Is it even possible to have multiple?"

"Well, that won't do." I guide her to the wall again, bending her over. I give her ass a slap and smile when a pretty shade of pink blooms on the curve of her cheek. "Time to remedy that. I'm going to broaden your horizons, sweetheart."

"What does that mean?" Maxine moans when I pull my fingers out. I push them back in her pussy, a methodical rhythm I pair with another touch to her clit. "*Oh.*"

"Feel good, angel?"

"Better than anything I've ever experienced. I feel it— it's everywhere and I—"

"And you're about to come while people pass us on the other side of that wall, having no idea you're being finger fucked just a few feet away. I wonder what they'd think if they saw you with your ass out for a stranger." My pace turns rougher, less gentle. My fingers are so wet, they almost slip out of her. "Not such a good girl after all."

She lurches forward. She cries out, my name a mangled exultation spilling from her mouth, then she's pulsing around me. Groaning and bucking her hips, greedily chasing the relief I bring her.

I let her ride the orgasm out, not stopping until her breathing returns to normal. When it does, I pull my fingers out of her. I grab her hips and turn her so she's facing me. Her back is against the wall. Her hair is messy, a few pieces sticking to her forehead and neck, and her skin is splotchy.

She's the most beautiful woman I've ever seen.

"That was nice." Maxine smiles, and it's dreamlike. Perfectly sated and adorable as hell. "Thank you for your service."

"I'm not finished with you. Have you ever tasted yourself?" I ask, and her eyelashes flutter closed, then open. She dips her head, and I hook my clean fingers around her chin so she has to look up at me. "Is that a yes?"

"It's embarrassing."

"I would never judge you."

"One time I used a toy to get off. After I finished, I, um, pretended it was… I gave it a blow job, and I tasted myself that way."

I groan. Imagining her in bed deep throating a sex toy is a hazard to my health, and I adjust my jumpsuit. Her eyes drop to the outline of my cock, and she reaches out to touch me. I take her wrist, stopping her, and she frowns.

"Tonight is about you," I say. "I don't need anything."

"Really?"

"Really." I bring the fingers covered in her cum to her mouth. I touch her bottom lip, and her mouth parts. I press down on her tongue, smiling when she closes her lips around me. "Clean me up. And don't leave a drop behind."

Maxine tips her head to the side, lapping at my fingers. Her tongue and teeth run over my knuckles, and watching her is mesmerizing. I see the determination in her eyes, the bob of her throat as she swallows down her arousal, and I could stare at her for hours.

She likes to be told what to do.

This could be so fun.

"That's perfect," I tell her, and her cheeks darken. She's pretty when she blushes. "How do you taste?"

"Good, I think. I don't have anything to compare it to. I've never—" She laughs, and I hiss when she bites the pad of my finger. "This is a first for me."

"My turn." I pull my hand back and get rid of the mask on top of my head. I push up my sleeves and drop to my knees, blinking up at her. I trace up her leg, stopping at the waistband of her underwear. "Can I? Please?"

"*Oh.* I'm not sure I'll be able to—it might take—"

"I won't complain. Can I eat you out, angel?"

"That would…" She laughs again. "Of course you can."

"Thank you," I murmur into her hip bone. "Can you help me out, sweetheart? Can you hold your underwear to the side with one hand? And with the other, I want you to use your thumb and finger to hold your pussy open for me."

"Like this?" Maxine does exactly what I ask, spreading her pussy lips and letting me look at her. She's pink and wet and the hottest fucking thing I've ever seen.

"Just like that." I lift her leg and put her foot on my shoulder, kissing the inside of her thigh. "You're so fucking gorgeous."

I keep my eyes on her as I lick her clit, unable to hold back my groan as I taste her for the first time.

We have a serious fucking problem.

I was already addicted to her, and this just sealed the deal.

I need to consume her. I need to have her in a million different ways. I need to make her *mine* with a ring and a house and five kids, and my cock leaks pre-cum in agreement. I've always liked being on my knees, but I just found my favorite alter. My new house of worship, and she's never going to be able to get rid of me.

"*Fuck*," she cries out. "Sorry. *Sorry*. I—"

"I don't give a shit about the consequences. Be as loud as you want, angel. I like to hear when I'm doing something right."

I have daydreams of waking her up in the middle of the night with my fingers inside her. Of falling asleep with her wrapped around me, her calf thrown over mine. She's exquisite. The best thing I've ever tasted and sweet as can be.

I lick and I suck, not bothering to come up for air.

I hope this is how I die.

"Why—how—" Max puts a hand on the back of my head, forcing me to bury my face between her legs. As if I wouldn't do it willingly. "It's never—"

"I know." I bite her thigh, kissing the small mark that blooms on her skin. "It is now."

"You might be my new favorite person." She threads her fingers through my hair, giving a tug. My cock hardens when she does it. "Two times in one night? You're going to walk around thinking you're God's gift to women with a huge ego."

"Women? Nah." I pull my mouth away from her pussy, easing two fingers back in her. She gasps and drops her head against the wall, her legs starting to quake. "Just you, baby."

"So charming." She sucks in a sharp breath when I bite her thigh again, timing it perfectly with a third finger.

"When you get home tonight, I want you to use that toy of yours," I tell her. "And when you do, I want you to pretend it's my cock when you fuck yourself. Can you do that for me?"

This moan of hers is the loudest yet, a splintered noise that practically shakes her whole body. I put my tongue against her clit and she explodes, her second orgasm hitting her stronger than the first. She squirms, alternating between whispers of *"it's too much"* and *"please don't ever stop."* I press my forearm against her stomach, not letting her pull away until I've licked up every drop she's going to give me.

"You're so beautiful when you come." I carefully pull my fingers out of her pussy and nudge her hands away when her body begins to calm down, fixing her underwear for her. I snap the waistband against her hip, wondering what her pain tolerance might be. Would she be okay with being tied up? How does she feel about nipple clamps? "It's too bad I don't have time to take care of you a third time."

"Three times might kill me," she says weakly. I shimmy her skirt down from her waist, covering her thighs, and she gives me a smile. "Thank you."

"Hopefully our time together isn't the worst part of your night like last time."

"Far from it." A piece of hair is stuck to her sweat-covered forehead, and she brushes it away. "Wow. I'm realizing I've never had a guy give me an orgasm without kissing me."

"Do you want me to kiss you?"

"That's okay. You don't seem like a man who—"

I step toward her, crowding her space. I put both hands on her cheeks, tipping her head back until my nose brushes against hers.

"You should know something about me, angel. If you want it? Ask. I'll give it to you. Do you want me to kiss you, Maxine?"

"I think I'd like that," she whispers, and I smile. "Please."

"With pleasure," I purr, crashing my mouth against hers.

Her lips are warm and full and they part, opening for me. I sneak my tongue in her mouth, brushing it against hers, and she wraps her arms around my neck. She hitches her leg up against my hip, surprising me when her teeth sink into my bottom lip. Each swipe of my tongue coaxes soft noises out of her, and I could listen to them all night.

When I break away from her, she's breathless.

So am I.

"That was…" Maxine trails off and touches her mouth. Her lips are starting to swell, and I hope I have some of her lipstick on me. A souvenir, along with her cum on my hand. What a lucky guy I am. "Wow."

Wow is fucking right.

I think my brain is fried after twenty minutes with this woman.

Heaven help me when I get a whole night with her.

"Be good, Maxine. And don't miss me too much." I kiss her forehead. "I'll find you again one of these days."

"Thank you for—well. Yeah." She clears her throat. "Goodbye, Hunter."

She slides away from the wall, slinking toward the path that will bring her back to the queue. With one more look over her shoulder, she gives me a small smile and disappears into the night.

I miss the fuck out of her already.

SEVEN

MAX

I'VE BEEN LIVING in a daze.

My feet are off the ground, and I can't stop smiling. Days have passed, but my head is still in the clouds. I've run through my encounter with Hunter so many times I have every single detail memorized. His burning gaze as he glanced up at me. Large palms, a commanding voice. My foot on his shoulder and his desire to take care of me.

Repeatedly.

This is a new side of sex I've never seen before. The confirmation I needed that I've been sleeping with the wrong people up to this point.

He set the new gold standard and didn't ask for anything in return.

So selfless, such a *man*.

I fall asleep thinking about him and wake up turned on, halfway to an orgasm and having to bury my face in my pillows so Skyler doesn't hear me moaning from down the hall.

There was something magical about the way he touched me. Possessive, but gentle. Rough, but sweet. He knew he had the power to fully control me, but he didn't. It was like he was being careful, treating me like I was important.

For as hot as the whole thing was, it was sweet, too, and butterflies flutter to life in my stomach.

I'm buzzing thinking about what other fantasies of mine he could help me live out given the chance. Wondering if he has any other masks he wears. If he's chased anyone through the woods and if he'd be willing to do it with me.

"Hey."

A knock on my classroom door pulls me from another replay of the night. I glance up and see my work best friend, Molly, leaning against the wall with a smile.

"Hi, Mols." I take a sip of water, trying to cool myself down. My body has been electrified since I left Fright Nights over the weekend, and I match her smile. Maybe orgasms are the key to world peace. The answer to making everyone happier. "What's up?"

"I'd ask if everything was okay, but it must be. You're practically glowing."

"Am I?" I touch my cheek. "Just distracted, I guess."

"I bet I know why. I saw Brian hanging out in the parking lot when I took the kids to recess. Did he bring you a surprise? Please tell me it's chocolate or flowers."

"What?" I frown and crane my neck, looking out the window behind my desk. I have a direct view of the visitor lot, but a quick scan of the spots doesn't show my ex's car anywhere. "No. Absolutely not. We broke up two months ago."

"You did?" Molly sits in the small chair across from me. "I'm so sorry, Max. I had no idea."

"It's my fault for not telling you. I was… embarrassed, I guess, of how things ended. I thought our relationship was more serious than he did. We were together for ten months, so I figured that meant we were exclusive." I snort and shake my head. "Joke is on me."

"Unless there's a conversation about a casual agreement, men should be giving you all of their attention. God. Leave it to the person with a dick to assume they can have their cake and eat it too." Molly's lips pull up into a smirk. "Okay, so it's not him who has you smiling, but it's *someone*. Judging from how hard you were blushing when I tried to call your name, I'd say it's someone bigger and better in every sense of the words."

"It's nothing serious. It's not anything at all, really. It was a two-time thing. Okay, more like a one-time thing. I don't even know who he is."

"A mysterious stranger? I love this for you. You're leaving it up to the universe to decide your fate. If you run into each other, it means you're destined to be together."

"I'm not sure about that. You're giving me a lot of credit, Mols, and making me feel more special than I actually am." I gesture up and down my paint-covered overalls and my untied shoe. "I'm a teacher who spends her afternoons doing after-school care, gets home at six, grades worksheets, barely has time to eat, then collapses in bed before getting up in the morning and doing it all again. I'm so boring."

"Knock it off with that self-deprecation. All I see is career woman who puts other people first and cares about her students. Your kindness is special, Max."

"Okay, well, now you're being too nice. Thank you, my sweet friend." I laugh and reach for her hand. My phone alarm chimes, letting me know I need to grab my kids from music class. "Come over this weekend? Skyler misses you, and I miss seeing you somewhere other than across the cafeteria."

"I would love that. Two months into the school year, and all my communication is with second graders and their parents. I need an adult conversation that doesn't revolve around unplanned absences."

"Sunday afternoon. We can watch movies on the couch after Skyler leaves for Fright Nights." I stand and grab my school ID. "We'll have fun."

"Can't wait." Molly stands too, fixing her sweater. "If I see Brian again, do you want me to let you know?"

"That would be great."

"You got it, babe. I'll text you."

Molly blows me a kiss, and I look out the window one more time, searching for Brian's blue BMW. Unease curls in my stomach when I can't find anything out of the ordinary, and the hair on the back of my neck stands up.

I don't like the feeling of being watched when I can't see who is doing the watching.

***

WEDNESDAYS ARE the only day of the week I don't have any duties after school, and I'm grateful to pull into my driveway just past four p.m. A yawn sneaks out of me when I kick off my shoes in the foyer. I walk down the hall, flipping on the lights as I go.

"Sky?" I call out. "Are you here?"

"My room," she answers, and I make my way to her bedroom. I nudge the door open and smile at her standing in front of her bathroom vanity with her makeup bag. "Hi, lovebug. How was school?"

"No vomit, no meltdowns, and we're another day closer to fall break. I'd say it was a success." I point to her bed, and she nods, stepping over to shove a duffle bag so there's room for me. I sit on her mattress and cross my feet at the ankles, happy when I grab her stuffed teddy bear and hold it close to my chest. "Something weird happened, though."

"Did you match with a parent on a dating app? Wait. Please don't tell me Tommy Dallworth's dad actually asked you out in the pickup line."

"No, and both of those things sound like a nightmare. I separate my personal and professional lives for a reason."

"You have to admit his dad is hot, though. In a nerdy, accountant kind of way."

"Because he *is* an accountant."

"Who knew khakis could be sexy?" Skyler joins me on the bed and rests her head on my shoulder. "What happened?"

"Molly came by while my kids were at music class and told me she saw Brian's car at school today."

"*Brian?* As in, your ex-boyfriend Brian?"

"That's the one." I frown. "I looked for his car in the parking lot, but I couldn't find it."

"Is she sure it was him?"

"I mean, I didn't ask for proof. She's met him and seen him drop off lunch for me in the past, so she'd know what he looks like. Knowing he was there creeps me out."

"Hm." Skyler drums her fingers on the sheets between us. "Any chance he's seeing someone else at your school?"

"Unless it's Phyllis, the librarian, chances are slim. The girl he cheated on me with is a bartender."

"Definitely weird then. Was there anything on your car when you finished for the day? A note? Something you left at his place?"

"No." My gut twists. I'm so confused, and that feeling of dread takes up residence in my stomach again. "We haven't talked in weeks. Why is he hanging around?"

"I bet he's trying to be a dick and intimidate you. Do

you want me to come volunteer tomorrow and keep an eye out for him?" she offers.

"I appreciate it, but it'll be okay. You have my location, so if things go off the rails and he kidnaps me, you'll be able to track me down."

"I would kick his *ass* if he touched you. I'd put my heel right through his chest. Maybe I'd step on his face."

"See? This is why you're my best friend. Because you're a total badass." I pat her hand. "Are you coming home tonight? Or are you meeting up with Dustin again?"

"Did he ask me to sleep over tonight? Maybe. Is it anything more than sex? Absolutely not."

"Permission to say something you might not like?" I ask. "As your best friend?"

"Granted, but only for twenty seconds," she answers, and I laugh.

"There's nothing wrong with enjoying time with some-one. If men are allowed to sleep with half the city and not be slut-shamed for it, women should be able to do the same. But you're also allowed to have feelings for a guy, Sky. It doesn't mean you're going to marry him. Just… you know. Let him cook you breakfast in the morning and hold your hand."

"I think I might be broken, Max. Dustin is a great guy. He texts me and asks how my day is going. He bought me Taco Bell on the way home from Fright Nights the last time we hung out. He even made sure there was extra hot sauce in the bag because he knows how much I like it. On paper, he's perfect. A stable job? His own home? A bed with a headboard?"

"Whoa. A whole ass headboard? Sweetie, you need to lock that down."

"He has curtains, too." Skyler giggles. "But then I think about being with the same person for the rest of my life, and I panic. We were cuddling after sex, and I felt like I needed to escape. It was… suffocating, almost. And I didn't feel like I had a way out."

"Have you talked to him about this?" I ask, and she's quick to shake her head.

"God, no. A friends with benefits agreement means no feelings and no emotions. It's *just* sex. Bringing up things like that is a surefire way for this to either tread toward *serious*, which I don't want, or *disaster*, which would mean not sleeping with him anymore. And I like sleeping with him more than I like sleeping with other people, so I keep my mouth shut."

"I'm never going to tell you how to live your life, Sky. But I *am* going to tell you that you deserve the world. Someone who treats you right, however that might look to you."

"True, but who needs a man when I have you?" Skyler leans over and kisses my cheek before hopping off the bed. "My best friend and ride or die."

I should be sitting here telling her about Hunter instead of my douchey ex, but I can't find the right way to mention I went back to the haunted house to see him. No part of her would *ever* judge me. We've seen each other through so many highs and lows throughout our lives, and we've never had any secrets.

She'd be happy for me.

Hell, she probably knows exactly who he is, but it feels like the second I admit this thing actually happened, that will be it. It'll give up the illusion I've created, and I want to keep the idea of maybe meeting him again somewhere down the road as a possibility for a little while longer.

I don't need to hear his story. I don't need to find out that he's a playboy or a womanizer who picks a new victim every night. By keeping my mouth shut, I can pretend I'm one of a kind. I can pretend he's somewhere thinking about me right now, even though I doubt he remembers my name.

"Right back at you, Sky." I toss a T-shirt her way. "How are things going with your archnemesis? I don't see you in a cast, which means he hasn't dropped you during the show yet. That's encouraging."

"He's as obnoxious as ever." She huffs and pulls on the shirt, pivoting in front of the mirror. "He walks around like he's god's gift to the earth, and I just *know* he has the world's smallest dick."

"There's an idea. Hate sex sounds like it would be a blast."

"Don't make me barf." Skyler gags. "Speaking of the show, a lot of the people in entertainment are having a bash at one of the bars outside Adventure Oasis next Tuesday. There's no Fright Nights, the drinks are free, and it's going to be really fun. Want to be my plus one?"

Entertainment.

Hunter is in entertainment.

Will he be there?

My heart races, and I do my best to keep my cheeks from turning bright red.

"I'd love that. What's the theme?" I ask. "I'll try to pull something from my closet this weekend or make a run to the thrift store."

"Sinners and devils," she says. "Very dark, very kinky, and I already have my outfit picked out. It's our last hoorah before Fright Nights gets too busy for the rest of the season. We go from five shows a night to six, and when I come home, I'm so depleted."

"Remember last year when I had to get ice for your knees at three in the morning because you were so tired? You were curled up on the sofa in so much pain."

"I refuse for that to happen again. I've been running six miles on the treadmill to build my stamina. I will not be defeated by a stunt show, even if my twenty-eight-year-old ass is starting to feel ancient."

"At least you're hot with a smoking body," I say. "And almost late. Don't you need to leave soon?"

"Shit. I should've left ten minutes ago." Skyler dumps her makeup bag in her duffle and tosses in her hairbrush and a change of clothes. "I'll see you in the morning, my sweet Max."

"Tell Dustin I say hi. And don't overthink things. You deserve it, remember?"

"I remember." She flips her hair over her shoulder and slides on her sandals. "Love you."

"Love you more," I tell her, but it doesn't get rid of the anxiousness I'm feeling.

EIGHT

HUNTER

"BEER?"

Leo holds a drink my way, and I shake my head.

"Nah. I'm good with water tonight."

"You're going soft on me, Wilder." He sits next to me on the couch and sighs. "You know I love our scare actor gig, but spending an evening with my best friend watching playoff baseball is my idea of a good time. How you convinced Janey to give us a Saturday night off, I'm not sure, but I'm not going to argue."

"Sold my soul to the devil. I consider it being a team player. There are guys who aren't getting a ton of shifts, while you and I are pushing fifty hours a week. Now we're sharing the love." I grin. "Dropping the dreaded *overtime* word helps too."

"Such a generous motherfucker compared to the multi-billion-dollar company who is terrified to overspend." He flips on the television and yawns. "They should be giving you the Nobel Peace Prize any day now."

"I deserve it for losing the hearing in my right ear over the years. And putting up with your ass."

"Easy, Hunt. If you want me to tell you about your haunted house girl, you'll have to be nice to me."

I sit up straight. I grab the remote from him and mute the baseball game. "You found out who she is?"

"Brennan in security is a sly asshole. I only have a license plate number, but it's a start."

"She came to see me again last weekend."

"She came *here*? And you didn't tell me?" Leo hits me in the face with the decorative pillow he purchased to make the living room look *homier*. There's a throw blanket draped over the back of the couch to add to the cozy ambience he was going for. A fresh candle on the coffee table and a picture frame of the two of us at high school graduation. I'm afraid they're going to be the next projectiles. "Some best friend you are. I could've made cookies."

"No, she didn't come here. It was at Fright Nights. She found me in the house." I rub a hand over my jaw, wishing my face was buried between her legs again. I've been thinking about her pussy nonstop. "I got her off. Twice."

"You did *what*? And you didn't get caught? You're shitting me."

"Nope. Hottest thing I've ever done, and nobody had a goddamn clue. *Fuck*. I wish there were security cameras back there so I could play it on repeat."

"I'm feeling very single and miserable and lonely." Leo scowls. "It must be so nice to have such a wonderful life."

"It is." I smirk. "Zero complaints."

"Well, since you're in a bragging mood, tell me about this girl."

"She's so… innocent. Like this pure, sweet woman who probably feeds the birds in the park and bakes dozens of cookies to hand out over the holidays. And I want to corrupt her so fucking bad. I want to find out what her limits are and push her there. It's been years since I've been with someone so—"

"Vanilla?"

I level him with a look. "Unaware of their fantasies. I started to tap into some when I was with her, and I want to do it again." I grab his phone off the coffee table and shove it his way. "I can't do that without knowing who she is. After we get her full name, you're in charge of using your background check database to find out as much information as we can about her."

"Do I have to?" he whines.

"You know I'm shit with computers. Remember that time I downloaded porn to my mom's desktop because I clicked on a suspicious link in my email?"

"Oh my god." Leo bursts out laughing. "She was so fucking pissed at you."

"I'll make it worth your while." I put a hand on his shoulder. "You know that girl who works in the house next to ours at Fright Nights?"

"The redhead?" He smiles shyly. "She's nice."

"That's the one. Janey is friends with her. I'll talk you up next time she's around to try and get her attention. I also promise to let you have a front row seat the night I invite Maxine over—as long as she's comfortable with being watched. I don't want to push her to do anything she's not fully onboard with."

"But you want to invade her privacy? I can't wait to be there when she realizes you broke a dozen laws to find out who she is."

"It's romantic."

"I'm sure every creep in history has said the same thing. I'm going to need more than that as a reward. I'm a good guy, Hunt. Cyberstalking isn't in my wheelhouse."

"What else do you want?" I ask. "Money? I have plenty. You know my side gig pays well."

He raises an eyebrow. "How much does a body disposal earn you, exactly?"

My lips twitch at his curiosity. Leo has always wanted to know the bare minimum about what goes on behind closed doors. He's aware of some of the logistics: the planning. The extensive cleanup to make the death look like an accident, but he doesn't want to be too involved.

I'm convinced he'd fold in a second during a police interview. He can't lie to save his life.

I don't walk around killing random people who cut me off in traffic. There's a vetting process. A waiting period between someone applying to the program, to the target being taken out. We need probable cause. A motive for the violence and assurance the world would be better without the deceased in it. Proof that their behavior is beyond fixing and no one would miss them if they were gone.

Only when all the boxes are ticked do we go in and perform the extraction. Our discretion comes with a heavy price tag, and I haven't told him about my compensation. He knows the pay is good because he's reaping the benefits of it. We've been in the six-bedroom, four thousand square foot home sitting on five acres for a few years now, and he didn't bat an eye when I paid it off fully in cash.

"You really want to know?"

"I need to make sure I'm offered fair compensation if I take the money route."

I smirk. "A hundred thousand a kill. Bonus if we leave the body, stage the crime scene, and no questioning is involved."

"And you've done—" Leo figures out the math in his head. "Damn. Here I was thinking I'd ask for a thousand bucks for my troubles. I need to add a zero or two to that."

"Ten thousand? It's yours."

"Nah. I want something better, money bags." He pauses, an idea coming to him by the way he grins. "The keys to your motorcycle so I can take it for a joyride. *Without* being your fucking backpack," he finishes before I can interrupt, and I scowl.

"No one is allowed to ride Ralphie except me."

"Looks like you're going to have to find someone else to help you."

"Fine. But you only get one afternoon with her."

"That's more than enough." Leo pulls up a text message and takes a screenshot. "You must really like this girl. Ralphie is your most prized possession."

Mentioning that I've been dreaming about Maxine would probably earn me a restraining order, but it's true. She's consumed all of my thoughts, and while I want to know everything about her, I also want to be respectful. Busting down the door to her house and demanding she give me her attention because I've missed her borders on extreme, so I'll have to get creative.

Luckily, thinking outside the box has always been one of my strengths.

"I do like her," I say, and I have to adjust myself over my gym shorts when I remember her jean skirt hiked up to her waist.

"Dude. Are you getting fucking *hard* right now? While I'm sitting next to you? Absolutely not."

"You would too if you had let her come on your hand."

"Tomorrow night I'm putting you at the exit and I'm taking all the house positions. The good stuff always happens to you."

"What can I say?" I tousle his hair. "The ladies love me."

"Love your dick is more like it."

"That too."

"I have her license plate, and I need to input it into the background check system so we can verify who exactly your mystery woman is." Leo grabs his computer off the coffee table and clicks a few keys, whistling. "Stop breathing down my neck."

"Sorry." I laugh. "I'm anxious."

"What's your plan here? Are you going to show up at her job? Randomly bump into her at the grocery store? Hope she comes through the line again?"

"I doubt she'll do that. She was nervous to visit the second time. The grocery store? Now there's a good angle."

"I read romance books. I know all about meet cutes. Bingo." He cracks his knuckles. "I really am letting my potential waste away by working in entertainment. My brain is fucking genius. I could crack nuclear codes in ten minutes."

"Wow, someone thinks highly of himself." I scoot closer to Leo. "What did you find?"

"Maxine Walters. Twenty-eight years old. No criminal record, no prior arrests. Wait." He looks up at me. "What does your record say?"

"What do you mean what does it say? It shows me being a model citizen because every person I've killed has been taken care of under the radar." I scoff. "Come on, dude. I'm not an amateur."

"Forgive me for being inquisitive. Okay, let's see. Maxine is currently employed at Orlando Elementary School where she teaches first grade. She's been there five years. Her last known address is 2586 Woodview Road in Orlando."

"Woodview," I repeat, pulling up Google Maps. I plug

in her address and look at the surrounding houses, glad to find a modest neighborhood in a good part of town. "Who does she live with?"

"Skyler Buchanan. Why does that name sound so familiar?"

I switch over to my Instagram page. I've stepped away from posting so frequently after some Fright Nights videos went viral two years ago. People found my social media accounts, and this time of year brings a constant bombardment of comments and requests for NSFW videos. I've had to turn off the ability for anyone on the internet to tag me in content they create. There's some scary shit out there.

My DMs are flooded with men and women shooting their shot for my attention, and as much as I admire their hustle, the C-level fame doesn't do anything for me. I'm more of a homebody. Someone who will share parts of his life but not give everyone the full picture, because I want to keep some things to myself.

"She's the main performer in the Fright Nights stunt show." I look at Skyler's profile boasting over forty thousand followers and a perfectly curated feed of filtered photos. "Shorter, blonde woman. Good smile." I turn my phone to Leo, and he hums.

"Oh, yeah. I've seen her backstage. She's hot. Those curves are sexy."

"The internet has too much information readily accessible. I don't like that anyone could find all of this out about Maxine. She wouldn't know if someone was following her until it was too late."

"And by someone, do you mean you?" Leo ignores me when I flip him off. "Doesn't say anything about a partner, but maybe you can do some more stalking—sorry, I mean *research*—when you see her Instagram page."

"You are a genius, Leo."

"I know I am."

Finding Maxine through Skyler's following list is easy. I click over to her page and smile at the public profile showing dozens of images of her.

I swipe past a photo of her volunteering at the food bank with gloved hands and a hairnet. I see another of her sitting in the middle of a classroom on a colorful rug, a wide smile and wrinkles in the corner of her eyes. A selfie at the beach with Skyler, the pair sitting under an umbrella and shielding their faces from the sun.

There's not a single man in sight, which is great news for me.

It only takes me a few minutes to put together an idea of who Maxine is: loyal and a good friend. A hard worker and someone who goes after what they want. I didn't think it was possible to like her even more, but here I am, grinning at my phone and happy as can be.

"Oh, no. You have a dopey look on your face." Leo sighs. "For real, Hunt. Can you promise me you're going to treat this girl right? I don't want you to go all in on something to break her heart three months down the road because you're not interested in her anymore."

"Hey." I frown. "I'm just fucking around. I mean, yeah, I'm bordering on obsessed over this woman, but if she tells me to fuck off and leave her alone, I will. Until then? I'm all in."

"I know you're not a monster. I've just never seen you so interested in someone before, and it's throwing me off."

"Because I've never been so interested in someone before." I drag my fingers through my hair, careful not to accidentally follow Maxine on social media. We'll get there, but for now I only want to observe. "She's made of magic, dude. My heart's been broken since Mom passed, but I think she might be the cure."

"Damn. Okay, Shakespeare. You tell her that and there will be a wedding by Christmas. I'm glad my romantic ways are rubbing off on you."

"Yes, Leo. This is all because of you," I say, and he gives me a thumbs up. "Enough flirting. What else can you tell me about her?"

He spends the next twenty minutes reading off where she graduated from college (the University of Central Florida) and her majors (early education and educational management). He shows me her Pinterest boards and action shots of her playing soccer in the NCAA championship, her gold jersey and black shorts showing off muscular thighs and long legs. There are photos from a pole dancing class he finds on a website, her beaming face front and center in a matching biker shorts and tank top set.

The more I learn, the more I want to know. What's her family life like? What's her favorite food? How many pillows does she sleep with? The questions linger long after Leo shuts his laptop, grabs a beer, and turns up the television so he can root for the Tampa baseball team having their best season ever.

One day, I tell myself.

I've always been a determined motherfucker. Someone who goes after what he wants, and right now, the only thing I need is Maxine Walters. I need her like I need air, and I'm not going to stop until she's mine.

NINE

HUNTER

MAXINE'S NEIGHBORHOOD is nice with tall trees and a sidewalk that loops around the block. The fenced yards and brightly painted doors are inviting, and I bring my motorcycle to a slow roll when I reach her house. There's a porch with some potted plants and multiple pumpkins on the steps. Two rocking chairs and a little table between them. I don't know much about her yet, but it seems very *her*.

I put the kickstand down and hop off my motorcycle, glancing around. It's the middle of the school day, so I know Maxine won't be here, and a quick look at Skyler's Instagram account from the fake profile I created tells me she's running errands until later this afternoon.

Plenty of time to do some sleuthing.

I told myself I was only going to pass by, but now that I'm here, I might as well look inside to make sure she's taking care of herself.

I whistle on the walk up the porch steps, stopping to straighten the welcome mat that's off center. There aren't any exterior cameras in place, and Leo didn't find record of the house registered to any security systems. I don't like that she doesn't have any protection in place, but that will be a project for next time.

The street is empty. There aren't any nosy neighbors looking out their window, and I wiggle the front door handle to get an idea for the lock I'm working with. I can tell the deadbolt isn't engaged—another thing I don't like—and I pull two paperclips from my pocket.

Bending them into a small hook shape, I carefully put them in the keyway, grimacing when I apply enough pressure to feel the pins inside the lock moving. Patience is crucial when you're doing something simple like breaking into a building, but when you've done it dozens of times like I have, it's like riding a fucking bike. When the lock pops open, I smirk.

Piece of cake.

I slip into the foyer and shut the door, taking time to kick off my riding boots so I don't track dirt inside.

I might murder people for a living, but I'm also a considerate guy.

Unbuckling my helmet and resting it on top of my shoes, I take my time looking through the house. I can't help but smile at how neat and organized it is. The walls are vibrant shades of yellow, pink, and blue. There are knickknacks here and there: a wooden figurine on the mantle in the living room. A plastic banana on the counter in the kitchen. A clay horse in the middle of the coffee table, and I laugh, having so many questions.

The hall is full of photos, and I stop to study them. There are several of Maxine and Skyler through the years. Individual shots and one of what must be Skyler's family. I touch a funny one of Maxine with a dog in her lap, her grin wide and her hair longer than it is now.

She's so fucking pretty.

The leather couch in the living room is large and positioned in front of a television. I wonder what side Maxine sits on when they watch movies together, and how many blankets she likes to use.

A stop in the kitchen tells me her fridge is almost empty except for some condiments and leftovers, and I frown.

Teachers don't get paid shit in Florida, and while the salary of entertainment workers at Adventure Oasis is modest compared to other positions, there's no way Skyler is pulling in a massive paycheck. I don't like the idea of either of them going hungry, and when I come back, I'm going to make sure the fridge and pantry are fully stocked.

Deeper into the house, I find two doors opposite each other down the long stretch of hallway. I pick the one on the right and pat myself on the back, instantly able to tell the bedroom belongs to Maxine.

Large curtains cover the windows and a bed with a fluffy comforter sits against the wall in the middle of the space. An attached bathroom is off in the corner, and the bookshelf to the left of the window is stacked with books arranged by spine color.

I pick one off the top shelf, curious. Inside are annotations and underlined sections. Notes are scribbled in the margins, and I trace over her handwriting. It's swoopy, neat, and I bet she's the kind of teacher who puts smiley faces on her kids' worksheets.

Her closet shows me folded jeans and T-shirts. The hamper is full of dirty laundry, a rogue sock hanging over the lip of the basket. If it's full again when I come back, I'm adding it to the list of things I'm going to take care of for her.

I'm great at being domestic.

There's nothing that stands out to me as being a threat to her in her room. I don't notice anything belonging to a guy, either. Maxine doesn't strike me as someone who would cheat on a significant other, and she never mentioned a partner or situationship, but I want to make sure I'm the only man in the picture. I play well with others on my terms, and two times with Maxine has shown me when it comes to her, I'm the only one allowed to play.

For as many murders as I've committed, this is my first stalking escapade, and it's fun as hell. I'm tempted to leave a note to let her know I was here, but I don't want to give away the fun too easily, so I compromise. I rip off a small piece of scrap paper from the corner of a notebook. I draw a tiny heart in the center then hide the love note in her desk. It's hidden enough where she'll wonder who put it there, but not so obvious where she'll know someone has been here.

I open a dresser drawer, grinning when I find a couple of vibrators tucked under a pair of sleep shorts. They're gently used, and I'd give just about anything to watch her touch herself with them. My eyes flick over to the bed, picturing her in it: hair across her pillows. Legs spread, a hand teasing across her stomach.

It's just missing me there by her side to help talk her through it.

My cock swells and I groan, so tempted to jerk myself off. I could do it into a pair of her underwear and bring them with me as a souvenir. Maybe I could take something every time I sneak in, collecting an entire drawer full of pretty lace before she notices what's gone.

I brush a hand over my tight jeans, willing myself to calm down. Jacking off and leaving drops of my cum behind might push the boundary of total creep behavior, and I don't want to be a bad house guest on my first of many visits.

Or make her afraid of me.

I peek into the bathroom and sort through her products, making a mental note of her favorite shampoo, conditioner, and body wash, just in case she ever spends the night at my place.

Another lap through the house has me searching the internet for the best interior and exterior home security cameras. Maxine and Skyler are beautiful, young, single women, which history has proven makes them a predator's favorite target. There are no weapons in the house. No guns, no knives that could cause real damage if they needed to defend themselves, and I know I'll be back soon to install something—multiple fucking somethings, let's be honest—so I can keep an eye on them.

I'm a protector. I always have been. When I saw kids getting picked on in school, I was the first one to put the bully in their place. As an adult, I know what happens to people—primarily women—when they don't have someone in their corner willing to fight for them.

I've spent less than an hour with Maxine, and I already know I'd torture anyone who laid a finger on her without her permission and enjoy doing it. I'd never consider a woman to be my property. I'd never fall into the bullshit *they must submit to me* alpha male rhetoric, but she's mine now, which means it's my responsibility to take care of her.

And take care of her I will.

Satisfied with today's snooping, I grab my gear and lock the door on my way out. A stroll to the backyard shows me a pool and a garden with tall sunflowers, and I'd like to see Maxine in a pair of overalls. A hat on her head, protecting her from the sun, and her hands in the dirt, planting something new.

The umbrella by the two lounge chairs looks broken, and it takes me ten seconds to fix the loose screw at the base of the stand to make it stop wobbling. Proud of my contributions to keeping her homeowner's insurance at a minimum, I blow a kiss to the house when I climb back on my motorcycle.

"I'll be seeing you, Maxine," I say, fastening my helmet's chin strap against my neck. "Don't miss me too much like I'll miss you until then, beautiful."

TEN
MAX

"UGH. I have pumpkin guts all over me." I laugh and hold up the seeds sticking to the back of my hand. "Disgusting."

"Remind me why we're carving six pumpkins again?" Skyler wrinkles her nose and sets down her knife. "Mine looks mutilated."

"Because the school needs them for the Haunted Harvest Festival. It's the field day we put together right before fall break when the kids are mentally checked out. We try to incorporate learning into the activities, but mostly it's four hours of them having a good time."

"Is one of those activities judging horribly decorated gourds? Like, look at this tooth I tried to cut out. It's so bad."

"That's a *tooth*? Jeez, Sky. You should stick to performing." I scream when she throws a handful of seeds at me. "Not in my hair! I take it back!"

"That's what you deserve for insulting all my hard work." She giggles and stands, jogging over to the hose to wash her hands. "A harvest festival sounds fun. What games do you play, and can I come?"

"Of course you can come. We do bobbing for apples and have a Halloween costume contest. Oh! There's also a dunk tank. I'm refusing to be one of the people dunked, but the kids love it. The fifth grade teachers use it as a science lesson. My first graders and I stick to the dessert table where we practice addition and subtraction with pieces of pumpkin pie." I laugh and wipe my hands clean with a paper towel. "This job has so many hard days, but things like this make it so worth it."

"You still have pumpkin strands in your hair, Max."

"Gee. I wonder why." I stick out my tongue and sit on the lounge chair by the pool. "I know we'll never get snow in Orlando, but for once I'd like it to be October and not feel like we're still living on the surface of the sun. It's hard to get in the seasonal mood when I'm sweating."

"Pop the umbrella open. That'll help."

"It's broken, remember?"

"Shit. You're right."

"The screw is—hang on." I scoot to the edge of the chair and lean forward. "That's odd."

"What's up?" Skyler looks my way. "Oh, god. Did you swallow some pumpkin seeds?"

"It looks like the stand is fixed." I stand and open the umbrella, securing it in place with a pin. Last week, it wouldn't open wider than halfway before tipping to the side. "What in the world?"

"That's fucking weird."

"Did you fix it?"

"How would I fix it? My handiness skills are nonexistent."

"Well, I didn't do it." I put my hands on my hips and look around the backyard, as if the answer to who is the mysterious umbrella fixer is hiding behind a hedge. "Wait. Look over there, at the edge of the pool deck.

There's dirt. Like someone walked from the side gate back here."

"Okay? And? It was probably an animal jumping from the fence. Or the pool guy!" Skyler snaps her fingers, proud of her deductive reasoning. "He was here the other morning cleaning the filter, and I bet he's the one that fixed it."

"He was? Oh, thank god. For a second I thought someone might be trying to break into our house." I sigh and sit back down, stretching my legs out in the shade. "Ever since Molly told me about Brian being at school, I feel like I'm being watched. It's really fucking unsettling."

"Shit, Max." She turns off the hose and hurries over to me. "One of the girls who performs in the show with me teaches a self-defense class. We should go to one and learn some moves. You can't trust anyone in this world, and you can trust men the least. I was honked at five times on my run this morning because, why? I'm in a sports bra? Fuck off."

"Wow. You're very passionate about this, aren't you?"

"We have to be. Like, Brian cheated on you. You broke up with him, which was a reasonable response. And now he's lingering around? For what? To make amends? No one likes you, dude. Move the fuck on."

I drop my head back and laugh. "I'm so glad I'm on the other side of that. Imagine if I married the guy? I'd be Max Fitzpatrick, and that just sounds like a fraternity president at a school who covers up hazing by calling it *learning opportunities*."

"Of all your exes, he's my least favorite."

"Mine too."

"Okay, but if you had to pick one guy from your past to sleep with again, who would it be?"

I clear my throat and reach for my water bottle. I chug

half the contents so I don't have to speak right away, even though the answer is obvious.

The hot scare actor who got me off in a haunted house, I want to yell.

I'm counting down the minutes until Tuesday in case it means I get to see him again, I almost add.

"That's a good question." I shield my eyes from the sun and offer her a shrug. "Maybe Andy? Remember him? I met him in that adult coed soccer league I played in a couple years ago."

"Oh, yeah. He was *cute*." She sits in the chair next to me and rests her hands on her stomach. "What are you doing the rest of the day?"

"Too much. There's laundry and worksheets and attempting to fix the faucet in my bathroom. It keeps leaking, and it's beyond obnoxious. When my to-do list gets long and chores pile up, being able to work from home so I could knock out a few things between meetings instead of leaving it all for my two days off every week would be nice."

"Dustin can come over and look at the faucet for you. He mentioned his dad was a plumber. Wait. No. An electrician? I forget. But he seems like a guy who knows his shit."

"Look at you having a man on speed dial who can fix household issues for us." I grin and toss my used napkin at her. She screeches and bats it out of the way, flailing her legs. "How the tables of turned."

"Shush. Out of the two of us, you're going to be in a relationship before me. You *love* dating."

"I don't love dating. I'm just a romantic, I guess." I sigh. "Which isn't always a good thing. It's weird to see people who went to high school with us on their second or third kid while I'm out here carving pumpkins for first graders who are going to throw a pie at my face."

"I think that's the nice thing about life. We're all doing things at our own pace, and one path isn't better than the other." Skyler slides her sunglasses over her eyes and turns her chin my way. "We haven't been single at the same time in forever, which means we need to find someone for you to hook up with at the party on Tuesday. Goodbye, Brian, hello hot guy who operates a chainsaw during Fright Nights."

"I don't—"

I snap my mouth closed. I was about to tell her I don't want to find someone to hook up with, because that's not me, but that would be a big fat lie.

And I've never liked liars.

"You don't do one night stands. I know, I know. A girl can dream on your behalf, though." Her laugh turns into a groan when she checks the time on her phone. "Dammit. I need to start getting ready for work."

"I can't believe how early you have to clock in. Your show doesn't start until eight."

"You're telling me. Doing a full rehearsal before the actual performance should be against the law."

"Hey." I rub the back of my neck, looking at the umbrella again. "This sounds so weird, but could you ask the pool guy if he did fix the umbrella? I'm just... I don't know. Maybe I'm being paranoid, but—"

"I'll call first thing in the morning." She takes my hand and gives it a squeeze. "Better safe than sorry, right?"

"Right. And we should sign up for that self-defense class. Brian couldn't find my clit, so I doubt he knows how to put someone in a headlock, but man this world has gone to shit these days."

"Amen. We'll be ass-kicking bitches who can fight our way out of anything."

"That's my girl. And speaking of ass-kicking, have a great show tonight. I promise I'll come watch your last performance on Halloween."

"You will?" Skyler squeals and throws her arms around me. "That makes me so happy. Thank you, Maxy Max. I love you."

"I love you too, Sky. Now go get ready so you can twirl and dance and spin those sticks of fire around."

"That's what we should get for self-defense. No one would come near us if they thought we were fire-breathing dragons."

"So true." I untangle our limbs and pat her cheek. "Have a great show, babe."

"Love you, my sweet darling." She pops to her feet and blows me a kiss. "See you in the morning."

I smile and wave, resting my chin on my knees. My eyes dart back to the umbrella then around the backyard, convinced I'm not here alone.

ELEVEN

MAX

"I'M SO glad we're going out tonight." Skyler wiggles with excitement in the seat next to me in our Uber. "I could use a drink. Or six. The bane of my fucking existence is pushing me to my breaking point, and I'm afraid the show is close to falling apart because of it."

"What's his name again?" I ask. "Derek?"

"Dominic, but it should be Domi-dick," she grumbles. "I swear his sole purpose on this earth is to make my life a living hell. We have this stunt we do together—you know the one where we're both on the silks and he drops me, but I catch myself?"

"How can I forget? My heart stopped when I watched that, Sky. I still can't figure out how you didn't hurt yourself."

"So many core exercises." She laughs and pats her stomach. "On Sunday night, Dominic looked at me and said, *sure hope I don't lose my grip.* And he let me fall two seconds earlier than what we've rehearsed. It took me by surprise, I almost hurt my ankle, and I'm currently plotting his demise. Arsenic might do the trick."

"*What?* The balls on him. What's his deal?"

"No clue, but he constantly antagonizes me. I wish he would break his leg so I could be free from him. Wait a minute." Skyler grins. "Maybe I should accidentally push him off the stage so that becomes a reality."

"I draw the line of retaliation at purposeful injuries. That would bring you down to his level, and you're better than that."

"I knew you'd use your teacher's voice on me. Fine. I'll behave, but I can't promise I won't knee him in the balls tomorrow night."

I laugh. "Now *that* I support. Maybe you remind him of an ex or something. That's why he's being such a jerk."

"Please. He doesn't have enough of a soul to have an ex, and if he did, I pity her. That man is the devil, Max, and I don't want to spend three more weeks with him."

"I'll sit in the front row and boo him."

"You're far too nice to do that, but I appreciate you saying it anyway."

Our Uber pulls up to the stretch of shops and restaurants outside Adventure Oasis, and when I climb out of the car, my mind wanders to Hunter.

It hasn't *stopped* wandering to Hunter.

Skyler always mentions how small the theme park world is. Gossip moves fast, and drama at one entertainment venue reaches the ears of the attendants working at a ride on the other side of the park by midday. Everyone knows everyone else, and with each step I take, my heart skips a beat at the thought of seeing him tonight.

Is this his kind of scene? Does he have a ton of friends? Is he the life of the party?

I bet he would be.

Did I spend extra time on my hair and makeup before we left the house in case he happens to be here?

Maybe.

He gave me the best orgasms of my life. What's a girl to do? Not hope she runs into the guy who got her off faster than any man has before?

"Are you okay?" Skyler loops her arm through mine and leads us to the security checkpoint. "You're jumpy. Did you have another Brian situation?"

"I'm fine." I flash her a smile, not letting myself scan my surroundings. I am not taking a deep breath in hopes I'll catch a whiff of his cologne. I am not rolling my shoulders back and fixing my shirt to show off my chest. "Just excited. I'm on fall break. We haven't had a night out together in what feels like months, and I can't wait to dance."

"That's my girl." Skyler drops her purse in the tray for security screening. She winks at the security guard when she walks through the metal detector, and I follow behind her. "How many shots will it take for you to get on the stage at the bar?"

"Too many. I'd be passed out before I made my first move, so I'll leave that to you. My ass doesn't shake like yours."

"But you have such a nice ass." She swats at my backside, and I giggle, jumping on the moving walkway that leads us toward the bar. "And that skirt shows it off. You look like a knockout, Maxine Walters."

"Thanks." I spin, grateful for the night air making me feel alive. The red leather skirt is far shorter than anything I would normally wear out, and I paired it with a black tube top, black leather boots, and a headband with horns. "Hey, did you call the pool company about the umbrella in the backyard?"

"I did, and the guy who worked on our pool says he doesn't remember fixing anything, but he was in a rush that day, so he can't be sure. I bet he popped the screw back in place and went on his way."

"Yeah." I nod, not liking the answer. I haven't been able to shake the feeling that something isn't right. "That's probably it."

When we get to the bar, Skyler flashes her work ID. A bouncer gives us wristbands and directs us to the top floor where other theme park employees are congregating. The lower level is packed with bodies on the dance floor, and we head straight for the alcohol.

"Gin and tonic," Skyler says.

"I'll take a rum and coke please," I say loudly to the bartender. "Sorry. I didn't mean to yell."

"Please. At least you're looking at my face and not my tits." She grins and grabs two glasses. "It's torture to be people's eye candy, but it's hard to argue with the tips I bring home to my wife every night."

"I love that for you." I dig into my purse and pull out two fives. "It's not much, but please accept this as my contribution to the wife fund."

"You're sweet." She slides over our drinks, then fills a pair of shot glasses with vodka. "An extra treat for being the best patrons tonight."

"Cheers." Skyler lifts her glass in appreciation, and we knock back the shots.

"That stuff is strong." I slide the empty glasses back to the bartender who disappeared to help the next customer. The man is looking directly at her chest, and I find another five in my wallet to add to the tip jar on his behalf. "Thank goodness we took an Uber."

"It's so much better than what we buy." Skyler stands on her toes and waves to someone across the room. "I see Delilah. She's one of the performers in the show. Let's go say hi."

We link hands so we don't get separated, but the crowd has grown. Two men push through our joined palms, making me lose her in the sea of people.

"Sky?" I call out, but the swell of a new song pulsing through the speakers drowns me out.

I spin and face the direction she disappeared in. I try to spot her, but I run straight into a firm mass of an object instead. Warm hands land on my shoulder and stop me from toppling over. I sway on my feet and reach out, grasping the closest thing I can find.

"Shit." Half my drink spills on the floor. "I'm sorry. I didn't see where I was going."

"Maxine."

I freeze at the achingly familiar voice. I bring my chin up, and I'm met with dark eyes. A devastating smile and messy hair with a strand that falls across his forehead.

Hunter.

"You're here," I say with a breathy voice.

"I told you I'd find you." His thumb brushes along the curve of my shoulder. My body reacts to his touch immediately, every inch of my skin heating under the press of his fingers. "It's not hard to do when you're looking for what you want."

"I'm sorry for running into you."

"I'm not." His eyes flick down to my outfit, and he grins. "You look good tonight."

"Thank you. So do you."

I had this idea he wouldn't be as attractive out of his costume. Maybe I fell into the guise of the mask and the knife, but looking at him knocks the wind out of me. His jeans fit his thighs perfectly. His plain white shirt shows off toned arms, more tattoos, and tan skin. His eyes twinkle, and there's the tiniest dimple on his right cheek.

God.

He's so hot.

The kind of man you look at and think there is no way in *hell* he'd ever talk to you, but here he is. Smiling down at me. Still touching me while my hand rests on his chest. And I don't know what to do.

"Are you having fun?" I ask, as if he's a friend, not a stranger who bent me over and used his fingers to fuck me.

"Always." Hunter spins me around so I'm facing the room and he's behind me. He points to a guy with red hair and a wide smile trying to get the attention of a redheaded woman sitting by herself at the bar. "I've been watching my roommate attempt to flirt. I love him very much, but I'm not sure he's going to score tonight."

"I hope he does. I always liked an underdog story. You're a good friend for supporting him in this endeavor."

"I thought so too." He traces down the line of my arm. "Are you having fun, Maxine? Don't tell me you're a new Adventure Oasis employee. I thought I knew everyone."

"Max," I say. "My parents call me Maxine, and I'm not a fan. I never have been."

His eyes flash with understanding, like he can relate. With a subtle nod he dips his chin to his chest for the briefest of seconds before returning to meet my gaze with the hook of a smile.

"I'm sorry. Max it is."

"That's okay. And, no. Nope. No scare acting for me. I'm here because my best friend and roommate works in the Fright Nights stunt show. I lost her a few minutes ago, but I'm sure I'll find her eventually."

"What's her name?"

"Skyler Buchanan."

"The blonde, right? Who does the silks?"

I smile. "That's her."

"If you track her down, I'd love to thank her for

bringing you to my haunted house." Hunter moves his hand to my face and cups my cheek. "My world has flipped upside down because of it."

It's far too romantic of a thing for him to say, but my silly, stupid heart falls for it anyway, and I have to hold back a grin.

"Are you here with anyone other than your roommate?" I ask.

I never considered what his relationship status might be, and I'm hesitant to hear the answer.

"I'm not. There are currently no women in my life, and cheating has never been a turn on for me. What about you, Max? Are you here with anyone other than your best friend?"

"No. I'm single. I broke up with my ex a couple months ago after I found out he was cheating on me. I haven't been with anyone since, and now I'm realizing I'm rambling and talking way too much. You didn't ask for my dating history." I take a long sip of my drink and let out a nervous laugh. "You're really intimidating."

"Am I?" Hunter stands in front of me. "Are you afraid of me?"

"Afraid? No. Not at all. You're just… way too hot to be talking to someone like me."

"The flattery continues." He flashes me a devilish grin. "You don't think you're attractive?"

"I'm not sure you want to hear about my lack of self-confidence, so I'll spare you the details."

"I'd like to hear everything you have to say, Max."

"Everything?"

"Everything," he repeats.

"Do you want to know about my childhood first?" I tip my head to the side and swirl my straw around in my drink, smiling when I catch him watching me intently. "Or what I do for work?"

"Let me guess. You seem helpful. I get the impression that you enjoy talking to people. Calm demeanor, but not afraid to speak your mind. Are you a nurse?"

"I'm a teacher. But I'll give you a half point because I considered going to medical school once upon a time."

"What made you change paths?"

"I can't handle the sight of blood, and it turns out that's a big component of being a doctor. I couldn't even look at the fake bodies at Fright Nights with their guts coming out of their stomach without gagging." I shiver. "Disgusting."

Hunter laughs. "You get used to it. What grade do you teach?"

"First, and I love it so much. I don't make a ton of money. I work long hours, but I'm fulfilled. Sitting in an office wouldn't bring me the joy I find in a classroom, so I've stuck with it."

"Teachers are superheroes. I have a lot of admiration for the people who had to put up with my obnoxious ass when I was a kid."

"You weren't a perfectly behaved child? I'm shocked."

"Behaved? Yes. Talkative, fidgety, and someone with too much energy? Also, yes."

"Ah. I have a few of those students in my class. They're also the smartest ones, and I have a feeling they're going to go on to be very successful."

"Do you want to take a walk?" He leans forward, keeping his eyes on me as his lips wrap around the straw in my drink. He watches me while he swallows a sip, a drop of liquor stuck to the corner of his mouth. "Maybe somewhere quieter?"

"Oh." I steal my drink back and finish off the alcohol, setting the empty glass on a nearby table. "I'd like that."

Hunter smiles and offers me his hand. I let him lead me through the throngs of people. He stops a few times to say hello to someone, but he makes it quick, his attention never straying far from me.

We turn the corner to a hallway tucked away at the back of the bar. There's no one else around, and I let out a deep breath, grateful for the break in the noise.

"How's this?" he murmurs, rubbing his hand up and down my back. "We can go outside if it would make you more comfortable."

"No, this is great. Let me send Skyler a quick text so she doesn't think I've been abducted, then you'll have my full attention."

"Take your time. We can't have her not liking me right off the bat. Or think I'm responsible for your disappearance."

I dig my phone out of my purse and smile, a new message from Skyler displayed on my screen.

SKYLER

It is way too crowded in here. Are you okay? I'm hanging out in the back of the main room with some people from the show. Come over here when you read this! xoxo

Hunter doesn't rush me, letting me fire off a quick response.

ME

Hi! We do we keep getting separated when we're together?! I ran into someone I know and we're catching up. I'm close by, so I'll come find you in a bit!

"Okay. We're all set." Tucking my phone away, I look up at him. "I don't know why more people aren't back here. It's so quiet and lovely. How do you handle being in the haunted house? There's so much screaming."

"Earplugs help. And after many years, I'm used to it."

"Many years? So that makes you—"

"An old man of thirty-five. How old are you, Max?"

"Twenty-eight. What was The Great Depression like?" I tease, and he surprises me by pulling me close. By tickling my ribs and making me squeal, a laugh whooshing out of me. "I take it back!"

"It's rude to insult your elders," he whispers, bending his head to kiss my neck. "How are you going to make it up to me?"

"How do you want me to make it up to you?" I put a hand on his stomach, relishing in the soft hiss he lets out when I play with the hem of his shirt. "I'd like to repent for my sins."

"You might be dressed like a devil, but I doubt you've ever sinned in your life. We could change that if you wanted to." Hunter folds his hand over mine, nudging my fingers to the waistband of his jeans. "Would you think I'm an absolute asshole if I told you I've been dreaming about fucking you?"

"No, because I've thought about it too." I swallow and fumble with the button on his pants, but I stop when I see movement out of the corner of my eye. I crane my neck and spot a couple up ahead, huddled close together. "We're not alone."

"We're not?" Hunter looks over his shoulder and hums. He moves my hand, sliding behind me. The light from the sconce above casts them in almost a spotlight. Her skirt is pushed up to her waist and his hands are in her underwear, pulling them to the side. "That's Shea and Polly. I worked with them in a house a couple years ago. Polly loves being watched."

I wonder how he knows that, but I don't have time to weigh his answer because she's lifting her head away from the wall. Polly catches me staring at them and my cheeks turn bright red. I try to look away, but she opens her legs wider. Moves her partner—Shea—to the left so I have a less obstructed view and lets out a groan.

"I've never…" I trail off, licking my lips. I squeeze my thighs together, turned on in a way that's new to me. "That's so hot."

"Do you like watching?" Hunter snakes his arm around my waist and my back presses flush against his chest. There's no one else around, so it doesn't feel wrong when I give him a small nod. When I admit one of the desires I keep locked away.

"I read a lot of books," I say softly. "To find out what I like. In, um, the bedroom," I add, waiting for him to make fun of me like Brian did. When he stays quiet, listening, I keep talking. "I've read a few where the characters watch other people together. I also like the ones when someone comes by the house and catches them in the act, but they keep going because she likes to be the one being watched."

"Exhibitionism," he says lowly, moving the hair away from my neck so he can kiss me there again. "It's a popular kink. Is that something you'd like to try?"

"I don't know." My entire body is alight with nerves, and the brush of his cock against my ass makes my nipples harden. "Yes. If the person I was with made me feel comfortable."

"That's the most important part of kink exploration. You never want to feel silly while you do it. It needs to be a safe space. Do you see how Shea is talking to her?" Hunter gestures in the direction of the couple, and I let myself look at them again without feeling like I'm intruding.

He still has his fingers buried inside her, but he's whispering to her too, a private conversation we'll never hear. He's stroking her cheek and nodding along when she answers, focused on her and her alone.

"Yeah," I say, mesmerized.

"He's checking in with her. Making sure she's okay with us being here. If not, he'll tell us to leave, because she comes first."

"Literally and figuratively?"

Hunter grins. "Exactly. If two people don't trust each other, it's never going to work. You should never feel uncomfortable when you try something new."

"What would you call it if one person wants the guy she barely knows to take her into a bathroom and fuck her?" I ask, the one drink and his pretty smile making me bold. "And if by person, I mean me."

"DIRTY GIRL." My smile grows. I grab her chin, and she gasps. "I knew I liked you, Max. Are you feeling adventurous tonight?"

"I am." Her eyes meet mine. "What are you going to do about it?"

"We don't need a bathroom. I'll fuck you against this wall if you want."

"Not the first time," she tells me, and my blood thrums at the idea of having her more than once. "I don't want… if I'm not very good or… I might not like the things you like, and—"

"Hey." I steer her out of the hallway and into a small breakroom off to our right. I shut the door behind us and lock it, wedging a chair under the knob so we can have some privacy. "Talk to me, angel. What's going on inside your head?"

"So many things." Max laughs and takes a step away from me, doing a lap around the room. She runs her finger over the edge of a wood table sitting in the center of the space and hesitates before speaking again. "I don't want to bring the mood down by talking about it. Can't we just have sex?"

"Not yet." I study her, paying attention to all of her movements. Her posture is rigid. Her shoulders are up by her ears, and her eyes keep flicking over to me, like she's seeking my approval of what she's saying. "If I didn't want to know, I wouldn't have asked."

"Of course you're a good listener. Do you have any flaws?"

"I have many wonderful personality traits, and I also have many flaws." I grin and sit on the edge of the table. I hold out my hand, glad when she takes it and slots herself between my legs. "Start talking, sweetheart."

"Fine." She sighs and touches my necklace. Her fingers loop around the gold chain and she gives it a soft tug that makes my cock twitch in my jeans. "This kind of spontaneity is new for me. Being here with you instead of hanging out with my friend is way outside my comfort zone, but I've been outside my comfort zone since the night we met. I have wild fantasies. Dreams I don't know how to put into words. Dark desires I want to indulge in. But for as much as I explore this new side of myself, I've only ever had vanilla sex. Missionary. No talking. No… accessories. I'm afraid I might be too boring for you."

"Why would I ever think you're too boring?"

"You strike me as someone very experienced, and I'm not."

"I am ancient, remember?" I tease, and she laughs, relaxing. "You're right. The list of things I've tried in the bedroom is exhaustive. If you name it, I've done it."

"You've had an orgy?"

"I've participated in a few, yes."

"Did you enjoy them?"

"I mean, I got off, so I didn't *not* like it. But there was too much happening for me to really have a good time. Lots of dicks and tits and hands. The logistics aren't easy." I bring my hand to the back of her head, twirling some of her hair around my fingers. "Go on. I know you want to ask me about something else."

"A… sex club," Max blurts.

I like that she's curious. I like that she wants to get to know me, but if I'm going to spill my secrets, I'm going to get her to share hers too. I want to know all about these dark dreams she has. I want to offer myself as a resource if she wants help. I want her to use me, to make me her toy in the name of learning.

"Have I been to one? Yes, and I think you'd like visiting one, to be honest."

"I would?"

"Mhm. It's a good way to figure out things you prefer and things that are off limits."

"How about—have you ever let a woman… you know." She reaches behind me and touches my ass. "Here?"

"Have I ever been pegged? Actually, no. But I have had fingers and toys used there, and I liked it." I cup her cheeks and kiss her forehead. "We could play this game all night, Max, if that's what you want. But for all the wild stuff I've tried, I've also had lots of sex without any frills and enjoyed it immensely. And I know it would be even better with you."

"How do you know that?"

"Because I got off to the thought of you last night." I kiss her nose, and her eyes flutter closed. I need to ease her into this, and I want to give her the affection she's looking for. "I came all over my stomach imagining you were in bed next to me. You don't even need to touch me and I'm worked up." I kiss the corner of her mouth and listen to her soft exhale. "That extra shit would be unnecessary."

"Really?"

"Really."

Max opens her eyes and shuffles back. She grabs her shirt and pulls it over her head, dropping it on the floor. Her hand moves to the zipper of her skirt next, and I watch her drag it down until the material loosens and slides over her thighs. The leather pools at her feet, leaving her in only a red lace thong and boots that come halfway up her calves.

"Fuck, angel." I bring my fist to my mouth and bite my knuckles. My dick is so hard, I can feel the pre-cum in my boxers. "You are exquisite."

The haunted house wasn't pitch black, but the dim lighting made it difficult to see her. The strobe effects didn't help either, but now that I know what she looks like under her clothes, I'm a ruined man.

Her breasts are the perfect size, and the rest of her body is just as incredible. Hips that fan out at her waist to give her an hourglass figure. The curve of an ass begging to be fucked and spanked and bruised. Soft skin on her stomach and the same strong legs I remember from the photos of her playing soccer.

I'm staring. My tongue is practically hanging out of my mouth, but I don't care. She deserves to be gawked at. To know the effect she has on me. She needs to know how gorgeous she is.

Slow, I tell myself. *Do not rush this.*

"Am I?" Max palms her breasts and squeezes them together. She keeps her gaze on me when she pinches her nipples and drops her head back, a quiet moan working its way up her throat. "Maybe you should do something about it."

"Come here," I say, and she moves toward me without hesitation. I curl my fingers around her wrists, pulling her hands off her chest and setting them on my thighs. "I want to touch."

"Please." She almost groans, and I lick the line of her throat.

"*Fuck*. You have such nice tits." I graze my thumbs over her hard nipples, stopping to give them a rough pinch. "I want to fuck them."

"You'll have to explain the logistics to me." Her laugh is soft, slightly embarrassed, but she recovers by dragging her nails up my thighs. She works a grunt out of me when she teases her hand over the zipper of my jeans. "It's unfair I'm standing here practically naked while you're fully clothed."

"What did I say about asking for what you want?" I lean forward and almost fall off the table. I bend my neck, sucking her nipple between my teeth. Max whines at the contact, her fingers digging into my legs. "Tell me what you want, and I'll give it to you. Should I take off my clothes, Max? So I can fuck you the way you're practically begging me to?"

"Strip," she says.

"With pleasure." I pull my shirt off by the collar. She wastes no time staring at my torso and the tattoos inked across the left side of my ribs, and I twist my fingers in the waistband of her underwear. "See something you like, angel?"

"Yes." Her throat bobs around a swallow, gaze dipping to my jeans. "I think I'd like it more if you took off your pants."

"This is a fun game, but we should up the stakes. For every desire you share with me, I'll take off an article of clothing until I'm naked." I put my hands flat on the table and lean back, making sure to flex my muscles so she knows what she's working with. "Then you can have your way with me."

"I told my ex some of the things I wanted to try. He laughed at me," she says, and rage twists in my gut. "It makes me want to be fine with average sex for the rest of my life."

"I say this with as much disrespect as I can muster, angel: fuck him and fuck his closed-mindedness. I promise I won't laugh. I promise I won't judge." I reach out and snap the waistband of her underwear against her hip. "If you tell me, we can try it the next time we're together."

"Next time? You want to see me again?" she asks.

"Baby, the second I sink my cock into your pussy, you're never going to get me to leave. Max's cunt. Population: 1. Me, the lucky motherfucker." I grin. "Even without that, I've become quite attached to you."

"I'll say." She rests her hand on my dick and gives it a squeeze. I jolt upright, groaning when her thumb brushes against the head through the denim. "Fine. A desire for your left shoe. I have this unsubstantiated idea that getting fucked by a guy wearing a mask would be unbelievably hot. I'd like not knowing who is in control of me."

"Really?" She kept staring at my costume in the haunted house, but I thought it was just the knife that turned her on. "What kind of masks?"

"I don't think I'd be picky." Max wets her lips, and I kick off my shoe.

"Give me an example."

"Um. A Ghostface mask? A motorcycle helmet?"

"How interesting. I have both of those at home," I say, and her eyes snap to my face.

"You do?"

"Yup. I have two motorcycles I love to ride and way too

many helmets to choose from. And *Scream* is one of my favorite horror movies."

"That… that is great information."

"Feel like taking a field trip to my place?"

"That's probably too far away. I need some instant gratification." She blushes and points at my right shoe. "I want to be chased. I want to think I'm not safe, and if I get caught, I won't like what happens to me."

"Angel." I groan and stand, pulling off my last shoe and ripping off my socks. "I'm starting to think you're a dream. That you're living inside my head. How are you saying the most perfect things? One more, Max. Tell me one more, and I'll make all of them come true."

"I want… I want someone to be rough with me. I don't want them to hurt me, but I want to have bruises on my ass. Marks on my neck and between my legs. I'm so sick of being treated like this gentle object who is going to break, when I'm a woman with needs and—"

I cut off her passionate plea with a sharp kiss. She moans against my mouth, and I fumble with the button on my jeans. Her arms snake around my neck and I yank off my pants, not breaking our contact until I've stepped out of the denim, left in a pair of black briefs.

"How long until your friend misses you?" I ask, scooping my hands under her ass and setting her on the table. I scoot her back until her feet can rest on the ledge, and I shove her legs open. "Do you think she'll try to find you when she realizes you're gone? Or will it take you screaming my name like the needy fucking slut you are for her to notice?"

"*Hunter.*" Max claws at my arms with sharp nails. Her eyes widen when I bend down to my jeans and pull out a pocketknife. "What are you doing?"

"I told you the real thing is more fun." I play with the

handle, my eyes never leaving hers. A gasp rushes out of her when I tease the blade against the inside of her thigh, bringing it all the way up to her underwear. I slip the knife under the lace and slice, cutting the thin fabric. "There. Now I can see your pretty cunt."

THE SIGHT of Hunter's very real, very dangerous knife scares the hell out of me.

It also makes me moan.

He drags it across my belly, teasing me with the blade. He dips it lower, between my legs, and brushes his mouth against mine.

Fuck.

My brain is screaming how wrong this is. He's touching me with a weapon, an object used to kill and to harm, but my thighs are opening wider. It's taboo, something I'd never, *ever* think to use in the bedroom, but I'm panting. Wondering what it would feel like inside of me and desperate to find out if that's part of his plan.

The competing sensations between his touch and the knife are overwhelming. I don't know if I want to push him away or ask him to get on his knees, but when he kisses me sweet and slow, my breath catches. I melt into him, savoring the taste of bourbon on his tongue and the glide of his hand along the curve of my shoulders.

"Do you always carry a knife with you?" I ask, my head

falling back when he drops his mouth to my neck. "Are you a vigilante stopping crime in our city?"

"No, but I am inspired." Hunter's teeth nip at my skin, biting the soft parts of my flesh and leaving a tiny mark behind. "Do you want me to put it away?"

"I-I—" I sigh, words failing me when he moves his lips from my collarbone to the swell of my breast. "No. I just don't want to hurt myself."

"I'd never let you get hurt, Max." He takes my breast in his mouth, tongue flicking against my nipple, and I swear I see stars. "I'm going to take care of you."

I don't know if he's talking about my safety or bringing me the best orgasms of my life, but I don't care. Both are fine with me, and the slow drag of his tongue down my body as he drops to his knees in front of the table is the closest thing I've ever had to a spiritual awakening.

I run my hands through Hunter's hair. He looks up at me, lust behind his gaze. His fingers dig into my knee, and I stretch my legs to accommodate his broad shoulders and wide frame. With his eyes on me and a hand on either one of my thighs, spreading me open for the whole world to see, he lowers his mouth and licks a hot swipe over my pussy.

"*Fuck.*" I grip the table and lean back on my elbows, the position giving him more space. "Hunter. I thought we were going to have sex."

"In a minute," he mumbles, sucking on my clit. "Want to get you off first."

"You're so kind." My laugh snuffs out when he slides two fingers inside me and curls them. "You've ruined orgasms for me. I'm going to be disappointed if someone can't make me come in less than five minutes."

"I'm the only one who's going to make you come. You don't need anyone else." Hunter grabs the knife off the corner of the table and rubs my clit with the handle in a slow, torturing circle. I gasp at the unexpected change in contact, the texture and pressure so different from his tongue. "I bet you'd look so pretty riding my knife, Max."

He said the same thing to me in the haunted house. It's obscene, but I'm picturing it, and I can't unsee it: the gentle press of the handle against my entrance and the brief flash of uncomfortableness that followed before it melted to delight. Hunter murmuring words of encouragement while he fucked me with the knife. Slow, deep, until he reached the start of the blade. Intoxicating arousal, the tease of danger. All while he watched me, a proud smile on his face while I took everything he gave me.

I've never wanted to be reduced to the vessel of someone's pleasure. I've always wanted to be an active participant, an equal partner, but imagining myself there, a mindless being at his disposal, is electrifying.

"What are you thinking about?" Hunter kisses my knee, my thigh, and my hip, reverence behind the press of lips. "Your pussy just tightened around my fingers."

"Nothing. It's *ah.*" I groan, the start of an orgasm sparking behind my eyes when he adds more pressure to my clit. Dirtier, dangerous. So close to sliding inside me. "I think I'd like that. I want to try."

"Next time. I'm not letting a knife fuck you before I do." He adds a third finger, and I cry out, the twist of desire zipping up my spine. "There you go, Max. You're close, aren't you? Let it happen, angel."

I'm so close. I'm on the precipice of blissful elation, and I realize every hour I've gone without seeing him has been utter agony. Nothing has ever felt this *good,* and I can't be bothered by the slick glide of his fingers as they work in and out of me. I don't care about the noises I'm making, each moan louder than the last. Anyone passing by could hear me and know exactly what was happening behind the closed door, yet here I am, about to scream his name.

"I'm going to come," My body no longer belongs to me when he pulls his fingers out of me and lifts his arm, bringing his hand to my lips. "Hunter. *Please.*"

He forces my mouth open, his drenched fingers resting on my tongue. I close my lips and lick his knuckles greedily, tasting myself. I collapse back onto the table, hoping for a reprieve, a moment to catch my breath, but he doesn't let me. Hunter grabs my ankle, placing my foot on his shoulder. I'm overwhelmed by the tantalizing pace of the knife handle, and my orgasm hits me like a freight train.

He doesn't slow down, not even when I beg him to stop because it's too much, and *this* is what I've craved. The depravedness. Handing over control to someone else and letting them be in charge, and it's the most wonderful thing I've ever experienced.

"You'll take all of it," he says, his voice a deep rumble that almost makes me come again. I whine when he teases the knife at my entrance, the hint of what could be, and I wish I could see how filthy it looks. "That's my girl," he adds, awe behind each word. I squirm, desperate for more friction, more... *something* to fill the void of being full from his fingers, but he drops the hand from my mouth to my stomach, holding me in place. "So greedy." A rough laugh, another kiss to my knee. "Jesus Christ, angel. You're so beautiful."

I feel beautiful, even with the sweat at my hairline and my chest rising and falling like I've been running for miles. I exhale, easing down from the high as the pleasure he brought me ebbs to complete happiness.

A giggle works its way free, and I smile. I'm drunk on affection when Hunter stands and cups my cheeks, kissing me.

"Gosh, that was nice." I nip at his bottom lip. He whimpers, resting his forehead against mine. The hard swell of his cock presses into my thigh when he helps me sit up and tucks a piece of hair behind my ear. "You left my boots on? I didn't even notice."

"Because they're sexy." Hunter closes the knife with the flick of his wrist and drops it on top of his jeans. He lifts my leg and drags the zipper of my boot down with his teeth before slipping off the right shoe, then the left. "Look at you. Naked and perfect."

I blush at the compliment and glance down at my body, smiling at the small marks he's left on my skin. It's like he's claimed me as his, and I touch the spot on my thigh where his fingers gripped me tight. "You did a number on me."

"Are you doing okay?" He kisses me again, gentler this time. "Did I go too far? Did I hurt you?"

"Not at all." My fingers dance over his jaw. "I loved every second of that."

"Good." Hunter rips the remaining pieces of my underwear away from my body, leaving me completely naked. His hand dips into his briefs and I watch him touch himself. "We have a slight problem, angel."

"A problem? What happened?"

"I don't have a condom. I didn't plan to take off your clothes tonight, so I didn't bring any protection."

"Oh." I bob my head and swallow. "What if we didn't use one? I'm on birth control." His hand stops mid-stroke. His eyes meet mine. Flushed cheeks, pupils blown wide, and I wonder if I said the wrong thing. "Sorry. That was stupid. I'm still turned on and not thinking—"

"I'll fuck you raw," Hunter rasps. "But if I do, you're going to be stuck with me for a very, very long time. No one else is going to touch you. No one else is going to have your pussy. It's *mine*, Max. Whenever and wherever I want it. And I'm going to want you in a million different ways." He hooks my leg around his waist and stares down at me. "Is that okay with you?"

God.

Am I allowed to shout *fuck, yes*? Should I get on my knees and thank him for saying exactly what I want to hear? For giving me the opportunity to learn and grow and be truly satisfied for the first time in what feels like forever?

I've spent years waiting for a moment like this. I've been patient, wondering if there was someone out there who understood what I wanted, and when I smile up at Hunter, I know I've found it.

This will probably only be a short fling. Something far from serious that will fizzle out in a week or two before we go our separate ways, but right now? Right now, I'm going to savor the hell out of every second.

I don't care that a more levelheaded woman might run or ask him to pump the brakes. I'm rational in every other part of my life, and I deserve to be free to explore every side of myself, no matter how reckless it might be.

"Yes," I whisper, and his groan is ragged. "That's okay with me, Hunter."

"I love when you say my name." He steps back and hooks his fingers in the waistband of his boxers. He yanks them off and kicks them away, showing off long legs. Strong muscles and a cluster of tattoos on the top of his thigh. "I got tested a couple months ago. Everything was negative."

"I got tested after I found out my ex was cheating." I stare at his hard cock and the glisten of pre-cum on the head. "I'm clear too."

"Can't believe anyone would cheat on you. You're the prize, baby." He moves toward me, gripping his cock and rubbing his thumb from the tip to the root. "I need you to open your legs nice and wide, angel, so I can fit."

"I've never been with someone so big." My throat turns dry when I study how long he is and the thickness of his length. My breathing quickens in anticipation of the pain I'm expecting. "You're huge."

"Your flattery knows no bounds." Hunter adjusts my position until my ass cheeks hang over the edge of the table. He brings my knees to my chest, one hand holding my thigh. "We'll go slow and make it fit." Three fingers are back inside me, and my back arches. "Perfect. Just like that, sweetheart. Let's get you ready for my cock."

He takes his time. He adds a fourth finger, and I moan, the angle letting him get deeper than before. It's even better now, my body used to him and appreciative of every jolt of indulgence he brings me.

Just when I'm on the cusp of another orgasm, his fingers fall away. I look down between my legs, watching him line his cock up with my pussy. I inhale sharply as he slowly pushes at my entrance, the stretch somewhere between mind-numbing pain and divine satisfaction.

"*Fuck.*" I close my eyes and gasp through the discomfort. Hunter freezes, waiting as I adjust to the new addition. "*Move*, Hunter. Please. I need—I want to feel you."

Hunter rocks forward, his chest inches above mine. I can feel the heat radiating from his body, can smell a hint of his cologne. One hand rests next to my head while the other moves to my throat, his long fingers pressing against my windpipe. My eyes fly open, meeting his questioning gaze, and I nod, conveying my approval when the touch at my neck tightens.

"Going to give you more," he slurs.

"Are you all the way in?" I ask, my voice cracking when his movements turn rough. "I'm so full."

"Only halfway, angel," he answers, and my laugh is splintered. "You're doing so well. We're almost there."

"Harder," I grit out. The hand at my neck squeezes and I moan, clawing at his back. "I can take it. And if not, death by your dick wouldn't be the worst way to go."

"Like this?" Hunter barks out a laugh and slams into me, and I almost black out. "Yeah. Just like that. Perfect fucking cunt taking every inch of me."

Everything he does is intentional, from the roll of his hips that allows him to bury his cock in me, all the way to the hilt, to the way he spits in his hand, the heel of his palm pressing against my clit. It's messy, desperate hunger in every bruising thrust. The hand at my throat moves to the back of my head, protecting my skull from bumping against the hard wood of the table when he drives into me with a particularly primal snap of his hips.

"Where should I come?" he asks through clenched teeth. "Your stomach? Your tits? Your mouth?"

"Why not in me?" I put a hand on the curve of his ass, urging him to increase the intensity of his pace to match my racing heart. He almost roars when I tease my finger along his crack. "Make me yours, Hunter."

I don't know what I'm saying, only that I want that more than I've ever wanted anything else.

"You *are* mine, Max." With a quick circle of his palm right against me, I break apart. My orgasm races up my spine as I cry out his name. "*Fuck.* Who does this cunt belong to? Tell me while you drench my cock, angel."

"You," I sob. A wave of emotion crashes over me, the aftershocks racking my body. "It's yours."

"That's right, baby. And you know what I'm going to do? I'm going to fill you up with my cum and send you back to your friend with it dripping down your leg."

A second burst of pleasure grips me, each word a

sparkle of ecstasy. Color bursts behind my vision. I watch the thorough way he fucks me, mesmerized when his thighs flex. My eyes snap to his face, relief in the hook of a small smile and the way he whispers my name.

"Give me all of it, Hunter. Make a mess of me."

That tips him over the edge, his body nearly collapsing onto mine. His cock pulses inside me, cords of warm release filling my pussy. His groan is guttural, yanked from him when he lets out a labored breath and buries his face in my neck.

"You've murdered me, Max, and I don't even have a will in place. So inconsiderate."

I giggle. "I'm sorry." My palms run across his back, rubbing circles over his shoulders. "Do you forgive me?"

"I'm about to give you the keys to my house, my motorcycle, and access to my entire bank account. Mercy." He nibbles on my earlobe, and I squeal. "Careful, angel. I don't want you to waste a drop."

Hunter stands to his full height. He puts a hand around his cock and pulls out of me, our groans simultaneous at the loss of contact. Stepping back, he looks between my legs, a smug grin sprouting on his mouth.

"Like what you see?" I ask, and he hums.

"Fucking love what I see."

"I have no clue what happens next."

"What do you mean?"

"This is my first time hooking up with someone in a break room at party. Do we walk out of here together? Do I pretend I don't know who you are? Is everyone going to know I just had the best sex of my life?"

"Best, huh? I've always liked being in first place."

"Okay, show off."

"I don't think you have anything to worry about, angel. Everyone out there is probably drunk as hell. They won't be able to tell why your lipstick is smudged. But I'll know you why." He touches the corner of my mouth and hums. "If you're feeling generous, I'd love your phone number. If not, I'll wait for the universe to intervene again."

I hold out my palm and he passes over his phone. I take a quick look at his home screen and the background, smiling at the photo hidden behind a dozen apps. "That's your friend from earlier," I say. "The redhead."

"Leo, yeah. We've known each other for years."

The image is of two teenage boys on either side of a beautiful woman with long hair and the prettiest smile I've ever seen. She has her arms around both of them, squeezing them close, and I can feel the love radiating through the picture.

"Who is she? She's gorgeous."

"My mom. We were fourteen there. She let us skip school and took us to Adventure Oasis. We rode roller coasters for hours then stayed for the fireworks. One of the best days I've ever had."

"Good days are nice, aren't they?" I pull up his contacts list, adding my name and number. Wanting to make it personal, I take a selfie. My eyes are closed. My hair is messy. I'm sticking my tongue out, but I smile when Hunter saves my information as *Max the Angel* with a heart after it.

"I promise I won't send any unsolicited dick pics," he says.

"You better not. I'm around children all day, and I don't get paid enough to have that kind of conversation with them." I hop off the table and find my clothes. My body aches, sore in ways it hasn't ever been, and a hot bath when I get home sounds like heaven. "I should find Skyler. I don't want her to worry. I guess I'll talk to you soon?"

"Very soon." Hunter loops his arm around my waist,

tugging my naked body flush against his. I sigh, happy and on top of the world from the orgasms and the sweet kiss he drops on top of my head. "Have fun with your friend."

"You too." I button my skirt and pull my shirt over my head, wishing I wasn't putting my clothes back on. "I hope your friend scored the girl he was after."

"So do I." He gives my ass a smack and I laugh, feeling unbelievably light.

"Until we meet again, Hunter."

"Looking forward to it." He swipes the knife off the ground and licks the handle, his eyes on me as his tongue runs up the black metal. "Stay out of trouble."

It's hard to drag myself away from him, but I stand on my toes and give his cheek one last kiss before I skip out of the breakroom. I take a deep breath when I reach the hallway, the noise from the party returning. My phone vibrates in my pocket and I pull it out, a text message notification in the center of my screen.

UNKNOWN NUMBER

Miss you already

Attachment: 1 image

I grin at the selfie of Hunter that comes through, his lips in a pout and his eyes closed. I hold my phone to my chest, sure this has been the best night of my life.

FOURTEEN
HUNTER

ME

Happy Friday, angel. Headed to school?

MAX THE ANGEL

Nope. I'm on fall break, so I'm off until Monday.

ME

That's exciting. Doing anything fun?

MAX THE ANGEL

Skyler and I are driving over to the beach this morning before she heads to Fright Nights tonight.

What are YOU doing?

ME

In bed, missing you.

MAX THE ANGEL

Can I see what your room looks like?

I GRIN and turn onto my side, FaceTiming her. The call rings twice before Max answers, her pretty face filling up the screen.

"Hi." She props her phone against a wall and brushes her hair, her attention flicking down to me. "I'm multitasking right now."

"I can see that. What beach are you going to?"

"Daytona. It's close enough for us to eat a Publix sub for lunch then head home."

"Damn. I love a Pub sub. I'm jealous." I stretch my arms above my head and she smiles at me. "Stop eye fucking me, angel."

"You're calling me without a shirt on. I can't help but look at you."

"You're right. I shouldn't complain." I sit up, letting the sheets pool at my waist. Her gaze travels down my body, and I smirk. "Want to take your shirt off so we can match?"

"No, because I'm already running behind. Doing that will distract me." Max sets down her brush and starts to braid her hair into pigtails. "What do your tattoos mean?"

"A lot of them are random. Stuff I got during my rebellious phase."

"And the dragon?"

"That one looked badass." I grin and hold up my palm, showing off the design. "Might need to get some pearls or a diamond on the back of the other hand so I can dress you up when I'm gripping your throat. A pretty necklace for my needy slut."

She drops the hair tie she's holding and blushes. She grabs the phone off the counter and slams the bathroom door shut, making me laugh when she levels me with a serious look.

"My roommate is down the hall. Keep your voice down," Max says, but she's fighting off a smile.

"Yes ma'am. Sorry for missing your pussy."

"You're unhinged. No filter, huh?"

"Baby, you have no idea." I flop back on my pillows and rest my arm behind my head. "Will you send me a picture of your bathing suit?"

"Only if you tell me your last name."

"We need to work on your negotiating skills. It's Wilder. What's yours, angel?"

"Walters."

"Look at both of our last names starting with the same letter. That'll be an easy transition when I get down on one knee with a big ring and propose. Max Wilder sounds nice."

"I'm going to need to know more than that before I'd even consider saying yes. What's your favorite food?"

"Besides your cum on my tongue?" I laugh when she flips me off. "Okay. I'll play. I love pasta. My family didn't have a lot of money growing up, and pasta was our go to meal. It's still my comfort food, I guess. Whenever I have a bad day, it's what I crave."

"Favorite sauce?" she asks.

"Not picky. Alfredo, maybe? But I love marinara. What about you? What's your favorite food?"

"Pancakes. I love to have breakfast for dinner with a cup of tea, and I can't say no to—"

"Max? Are you still in there?" There's a knock on the bathroom door and a voice on the other side. Max's eyes meet mine. She points at me then mimes zipping her lips, and I get the hint. "Are you talking to someone? Please don't tell me it's Brian."

"It's just a video I'm watching," she answers. "I'll be right out!"

"'Kay. I grabbed some Pop-Tarts for us to have on the drive over."

The other voice disappears, and Max's shoulders sag. "Sorry. That's my roommate, Skyler."

"Am I your dirty secret, angel?"

"Not intentionally and not because I'm embarrassed of you or anything." Her blush deepens. "I'm going to tell her. It's just nice to enjoy the moment, you know?"

"My roommate knows about you," I say, and her mouth pops open. "What? I've been talking about you nonstop since the first night you stopped by my haunted house."

"You have?"

"I told you I'm obsessed with you." I flash her a grin. "Who's Brian?"

"My ex-boyfriend. The one who cheated. A girl I work with told me his car was in the parking lot at school recently, and I swear I saw him drive by our house last night. It was dark, though, and I can't be certain."

"Huh." I frown, not liking the sound of that at all. "That's odd."

"Very odd, but I'm probably imagining things."

"Do you have a security system at your place? Cameras? An alarm?" I ask, even though I know the answers.

"No." Max shakes her head. "Sky and I keep saying we need to install something, but I haven't had any time. It's on my list to get to during the holiday break." She smiles and looks at the camera. "I should go."

"Make sure you wear sunscreen."

"Okay, daddy." She rolls her eyes, and my cock twitches under the sheet. "If you say so."

"Sorry for caring about your wellbeing. It would be a

shame if I had to put you over my knee and teach you a lesson."

"And what lesson is that?"

"Talking back to your elders."

Max laughs. "Have a good day, Hunter."

With one last smile my way, she waves and ends the FaceTime call, and I stare at the ceiling, positively smitten.

<hr>

"IT'S about time you got up." Leo slides a bowl of cereal my way when I make it into the kitchen and taps the milk sitting on the counter. "I'm too tired to make something special."

"What are you talking about? Cheerios are the way to my heart." I cover the cereal in milk and join him at the island on one of the barstools. "How are you able to get through the day without drinking any coffee? I feel like I need to submerge myself in a gallon of caffeine just to eat my food."

"Pure adrenaline, baby." He shovels down half a blueberry muffin, crumbs spewing from his mouth. "You're on the late shift tonight, right?"

"Yeah." I yawn and drop my chin in my hand. "I don't clock in until six, but I'm going to be busy all day."

"With?"

"Max."

"Oh, shit. Is she coming over? Are you spending the afternoon together? Do I get to meet her? Please tell me you're taking her on a date and not fucking her on another table. *Wooing*, Hunter. Remember?"

"I remember." I take my time eating a bite of cereal. "I'm doing none of the above. This requires things more along the lines of breaking and entering."

"Of course it does. What grand gesture do you have up your sleeve?"

"It's not so much a grand gesture as curiosity. She just told me her ex-boyfriend showed up to her school. He also drove past her house last night. I'm going back over to her place to install a camera on the exterior of the house and maybe one in her bedroom so I can keep an eye on her."

"Right. Totally normal behavior for a woman you just met." Leo blinks. "Wait. What do you mean by back over to her place? Hunter fucking Wilder. Have you been to her house before?"

"Maybe," I say innocently, and Leo groans. "What? You gave me her address! I simply drove by, accidentally picked the lock and…" I trail off with a grin. "Stumbled inside. I have no clue how it happened."

"Absolute maniac," he mumbles. "So, what? You're literally going to watch her sleep? And not tell her you're doing it?"

"In my defense, it's to keep her safe."

"Oh, this will be fun. Keep her safe from who? The monster who lives under her bed?"

"The ex. Anyone else who might want to harm her." I stir my spoon around the cereal and shrug. "She seemed creeped out by him, and when I stopped by their place the first time, they didn't have any security systems in their house. They didn't even have the deadbolt in place. And don't get me started about the lack of weapons to defend themselves."

"Shit. Do we think this guy is bad news like you're used to handling? Is he a rapist? An abuser? Have you looked him up?"

"Not yet, but I'm going to. If there's even a *blip* on his record, I'm buying Max a knife she can sleep with to protect herself. Fuck. I might buy one for her anyway."

"Okay, well, it's hard to call you a creep when you're being all noble and shit, but don't watch her sleep. That crosses a line."

"No promises." I finish off my breakfast and stand, dropping the empty bowl in the sink. I move to the coffee maker and hit brew, waiting for the pot to fill up. "But I'll do my best to behave."

"When she gets mad at you, I want you to tell her I had no part in this," he says.

"Yeah, yeah. I'll make sure your good name stays clean."

I give him a salute and turn for my bedroom to get changed, knowing I'm going to be taking my coffee to go. There's a long day ahead of me, and all I can think about is doing everything I can to protect Max from the shitty people who might want to hurt her.

MAX'S FRIDGE is still empty, but there's a loaf of bread on the counter. Her laundry hamper is full again, and I wish I had more time to hang around and help her with some of her chores, but I'm already running behind.

Picking the right cameras were a longer process than I thought it would be. I added upgraded features and premium services. I paid more for the app so I can watch both camera feeds on two separate devices at the same time. I went all the fucking way in, and I stare at her bookshelf, wondering what book I'm going to sacrifice so I can hide the camera out of sight.

One at the top catches my eye, and I pull it off the shelf. It looks used, like it's seen better days, and I promise myself I'll buy her a new one if this ends up being a favorite.

I make a hole in the spine of the book and attach the camera between the pages, careful when I set it back in place. I pull up the app connected to the live stream and wave my hand in front of the camera, glad when the mirror image shows on my phone.

I turn the book slightly to the left to give the camera a better angle of the whole room, and I grin. I *will* be able to watch her sleep, and Leo is going to be so fucking mad at me. The camera is tiny, unnoticeable when I take a few steps back and look at the shelf up and down, and there's no way Max is going to realize it's there.

Satisfied with the placement of the first camera, I head outside, surveying the house for where I'm going to put the second. I do a full lap, laughing when I get to the backyard and see the umbrella I fixed standing upright.

"You're welcome, angel," I say, making my way back to the front.

The porch has less places to hide something, and I settle on placing the camera on the back of a sconce attached to the brick. It's not as discreet as I would've liked, but beggars can't be choosers. Not when this is her safety we're talking about. Something is better than nothing, and I curse when I burn myself on the warm glass.

"Motherfucker," I mumble, blowing on the tips of my fingers.

I hop off the chair I'm standing on and put it back in place, not wanting my presence to be noticed. I check the feed on this camera and give myself a pat on the back, happy when everything seems to be working correctly.

Our FaceTime call wasn't the first time Max mentioned her ex. She told me he cheated on her when we ran into each other at the party on Tuesday, and now my guard is up. I don't know who the fuck this Brian guy is, but I do know I'm going to keep my eye out for anything suspicious. The second I see anyone lingering around, doing things they shouldn't be doing, I'm going to take care of them.

If I was a nice guy, I would let Max know I installed the cameras. I'd make sure she knew she was being watched, but I'm going to keep this secret to myself. The less people who know, the less have to be involved if and when I need to take matters into my own hands. I'm careful to not leave a paper trail in my other job, and I'm going to treat this the same way.

One wrong move from this ex-boyfriend of hers, and I'll end him with a quick snap of his neck.

I haven't used that move in a while. I bet it could be fun.

I blow another kiss to the camera even though Max can't see it and make sure I pack away all my tools.

"Until we meet again, angel," I say, making sure the camera app is hidden in a folder on my phone labeled TAX STUFF. Technically, the purchases *are* a write-off, so I'm not totally lying. "But I'll see you well before you see me."

FIFTEEN
MAX

HUNTER

Happy Monday, angel. I hope you have a
good day.

ME

What do you do on days when you don't
have Fright Nights? Sleep until noon?

HUNTER

A little bit of everything. Today is going to
be yard work.

ME

Do you own or rent?

HUNTER

I own. Leo, my best friend, lives with me.
Six bedrooms, five acres. The property
backs up to the woods, and there's no
neighbors around for miles.

ME

Sounds like that start of a slasher film!

Five acres? Are you some trust fund nepo baby?

HUNTER

Far from it. I pick up odd jobs here and there to make some extra money.

Are you busy tonight?

ME

No. Why? Do you want to do something?

HUNTER

Feel like taking a ride?

ME

To where? The slaughterhouse you have on your one million acres?

HUNTER

You're funny. I can confirm the property is slaughterhouse free.

ME

A ride sounds nice. Skyler has plans this evening, so she won't be around.

HUNTER

Keeping me your dirty little secret, baby?

I'd be honored, but it can't be that. I remember you saying I was very big. HUGE.

ME

Wow. You know what? I think I'm busy tonight.

HUNTER

I'm just kidding, angel!

Forgive me?

ME

I don't know. You might need to get on your knees and beg.

HUNTER

On my knees? There's something I'm very good at.

Text me your address?

ME

We'll see.

I CAN'T HELP but smile at the knock that comes later that evening. I skip down the hall and wrap my hand around the door handle, bursting out laughing when I see Hunter kneeling on our welcome mat with his hands clasped in front of him.

"What are you doing?" I ask, leaning against the door frame.

"Repenting for my sins." He looks up at me, and I realize he's in a white motorcycle helmet, bulky jacket, and dark jeans. His voice is muffled, and I can't see his eyes until he flips open his visor and winks at me. "Do you forgive me, angel?"

"Of course I forgive you." I reach for his hand and tug him to his feet. He wraps his arms around me and gives me a tight hug, and I can't help but grin when he rests his chin on top of my head. "I'm guessing you rode your bike here?"

"Whoa, okay. Easy, Max. My Ralphie isn't a *bike*. She's a goddess."

"Do I have competition?" I squeal when he presses his fingers into my ribs and tickles me. "Show me the other woman so I know what I'm working with."

Hunter leads me down the porch stairs and stops in the middle of my driveway. He points to the blue bike with silver rims and unbuckles his helmet. "Here she is. I've had her for two years, and I thought I could take you for a spin."

"*Me?*" I shake my head and step back. "No way. I'm a four-wheels-on-the-ground kind of girl. A motorcycle is too dangerous. I have too much to live for."

"I got here safely."

"You're wearing proper gear. And you're experienced."

"You don't think I brought a helmet and jacket for you?" He walks to the bike and holds up a black helmet sitting on the leather seat. "Gotta make sure my girl is protected."

My stomach swoops low at the *my girl* declaration, but I still hesitate. "Can I think about it?"

"Of course." Hunter smiles. "Ralphie would love to have you anytime."

"Are you going to tell me what Ralphie means? Is it short for Rapunzel?"

"No. The bike is a Kawasaki Ninja." He pulls his helmet off and shakes out his hair. "There's a hockey player in Washington DC who rides the same one. He named his Donatella, after the Teenage Mutant Ninja Turtles, and I thought it was a great idea. So, I went with Ralphie. Short for Raphael, but I call her Raphaella."

"Boys and their toys." I shake my head. "Do you want to come inside? I can give you the tour."

"Sure." Hunter follows behind me, slipping into the foyer and unlacing his boots. "Your place is nice. How long have you lived here?"

"Three years. Skyler and I were renting before, but this place became available, and we took it. It's close to Adventure Oasis and my school, and the neighborhood is great. It's very close-knit. There is a block party on Halloween and caroling during the holidays."

"Sounds fun." He unzips his jacket and neatly folds it, setting it on top of his boots. His gloves come off next, and I frown when I see a cut on the back of his hand. I take his palm and examine it.

"Are you okay?"

"You don't need to worry about me. Just a scratch from a stick."

"And your cheek?"

"Courtesy of a tree branch."

"Do you want some ice?" I touch the small red mark under his eye, and he winces. "That looks like it hurts."

"I'm fine, angel, but thank you for offering to take care of me." Hunter flashes me a grin and puts his helmet on the small foyer table. "Where's Skyler tonight?"

"She's hooking up with this guy who—wait a second! You know him!"

"I do? God. Is it my roommate? I hope so. He needs some love and affection."

"No." I lead us to the living room, taking a seat on the couch. "It's Dustin, the guy who works at your haunted house."

"*Dustin?*" He lifts an eyebrow and sits next to me, pivoting my hips so my legs drape across his lap. "I had no clue he had any game. Good for him."

"He does, apparently. I thought he would tell Skyler he saw me at the haunted house a second time, but I guess he's been too distracted."

"Men are weak creatures." Hunter presses his thumbs into my calf muscle, and I sigh. "If you flashed me your tits, I would be speechless. Incapacitated for the rest of the day."

"Please. You're not that pathetic."

"Oh, Max. When it comes to you, I'm pitiful."

"Will you tell me more about yourself?" I blush and hug a pillow to my chest. "I feel like we're working backward after having sex, but there's normally at least dinner before I take my clothes off."

"Do you want the Hunter Wilder memoir? I'm pretty boring." He smiles my way. "I'm an only child. I'm born and raised in Orlando. Leo and I are co-dependent. I like long walks on the beach and getting caught in the rain."

"Such a romantic." I lean my elbow on the couch cushion and look at him. "Do you work at Adventure Oasis year round? Skyler is in the Mardi Gras parade too. Have you two ever crossed paths?"

"When I was younger, I did other things around the park, but now I'm strictly seasonal to Halloween. This is my last year. I've loved it, but I'm ready to take a break."

"Anything exciting on the horizon?"

"Hoping I can keep this cute girl around when I don't have my mask and knife with me," he teases, and I dip my chin. "Besides that, I have a few things I do that pay the bills."

"Mysterious." I shift my position, leaning against his shoulder. "Do you work for the FBI?"

"Fuck, no. I'm not a fan of authority." Hunter runs his fingers through my hair, and I relax into him. "Are you going to tell me about yourself, angel?"

"I'm also an only child. Born and raised in Orlando. My parents divorced when I was younger, and I don't see my dad a lot. My mom likes to travel, so I don't see her a lot either, but for different reasons."

"When's your birthday?"

"Don't tell me you're into astrology."

"I could be for you."

I laugh. "My birthday is in July, and I have no clue what my astrological sign is."

"I'm a February baby. Valentine's Day, actually."

"Wow. You must be so full of love."

"For the right people." He kisses the top of my head. "Can I have a tour of your place?"

"Is that code for wanting to see my bedroom so I'll take my clothes off?"

"I have other interests besides your body, angel."

"Oh yeah?" I poke his side, grinning when he takes my hand in his and kisses it. All of this feels so natural, like we've done it a hundred times before. "Like?"

"Baseball. I used to play on a little league team when I was younger."

"Baseball? Huh. Arguably the most boring sport."

"Jesus Christ, Max." Hunter groans and puts a hand over his chest. "You wound me."

I laugh again and stand, pulling him to his feet. "Will showing you my room make up for the pain I've caused?"

"Oh, without a doubt, sweetheart. I think I also need to try out your bed."

I lead him down the hall, telling him about the pictures hanging on the wall. He asks questions here and there, wondering about my soccer career and what position I played, genuinely interested in hearing what I have to say. When we get to my room, I pause before opening the door.

"I have to apologize," I say, and Hunter lifts an eyebrow.

"Are you the one with the slaughterhouse?"

"No way. I hate blood, remember?" I huff and cross my arms over my chest. "My room is messy. Teaching takes a lot out of me, and I also handle after-school care for students who don't get picked up until late in the day. I haven't had time to clean up."

"Hey." He cups my cheeks and tilts my head back. "You don't need to do anything to impress me, Max. I don't care if there are clothes everywhere and dirty towels on the floor."

"What about cockroaches?" I whisper, and he grins. "Or spiders?"

"From all the haunted houses I've worked in, nothing phases me anymore. I hope there are rats too."

"Are you sure?"

"Positive."

"If you say so." I open the door and hold out my arm. "Welcome."

"Wow." Hunter steps across the hardwood floor in his bright pink socks and surveys the space. Never in a million years did I think he'd be here after our first encounter, but I'm glad he is. "I like it."

"Thanks." I move to the bookshelf and stand on my toes, fixing a book with a dark spine that's out of order. "Can't forget the bed you're so eager to see."

"Feels like I've been waiting my whole life for this." Hunter flops on the bed and frowns. "This mattress sucks."

"It's not the best, but it was cheap, and it gets the job done." I join him on the bed and wiggle on the comforter. "Okay, yeah. This does suck."

"You sleep on this every night?"

"Where else would I sleep?"

"The floor might actually be more comfortable."

"It's not *that* bad." I rest my hands on my stomach and look over at him. "I'm getting a raise at the end of the school year, and I'm planning to put some of that money toward a new mattress."

"The end of the school year is months away."

"It is, but I've survived this long, and I'm doing just fine."

Hunter hums, and I rest my cheek on his chest. "You deserve to be spoiled, Max."

"I'm a simple girl," I say. "It doesn't take a lot to make me happy."

"That was before you met me." He scoots out from under me, letting my back press into the mattress. He holds himself above me, a lock of hair curling over his forehead. "When I'm around, I'm going to take care of you, okay?"

"Okay." I smile up at him. "If you insist."

"I insist, angel."

My eyes flutter closed when he strokes my arm with his knuckles. It's a gentle caress, something sweet and soft and so *right*, and the attraction I've been feeling for him bubbles to the surface. I need to remind myself to keep my feet on the damn ground. It's too soon to be so enamored with someone, but he's magnetic. Pulling me toward him, and I'm not doing anything to stop it.

"Do you have any plans the rest of the night?" I whisper, my breath hitching as his thumb moves to trace along the underside of my breast. Sensual, teasing. Enough to make me squirm. "Or can you stay?"

"My only plans involve you." Hunter dips his head, pressing a kiss to my cheek, my neck. "I told you I'm pitiful, Max, and entirely at your mercy."

He brings his mouth to mine, kissing me, and it's far different from the other night. He helps me out of my shirt, delicate when he unravels my hair after it gets caught in the sleeve. My shorts come off next and so do his pants. His hands wander and he takes his time kissing down my body, learning every curve, every inch. It's slow, patient, exactly like the no-frills sex he said he's had before, but it's absolutely perfect.

SIXTEEN
HUNTER

I PUNCHED my ticket to hell a long time ago, and I can't bring myself to have an ounce of guilt while I watch Max on the camera I set up in her room. Seeing her wake up has become the best part of my morning.

I prop my laptop on a pillow, grinning when she stretches her arms above her head in her bed. She rolls to her side and yawns, the strap of her tank top slipping down her arm with the movement. She doesn't bother pushing it up, and her hard nipples are obvious through the thin material.

Fuck.

I wish I was there with her right now.

I rub a hand over my cock and pull up my texts, firing off a message to her.

ME

> Dreamed of you last night. How did you sleep?

Her phone lights up on the sheets. Max reaches for it, a

smile bursting across her face when she reads the notification. She sits up, back against the pillows and her fingers flying across the screen, and I wait impatiently for her answer.

MAX THE ANGEL

Good morning. Not bad. What were these dreams you speak of?

It's my turn to smile. I dip my hand below the waistband of my boxers and grip my cock, giving myself a slow stroke while I type a message back.

ME

You were tied up in my room. Your legs were spread wide. Your pussy was drenched. I ate you out until you screamed, and then I did it a second time.

Max's eyes widen. She scoots down the pillows, and I see her hand disappear under the sheets while her head drops back. I stifle a groan when she uses her other hand to peel off her shirt and drop it on the floor, her chest on display in the early morning light.

MAX THE ANGEL

Can I tell you about the dream I had last night?

ME

I think I might die if you don't.

There's a long pause on her end while I watch her set her phone down on the sheets. She throws back the covers and shimmies out of her tiny sleep shorts, letting them fall on the ground too. Her arm reaches for her bedside table, rummaging through the drawer before she pulls out a toy and drags her fingers over the length of it.

It's impossible to look away when she clicks the toy on, soft vibrations filling the room. I've never been so happy to spend money on top of the line equipment in my life; getting the camera package with the microphone was the best purchase I could've made.

"Shit," she whispers, parting her thighs.

The toy rests against her clit, pulsing in a way that makes her back arch. I'm scrambling to bring the laptop closer, not wanting to miss a second of this one-woman show. I can't wait for the fire in the Underworld to burn me alive.

Max slides her feet up the sheets, bending her legs. I know she doesn't know the camera is there—she'd kill me if she did—but I wonder if she has an inkling, because she's angling herself toward the bookshelf. She's propping herself up on an elbow, her free hand reaching for her phone. Three dots appear in our text message thread, and I slow my stroking so my dick doesn't fall off with anticipation.

MAX THE ANGEL

It's really dirty.

ME

Tell me, baby. How bad were you?

Her lips curl into a smile and she clicks up the speed on her toy. The moan she lets out is loud, more urgent, and she rests the phone on her stomach so she can pinch her nipple. Pre-cum soaks my boxers, and I pull them off completely so I can pretend she's next to me, mouth open and ready to wrap around my shaft.

Max types her response, and when the text comes through, I almost come on the spot.

MAX THE ANGEL

> We were at a sex club together. I did something you didn't like, and you made me sit in a chair in front of everyone. You let them watch while you teased me, but didn't let me come. Except, I accidentally did come, and you weren't happy. You found two people to help hold me down while someone else held a knife, and they took turns fucking me. You watched, and when you were ready, you fucked me in front of the crowd.

> I woke up in the middle of the night so turned on. I've never had a dream that vivid before.

My imagination is running wild. I can't stop picturing her agreeing to all of those things, and I spit in the center of my palm, jerking myself off. I groan with every rough glide of my hand, wishing it was her pussy instead of my fingers.

On my laptop, Max is just as worked up. She's squirming on her bed, the toy pulsing against her clit, and I don't want her to think I'm ignoring her. Not when she revealed a secret I'm sure she's embarrassed to admit.

ME

> That's so hot, angel. I wish I was with you right now. You could reach over and ride my fingers. I'm at your disposal, Max.

Real life Max drops her phone and pushes three fingers in her pussy. Her legs are opened so wide, I can see the damp spot on her sheets. She throws her head back, an orgasm sinking its claws in her as she comes undone.

It doesn't take long for me to follow her over the edge, drunk off the sight of her pleasuring herself. I muffle my grunts with a pillow over my face so Leo doesn't barge in and think I'm dying, but even if he did, I wouldn't care. Warm cum covers my hand and my bare stomach, and holding back my roar is almost impossible.

"Jesus Christ," I pant, hurrying to see what she does next.

It takes a handful of languid movements and the slow flex of her legs before she climbs off her bed, a sated smile on her face. She swipes her phone off the sheets, hips swaying on her walk to the bathroom where she disappears out of sight. A message is waiting for me when I clean myself up with a dirty shirt I find on the ground.

MAX THE ANGEL

What a way to start my morning.

ME

And how's that, baby?

MAX THE ANGEL

Getting off to the thought of you. Now I need to go shape the future great minds of America.

Have a good day, Hunter.

ME

I'm thinking about you, Max. It's already the best day.

"YOU HAVE BLOOD ON YOUR SWEATSHIRT." Leo squints at me from the kitchen table. "Yuck."

"I do?" I look down at the hoodie I threw on after a

cold shower and sit next to him. "Whoops. Leftover from last night's job. The fucker wouldn't go down without a fight."

"Seems like you took care of things. You're glowing." Leo shoves a coffee mug my way and I smile. "Care to share with the class what's got you all excited? Is it the big ass paycheck that got deposited in your account?"

"I got to see my favorite show this morning."

"What the hell is your favorite show?"

"Watching Max get off on the camera I installed in her room." He chokes on his orange juice, and I pat his back. "Swallow, Leo. It's not that hard."

"You're sick."

"I'm resourceful." I sip my coffee and sigh, happy. "Hey. Could you do me a favor? I need help looking someone else up."

"Is it the number for a psych ward? Because I have a feeling the jury is going to find you guilty of stalking, my friend. I promise to visit you in jail."

"It's not stalking if she doesn't realize I'm doing it."

"Oh, boy. Your comprehension skills are nonexistent."

"I'm glad to know your moral line isn't killing people. It's watching the girl I like finger herself."

"You know what?" Leo holds up a hand. "It's a beautiful Wednesday morning, and I don't feel like arguing. How can I assist you, Hunt?"

"I want to find some information on Max's ex."

"Why?"

"My gut tells me he can't be trusted. That's the point of the cameras, remember?"

"Cameras? As in more than one? Why am I not surprised?" He grabs his laptop and opens his background check software. "What do you know about him?"

"His name is Brian," I say.

"That's it? You're giving me nothing to go off of. I need more than that. There are a million former frat bros out there with the same name."

"Hang on. Let me try social media."

I pull up Instagram and find Max's page. I doubt she's still following him, so I scour through old posts. There's a photo from eight months ago of her on a golf course, squinting and smiling at the camera. I check the likes on the picture and find one from a username listed as Puttin-OnTheFitz.

Seems like a douchey enough handle that it could belong to him, and it's a good place to start. Clicking on the profile, I see Max has liked some of his older posts and I pump my fist, excited.

The names match, and this has to be the guy.

"Brian Fitzpatrick, located in Orlando, Florida," I say.

"You don't need me at all." Leo taps his keyboard and hums, waiting for the information to populate. When it does, he frowns. "Huh. That's weird."

"What?" I scoot my chair closer to his and glance at his screen. "No results found? What does that mean?"

"It means there's not a Brian Fitzpatrick in Orlando who fits the parameters I put in. There's a Connor Fitz-patrick." He clicks the profile and zooms in on the photo plastered on the screen. "Is that your guy?"

I cross-reference the Instagram profile with the picture on Leo's computer. The two men are spitting images of each other, and I'm confused as hell. "That's him. Does he have a twin brother?"

"*Fuck.*"

"What?"

"I'm guessing your guy uses a different name on social media because he's been arrested for domestic assault in the past."

I grab the computer and yank it toward me, gaping at the arrest report on the screen.

There's a restraining order. A battery charge. Possession of a deadly weapon and another domestic assault case that was apparently settled outside of court. My blood boils as I read through the list.

"Motherfucker," I whisper. "How the fuck is this guy not locked up?"

I blink, but all I can see is red. Rage like I've never experienced before grips me, and I have to do a lap around the kitchen to stop myself from breaking the laptop in half.

"Hunter?" Leo asks.

"I'm going to kill him," I whisper. "If I find out he ever hurt her, I'll murder him with my bare hands and smile while I do it."

"Do you think Max knows?"

"No. If she did, she'd be more freaked out that he's not totally out of the picture." I gulp down a deep breath. I can't stay calm. "*This* is why I put up fucking cameras. I knew this guy was trouble."

"What are you going to do?" He stands and grabs a cup of water, shoving it my way and forcing me to drink it. "You're not going to confront the dude, are you? He could be dangerous, Hunt."

"Everyone I deal with is dangerous, but I'm not going to confront him. Not until I find out everything I can about him. The second he's near Max again, I'll make sure he knows I'm watching him. One toe out of line, and I'll smash his skull in."

"Christ." Leo groans. "Why can't men just fucking behave?"

"Behaving is the bare minimum, and this guy doesn't even have the decency to do that." My fingers curl around the cup, and I almost break the glass. "Keeping her safe is my sole purpose for living from here on out."

"What do you need from me?"

"Nothing." I look over at him with a wicked smile. "Just know if I go down, I'm going down fucking fighting for my girl."

I HAVEN'T MENTIONED anything to Max about who her ex really is. I know I should. I know it's shitty to keep such big fucking news from her, but I need more information. Substantiated evidence that would hold up in court if he tries anything with her, and I want to keep enjoying her without the worry of someone from her past looming over our heads.

Max is a dream, and for as good as the sex is, just spending time with her is the highlight of my day. She slept over last night and met Leo, the two becoming fast friends while they laughed at the mess I made in an attempt to do homemade spaghetti sauce for dinner.

The three of us shared a bottle of wine with our food and watched a scary movie with the lights on. Max hid her face in my shoulder whenever something popped up on the screen, and I was glad for an excuse to have her in my arms.

I gave her a tour of my room after we said goodnight to Leo, and we stayed up for hours talking about our childhoods and favorite things. She fell asleep wrapped around me, and I've had this dopey, stupid smile on my face since she left early this morning. Maybe that's the reason why I'm back at her house while she's away, busy setting up a third camera at the back door: because I can't fucking stay away.

"I dare you to try something now, motherfucker," I grumble, checking to make sure the camera feed is synced with the app. "I will fucking end you."

With everything working correctly, I grab my toolbox and stroll into their house, stopping to wash my hands. It's empty and quiet inside with Max at school and Skyler at a yoga class and a doctor's appointment, and I savor their absences. It means I have a couple of uninterrupted hours here to do whatever I want, and I call Leo after I dry my hands with a hand towel decorated with dancing skeletons.

"What's up, Hunt?" he pants from the other end of the line. "Are you in jail?"

"Would I be calling you from jail on my cell phone?"

"With you, I'm not sure. You'd probably find a way to charm the cops."

"I didn't get arrested." I laugh at the noise Leo makes. "Why are you grunting and groaning? Are you fucking someone while you're talking to me?"

"I wish. I'm at the gym and feel like I'm dying. Might stick with my dad bod forever, because lifting weights sucks."

"You might have a future in erotica audiobook narrating, dude. And for what it's worth, I like your dad bod."

"I can always count on you to boost my self-esteem. Hang on." There's the click of a couple buttons and a labored breath. "Okay. I'm free from exercise hell. What's up?"

"When you finish, can you place a big grocery store order for pickup? Anything and everything you can think of: vegetables. Fruit. Snacks. Meat. Bread. Eggs, no matter how fucking expensive they are these days. My card is still saved under your Apple Pay. Charge it all to my AmEx."

"Am I bringing them to the house? I just bought a ton of shit two days ago."

"It's for Max. I'll text you the address."

"We should change your name to Hunter Loverboy Wilder, because you're fucking smitten, dude," Leo sings. "Give me an hour, and I'm there."

"Add paper towels and napkins to that list." I open the pantry and shake my head at the bottle of soap that stares back at me. "And toilet paper."

"Can I throw in a candle? Oh! How about Oreos? Girls love Oreos."

"Only if they are Double Stuf. They're superior."

"What about the Halloween Double Stuf? Talk about festive."

"Get whatever you want. Thanks, man."

We hang up, and I head for Max's room. I grab the laundry basket tucked away in her closet and search for the laundry room, finding it in the back of the house next to a small half bathroom that smells like flowers.

I separate her items and dump the first load of clothes in the washer, starting the cycle and flipping off the light before making my way back to the living room. Knowing I have some time to kill, I go into deep cleaning mode.

I scrub down all the surfaces throughout the house. I empty the trash from the bathrooms and bedrooms, taking two garbage bags outside and tossing them in the barrel on the side of the house. I only stop working to open the door when I see Leo struggling on the porch.

"My arm is going to fall off," he whines, showing off the dozen bags he's carrying. He sighs in relief when he sets them on the kitchen counter and touches his skin that's turned pink from the weight of the groceries. "I'm pretty sure I spent your entire paycheck on this stuff."

"Worth it." I pull out a carton of eggs and slide them in the fridge. "This place is barren. You saw how much Max ate at dinner last night. I'm stocking up so she and Skyler can have plenty of food."

"I wanted to talk to you about that." Leo hands me a gallon of milk, and I lift an eyebrow in warning. "Calm down. I was going to say I fucking *love* her, Hunt. She's perfect, and she's so into you."

I grin. "You think so?"

"It's so obvious. She couldn't stop giggling at your stupid jokes that weren't even funny, and I swear she looked at you all night."

"Shucks." I run a hand through my hair, glad to know these feelings aren't one-sided. "She's beautiful, isn't she?"

"Hot. Goddamn gorgeous. You two are going to have adorable kids, and I can't wait to be the lonely godfather that sneaks them candy when your strict ass isn't around."

"That might be moving a little too fast." I laugh and unload a bag of carrots and some green peppers. "I'm all in, but all we do is fuck. I haven't taken her on a date."

"Maybe you should've started with a date instead of trespassing."

"Too late for that now." My phone chimes, and I tap the screen. "Lovely. The mattress delivery just arrived."

"*Mattress delivery?*" Leo almost drops a jar of salsa. "Christ on a fucking cracker. How many times have you been here? Please don't tell me you sleep in her closet."

"This is only the second time." When he glares at me, I give him an innocent shrug. "Okay, maybe it's my fifth, but it was only to make sure the cameras I set up were still working after some technical difficulties. But thanks for the closet idea. That sounds hot."

"A mattress. Unbelievable." He unloads the rest of the groceries and shakes his head. "As if she's not going to notice *that*."

"I'm sure I'll think up something to tell her." I jog to the front door, welcoming in the delivery guys and directing them to Max's bedroom. "I'm going to switch the laundry. I'll be back in a second."

By the time I make it back to her room, the old mattress is out in the hall. I help the guys position the new bed on the frame then hand over a hundred bucks to each of them to thank them for their quick delivery.

I don't want to push my luck by sticking around for too long, and Leo and I make the bed with her same sheets so the switch isn't obvious right away. I'm banking on her assuming Skyler took care of the food and her clothes, but a mattress is trickier. I don't think I'm going to be able to fool her with that one, but I'm going to try.

An hour and a fully stocked fridge later, I fold the last of Max's clothes. I set the shirt on top of the neat pile I've made in the middle of her bed and smooth my hand over the wrinkles, hoping everything looks okay. I track down a sticky note and draw a heart on it, placing it on the toe of a white sock and smiling at my handiwork.

"You should put the candle on her desk to really bring the insanity all together." Leo hands me the last of the purchases and taps the top. "Crisp leaves is the scent, and it smells like cozy fucking sweaters and apple cider."

"I like that." I give it a sniff and hum. "Perfect, Leo. Your future as an interior designer is bright."

"I'm good, aren't I?" He puts his hands on his hips and surveys her room. "What are you going to tell her when she asks if you did all of this?"

"I'm very good at playing dumb. Besides. I was with you all day at the house. It couldn't have been me."

"Now I'm being roped into this? Fine. But I get another day on Ralphie."

"Once was enough."

"Was it? It's a good thing Max gave me her phone number so I could text her and tell her about the weird guy who just *stole a pair of her underwear*. Hunter. Put it back."

"I'm not a dog." I pout and pull the lacy thong out of my pocket, mad he caught me. I was going to jerk off to that later. I drop the underwear and groan. "And you're no fun. Fine. You can have my motorcycle one more day."

"Good boy." He snorts and stands on his toes to pat my head. "Let's go. We have that staff meeting before we clock in to talk about the last fourteen days of Fright Nights and the capacity numbers we want to hit—*blah, blah, blah*. I don't need Janey ripping us a new one for being late."

"You need to live a little." I snag another book off her shelf and tuck it under my arm. "What are they going to do? Fire the best scare actors two weeks before Halloween? Please." My phone chimes, and I sneak a peek at the screen, hoping it's Max. When I don't see her name, I pout again, missing her.

"Anything important?"

"A job for next week. Serial rapist who walked free after the jury said there wasn't enough evidence to find him guilty of raping his girlfriend's four-year-old daughter." I gag and put my hand over my mouth. "He doesn't deserve a kind death."

"People are sick." Leo looks over at me as we walk down the hall. "I know not everyone would agree, but what you're doing, Hunt? Getting these pieces of shit off the street? It's heroic. Your mom would throw a *fit* if she knew this is the path you went down, but she'd come around eventually."

"Sometimes I feel like it's not enough. There are thousands of predators just like this guy walking around, and no one will ever know. They won't ever be punished for their crimes."

"But one less person is better than one more person, and that's what's important." He does a sweep of the kitchen, making sure all the food is put away. "Does Max know what you do?"

"No." I smile at the flowers Leo bought and put on the kitchen table. "I'd like to hope she won't care when she finds out."

"Probably shouldn't keep it a secret for too long, dude. That's kind of first date level information. Might be too late to share that you're a murderer."

"Or maybe it's the perfect time." I grab my tool bag and smile. "Ready to roll?"

"Let's go before you do something even crazier like hide an engagement ring in her teacup."

"That is *brilliant*. When the time comes, I'll make sure to give you credit."

"Jesus." He sighs. "You're something else."

"And you're still sticking around." I shut the front door behind us and lock it with the copy of the key I made. "I can't be too terrible."

"You're not, which is really fucking obnoxious."

We say a quick goodbye, and I look up and down Max's street, searching for anything of the ordinary. I smile, knowing she's in good hands.

I've got you, angel.

SOMEONE HAS BEEN in my house.

I can tell the second I walk through the front door something is wrong.

I freeze and scan the living room, trying to pinpoint what's out of place and—*there*.

The rug that leads to the kitchen is uneven. Up ahead, the bedroom door I shut before I left for school is halfway open.

What the fuck?

"Hello?" I reach for the small pepper spray attached to my keychain. Closing the front door behind me, I grab a book sitting on the foyer table. I refuse to be the idiot in the horror movies who doesn't protect herself, but there's no answer as I tiptoe down the hallway. "Sky?"

The kitchen is empty, but there's a glass of water next to the sink and a vase of gorgeous sunflowers on the table. I walk toward them, checking for a note but not finding one.

Nothing is missing or out of place in here. The knives are all in their wooden block, and the pots and pans are where they belong. The back door is locked. There's no blood, no mess that shows any sign of forced entry, and I blow out an exhausted breath.

It's been a long week at school. Fatigue is setting in, and everything could be explained if I took a second to think clearly. Skyler probably went in my room to borrow something and didn't close the door behind her.

No big deal.

The rug is messed up because she was in a hurry to get to work, and I set the book on the counter, reassured.

All is well, I tell myself as I open the fridge to grab a bottle of water.

Except...

The shelves are lined with food. There's chicken and vegetables and a whole watermelon. Ears of corn and a fresh jar of jam. There are even apples and carrots, and I'm fucking baffled.

Skyler knows I hate carrots after almost choking on one in high school. I whip my phone out to fire off a text to her.

ME

> Hey. Weird question. Did you buy a ton of groceries? If so, let me know how much I owe you!

The message that comes through seconds later makes my heart sink to my toes.

SKYLER

> I haven't been home since early this morning. Wasn't me. Did your mom stop by? Sounds like something she would do!

It *does* sound like something she would do, but she's out of town on a girls' trip with her college roommate. It's not possible she swung by while I was at work when she's in San Diego, which means someone else has been here. Dread settles in my stomach, and I take a deep breath.

ME

I didn't even think to ask her, but you're right. She totally would do that. When you get home, there's tons to eat.

I swipe out of my conversation with Skyler and dial 911. Calling the police is the smart thing to do. They could come and dust for fingerprints or review security footage from my neighbor's doorbell cameras. It would establish a paper trail. The complaint I'm filing now would be documented in case this turns into a problem bigger than odd grocery shopping.

A noise from down the hall steals my attention.

I hold my pepper spray in front of me, heading for my room. It's empty in here too, but there, in the center of my bed, is all my laundry that's been piling up.

Folded.

Neatly stacked.

Arranged by category.

And a small sticky note attached to one of my socks.

I rush forward and rip it away from the fabric, gaping at the small heart doodled on the paper.

This is all too bizarre. Deeply unsettling, and I hate that I'm here by myself.

Hunter will know what to do, my mind screams. I fumble with my phone, begging the universe to let him pick up. When the call connects after two rings, I almost collapse with relief.

"Max," he answers. "Hi, angel. This is a nice surprise."

"Hi." I put a hand on my chest, telling myself to calm down. My heart is racing. My lungs feel like they are going to explode at any second. I check to make sure my window is locked, and everything is securely bolted. "Do you have a minute?"

"For you, I have all the minutes in the world. What's up?"

"I just got home from work and found my fridge, which was empty when I left the house this morning, full of food. Skyler didn't stock it. I didn't stock it. Who the hell did?" I bend down and check under my bed, grateful when all I find is a dusty sock and not an intruder. "My laundry is also folded." I swallow and rub my forehead. "I-I know how this sounds, but I think someone has been in my house."

"Is anything stolen? Are you in danger?"

"I'm fine. Totally fine. And I haven't done a deep dive to see what might've been taken, but it looks like they only —" I sputter out a laugh. "Whoever was here, it's clear they wanted to help me. Food? Laundry? Flowers? It's really fucking weird."

"Is it possible Skyler did your laundry for you?" Hunter asks, and I pace around my room. "She probably had to wash clothes for work. Your stuff might've gotten thrown in too."

"Yeah." I nod. "I guess that could be right. She's done that in the past."

"I do Leo's laundry when I'm feeling nice, and his sweaty work socks are *revolting*." There's a muffled string of curses on the other end of the line, and I giggle when I hear Leo arguing. "I'm sure your shirts are much more pleasant."

"That explains the clothes, but what about the fridge?"

"You said Skyler and Dustin are hanging out, right? Has he been to your place? He might've been the one to do it. Men are weak, remember? I bet Skyler mentioned she was hungry, and he decided to buy one of everything at the grocery store to feed her."

"He was here the other day. Maybe he stopped by this morning."

"Or last night when you were at my place. See? A totally logical explanation."

"Thank you for listening. For a second there, it felt like I was losing my mind."

"I'm happy to help," he says.

"Now I can actually relax instead of calling the police." I smile and sit on the edge of my bed. "Is Fright Nights going to be busy tonight?"

"Yup. The event is at capacity. We'll have a three hour wait for our house, which means I won't get out of here until close to four in the morning." Hunter sighs. "Miss you, gorgeous. Wish I was with you instead."

"Me too." I lean back on my pillows and frown. "What the hell?"

"What?" There's urgency in his voice. "Are you okay?"

"I'm fine. It's just—my bed." I bounce up and down. The mattress is more cushioned than I remember it being. It sinks under my weight, almost like it's molding itself to my body. "Okay. I'm officially losing it. This doesn't feel like my bed. Like, I know it's my bed. It's in my room. But it's way too comfortable."

"You've had a long week, angel."

"It's Wednesday, Hunter."

"Exactly. You're tired. You've had a lot going on, so your mattress probably feels nicer than usual. Why don't you take a bath and relax the rest of the night? Better yet, I'll order you a pizza. No cooking required."

"Does Dominos come with wine?" I reach for the sticky note again, looking for a clue about who it might be from. "Because I could use a whole bottle."

"Probably not, but I'll see what strings I can pull. Red or white, angel?"

"White. *God*. I don't know who the hell could've done all of this. Unless…" I trail off and giggle. "Did *you* break into my house, Hunter?"

"Sorry, good lookin'. I've been with Leo all day. You should hear the sounds he makes when he's at the gym."

I bite my lip, almost wishing it *had* been Hunter who did all of this. It would help me sleep better tonight knowing he was trying to be a nice guy, but there's no way I'm going to be settled until Skyler gets home. Being alone is the last thing I want.

"What would you suggest as a good tool for self-defense?" I ask. "I don't want a gun. The loud noise would scare the shit out of me."

"How about an ax? Or a knife."

"An ax sounds like a good idea. I'm sorry to bother you before work with all of this. I might need a vacation."

"You're never a bother, Max. And if you want to take a vacation, the second Fright Nights ends, I'll whisk you away."

"Where would we go?"

"Anywhere you want."

I smile. "Thank you for listening to me."

"You'll let me know if you notice anything else that makes you uncomfortable?"

"I will. Do I get to see you in hero mode?"

"You don't want to see me in hero mode. I'd burn the city down for you."

A blush creeps up my cheeks. "Have fun at work, Hunter."

"I'll be thinking of you the entire time."

We hang up, and I pull up a search for the best axes to use for self-defense. The options are overwhelming, and I fire off a text to Hunter asking him to pick one for me. He answers immediately with a tracking number, telling me a package will be here the day after tomorrow.

Thirty minutes later, the doorbell rings. I carry my pepper spray with me as I check the peephole, laughing when I see it's a pizza delivery with a bottle of chardonnay.

When I settle into my bathtub with two slices of pepperoni on a plate and a generous pour of wine, I decide I need to relax more. After a thorough search of my house that shows no one is hiding in a closet waiting to attack me, I climb into bed and sleep soundly through the night, convinced I'm overreacting.

NINETEEN
HUNTER

AM I a dick for gaslighting Max into thinking no one broke into her house?

Completely, but it was for selfish reasons.

I like seeing her on the camera, and letting it slip that I was there after denying it originally would probably take away my access to her.

And I don't want *that*.

I'm having too much fun watching her fall asleep and walk around her room in a towel after her shower. It's all so thrilling, and I need to be very fucking careful.

It's easy to see why people get addicted to this lifestyle, and I'm glad it's *me* observing her. Anyone else would've done something unhinged by now, but I'm not that guy.

I'm only hiding in her closet so I can check on her.

There's a difference.

I stretch out my legs and drop my elbow on a pile of sweaters, waiting for Max to get home. She's at dinner with a teacher friend from school, but her last text to me mentioned she was finishing up. She should be heading this way soon, and I fucking miss her.

My phone lights up with a notification from the camera app, telling me there's movement at the front door. I tap over to the feed and see Max's Uber pulling into the driveway. She hops out of the car in a jean skirt and a sweater that hangs off her shoulders. Her hair is down, and I smile when she skips to the porch and unlocks the door.

She appears in her room a few seconds later, tying her hair up in a high ponytail. She sits on her bed and pulls out her phone, holding back a smile as she types something on the screen.

My own phone buzzes a second later with a text from her. I wait before reading it, adjusting my position so I can keep an eye on her through the closet door that's slightly open.

MAX THE ANGEL

I'm home! Hope you're having a good night.

ME

I'm on break right now. How was dinner, baby?

MAX THE ANGEL

Delicious. I might've had a touch too much to drink.

ME

Uh oh. Is my girl drunk?

MAX THE ANGEL

Tipsy. And horny.

I crane my neck to look at her. She unbuttons her skirt and shimmies out of the denim, tossing it to the side. I bite my knuckles to keep from groaning when she peels off her shirt next, leaving her in a pretty red bra and lacy underwear.

Fuck.

This is so much better than watching her on the app. I type out a response to her with one hand, using the other to quietly unzip my jeans and pop open the button at the top of my pants.

ME

> Wish I was there to take care of you, angel.

MAX THE ANGEL

> So do I. Should I record a video touching myself and send it to you?

ME

> Imagine me on my knees in front of you begging. Please, please, please.

Max giggles and stands. She pulls back the curtains and relaxes on the bed, her head propped up on the pillows.

MAX THE ANGEL

> I'm going to pretend you're watching me from outside my window. It's dark, and my light is on, so I wouldn't be able to see you. But I'd know you were there.

ME

> You want to put on a show, don't you? You want to be on display.

She unclasps her bra and lets her tits spill free. Her underwear comes off next, leaving her gloriously naked, and my mouth pops open. She grabs three books off her nightstand, setting them at the foot of the bed and propping her phone against them. She starts recording, and I can't help but inch toward the door so I can have a better view.

"I've never made a video for someone before." Max rests a hand on her breast and rubs it across her chest. She sighs, thighs parting as she pinches her nipple between her thumb and forefinger. "I hope I do this right."

It's going to be the best thing I've ever seen I want to shout. I almost crawl out of the closet and take the spot on the mattress next to her so I can reassure her as her low moans fill the room. Her free hand snakes up to her throat, touching her neck and applying pressure against her windpipe.

"I like when you do this to me. I know you're not going to hurt me, but I like it when you're rough. The hint of danger is fun."

I adjust my briefs so my cock is free, slowly stroking myself. I want her in so many ways, and it's hard to be patient. I want to yank her by her ankles and shove her legs apart. I want to leave bruises on her ass so it hurts to sit down. She trails her hand down her body, teasing across her stomach with a smile that's sharp and cunning.

"When I'm with you, I like how fast you get me off. But when I'm by myself, I like to take my time."

Her palm dips between her legs, and I bite my collar to keep from groaning when she slides two fingers inside herself. Her back arches off the bed as she plays with her clit, and I study the circles she's using. She does like to draw it out as long as possible, teasing herself, and I'm going to try that the next time we're together.

Max is quiet, finding the rhythm she likes, but a moan tumbles out of her. I wonder if anyone driving past is slowing down so they can see her.

I would.

She's fucking *begging* for someone to watch her and give her attention.

I could stare at her for hours, especially when she

pinches her nipples again and fumbles with the drawer on her nightstand. She pauses to pull out a pink vibrator, and my cock practically leaks with pre-cum.

I bought a couple things to use on her: a butt plug so I can start getting her ass ready for my cock and another that I can control, setting the toy to different speeds and stopping when she gets too close to coming.

But she doesn't need me. She's gorgeous by herself, holding the vibrator on her clit and changing the speed so it pulses against her.

"I like sex, but I think I like this more," she says, gasping when a jolt of pleasure hits her. "It feels so fucking good, Hunter."

Her moan fills the room, and I swear to fucking god she says my name again before she pushes the toy inside her cunt. She's filling herself, spreading her legs open so I get the perfect view of her stuffed pussy.

It's a wonder she can't hear the noise I make, and I think this is how I die: watching her touch herself and knowing I'm going to relive it all over again when she sends me the video.

I'm a lucky fucking bastard.

"I'm already so close. It's probably because I'm thinking about you." Her laugh is soft, easy, and she hums when she increases the speed of the toy. "This is so silly, but I used to think all those multiple orgasms were bullshit. How could it be possible for something to feel so good so many times in a row?" Her eyes lift, and she looks at the camera straight on as she buries the toy all the way inside her. "But it's that good with you. Which means I'm sure your ego is fully inflated by now."

I jerk my cock up and down. I'm going to make a mess on myself when I come like I haven't done in goddamn years, but I can't bring myself to care. My shirt is a willing sacrifice when she lifts her hips and cradles the base of the toy, fucking herself.

"Christ," I whisper, my shaft thickening in my hand.

Max pauses. Her eyes dart around the room, studying the closet for the briefest of seconds. I bite my lip so hard, I taste blood on my tongue, and I haven't dared to breathe.

"Now I'm really losing my mind." She smiles and rubs her clit, knees bending and hips lifting so she can reach a new, deeper angle. "You're not here, but I'm hearing things that sound like you. Maybe I'm tipsier than I thought."

I keep the stroke of my hand quick, matching her pace. Hard, fast, she doesn't relent, squirming on the sheets until she groans, loud and long.

"*Fuck*," she lets out, touching herself through her orgasm. My balls tighten. Sweat forms at my hairline. I'd give all the money I have to lick her clean, and when she pulls the toy out of her pussy and runs her tongue along the length of the silicone, I splinter into a thousand pieces.

Warm cum covers my fingers and my shirt, my hips convulsing as she deep throats the vibrator. She keeps her eyes on the camera as she does, an innocent look behind her gaze while her lips suck her arousal off the toy.

Holding back a yell is the hardest thing I've ever done, and I collapse into a pile of jeans when she pops the vibrator out of her mouth and giggles.

"That was fun." Max touches her cheek, a smudge of her lipstick right in the corner of her mouth. She rolls onto her stomach and cradles her chin in her palm, smiling at her phone. "I hope you like that. If you do, will you send me a video back? I'm sure I sound silly, but I like knowing you're excited by what I share with you."

Baby, I'll live stream it so everyone can see what you do to me.

"I'm going to shower. I hope work goes well. Don't let

anyone else watch this." She gives the camera a stern look and follows it up with a kiss. "Talk to you later, Hunter."

Max sighs, ending the recording. She swings her legs off the bed and saunters to the bathroom, showing off the beautiful curves of her ass. With one last look over her shoulder, she closes the door behind her, and I finally let myself relax.

"Fucking angel." I groan and grab a rogue pair of black tights I find underneath a basket. I use them to wipe off my hand and tuck them in my pocket, vowing to buy her a new pair.

The water turns on in the bathroom. Max yanks the shower curtain open, and I know now is my chance to escape without being seen.

Standing on shaky, post orgasm legs is really fucking difficult, but I tuck my dick back in my pants. I zip up my jeans and slide out of the closet and into her room. I see the sticky notes on her desk and pull one off the top, scribbling out a quick note for her to find.

Thanks for the great show.

With another heart under it.

Feeling ballsy, and like I'm testing my luck, I pick up her discarded vibrator. I lick it and moan, my cock twitching at the taste of her cum. She's so fucking sweet, and I want to take it home with me. That would be too obvious. A dead giveaway and playing with fire, so I set it back on her comforter with my love note attached to it.

I press my ear against the bathroom door, smiling at Max singing a song badly out of key. I kiss the barrier that separates us and sneak out the front door just as the water shuts off and her bedroom door opens.

The walk to my motorcycle parked up the street and around the corner is torture. The last thing I want to do is leave her, but the text that comes through with a video attached makes me grin.

MAX THE ANGEL

For you. xoxo

Attachment: 1 video

Soon, I tell myself.

I'll let her know about my voyeurism soon.

Until then, I'm going to watch this video on repeat and miss her every second we're apart.

TWENTY
MAX

"OKAY. ONE MORE TIME." Skyler crosses her legs on my bed. "You recorded a video, got in the shower, and when you came out, this was here?" She gestures to the note she's holding, and I nod. "Which implies someone saw you recording said video."

"Yeah." I pull the blanket draped around my shoulders tight to my chest. I've called in sick to work the last two days, too freaked out to leave the house out of fear someone will break in while I'm gone. Or follow me into a dark alley and hurt me. "They were hiding in the house without my knowledge, and I want to throw up."

"Have you thought about going to the police?" Skyler reaches for my hand. "This goes well outside the scope of the true crime podcasts I listen to."

"I'm afraid they're going to say it's all in my head. That I'm being dramatic."

"There is literal *proof* that someone invaded your privacy, Max."

"Yeah, but I can see exactly how that conversation is going to go. They'll say it's someone making a joke. They'll justify it as the note being there for days. Look at the number of rape or assault reports that never result in charges. People love to silence women and call us crazy, and frankly, I'm starting to feel like I've lost my fucking mind."

"You haven't lost your mind. I believe you. Between the fridge being stocked, your clothes being folded, and a *note* left for you? Someone else has been here."

"I just wish I knew who." I look out the window. My stomach rolls, wondering if whoever is watching me is out there right now. "I don't think it's Brian. He was never good at being sneaky. I literally caught him sexting someone else while he was next to me, and he doesn't have a key. Are you sure it wasn't Dustin?"

"Nope. The only time he's been over, I was here with him. For as good looking as he is, I don't think he's smart enough to know how to break into someone's house. And that doesn't explain the note."

"I'm missing a clue that would pull all of this together, and I can't figure out what it is."

"I wish I could stay and help you, Max, but I need to leave for work. Do you want to come with me? You could hang out at one of the restaurants until I get off work and we can drive home together."

"No. I'm determined to get to the bottom of this." I point to the ax that's within reach of my bed. "I can protect myself, and when I find out who is responsible, I'm going to make them pay."

"Will you text me so I know you're okay?"

"I will. Call me when you're coming home so I don't throw a weapon at your head."

"God. That wouldn't be fun." Skyler gives me a hug and sighs. "Because I know you're okay, I'm going to say this next thing and hope you won't get mad at me."

"What's that?"

"For as creepy as this whole situation is, at least they aren't hurting you. They've been in the same house as you. They had the opportunity to harm you. Going the grocery and laundry route is… well it's not *cute*, but it's kind of sweet, isn't it?"

"This is Stockholm Syndrome," I deadpan. "And I'm not falling for it."

"Just an observation. You don't need to be in love with them!" She pinches my cheek and climbs off my bed. "I'm serious, Max. Keep me updated."

"I'm going to deadbolt the door once you leave. Maybe I'll put a chair under the handle too." I stand and let the blanket fall away from my body. "This fucker is going to have to jump through hoops if they want to keep messing with me."

"That's my girl." Skyler grins, and I follow her down the hall. I check behind every corner and grab the biggest knife from the wooden block in the kitchen. "I love you, Max. We're going to figure this out. And when we do, I promise I'll testify in your favor in court."

That makes me laugh, and I hug her. "I love you too, Sky. Break a leg tonight."

"Call me if you need *anything*. We have alternates ready to fill in if I need to leave early."

I lean against the door frame, watching her get in her car. When she pulls out of the driveway, I sigh and close the door, checking that it's locked.

A thorough walk through the house doesn't turn up anything out of the ordinary. When I get back to my room, I stop short.

There's a flower on my bed with another note attached to it.

That wasn't there three minutes ago.

I grip the knife tightly and reach for the note, a choked gasp leaving me when I see what's written there for me.

I'm sorry for scaring you.
I thought you'd figure it out by now.
Let me know when you want me to come out and play.
Forgive me?

There are angel wings around the word *now*. At the bottom is another heart, this time with an arrow through it.

My blood runs cold.

I grip the wall to keep myself from falling over, and my eyes prick with tears.

Hunter.

Of course it's him.

It's been in front of me this whole time.

I *knew* things with him were too good to be true.

He broke into my house, went through my stuff, *watched me* without permission, and I'm not calling the police because… *why?*

Something is fucking wrong with me.

I'm so furious. The second I see him, I might strangle him. Or carve out a piece of his flesh and roast it over a fucking fire so he can feel violated like I've felt violated.

I dial 911, my fingers hesitating over my screen before I complete the call. Hunter's name pops up, a text message coming through, and I drop the knife on my bed as fury rips through me.

HUNTER

Do you really want to get the police
involved?

ME

What the FUCK is wrong with you? How did
you get into my house?

HUNTER

Magic :)

ME

Are you following me?

HUNTER

Define following.

ME

Watching me when I can't see you?

HUNTER

Maaaaybe.

By the way, that dress looks beautiful on
you, angel.

I turn my attention to the bathroom. I pick the knife
back up and wrap my hand around the knob of the half
ajar door, shoving it fully open. I pull back the shower
curtain and lower the hand holding the knife, stabbing
the air.

"Got you, asshole," I seethe, but the bathtub is empty.

My phone buzzes with another text, and my chest
heaves with adrenaline.

HUNTER

The shower? Really? Way too obvious. I
have to make you work for it.

ME

I'm going to kill you. This behavior is so inappropriate.

HUNTER

Is that why your nipples are so hard right now?

"Motherfucker." I look down and cross my arms over my chest. "I'm not kidding. I will murder you and make it look like an accident. Everyone will believe me, and you'll rot in hell."

HUNTER

You don't want to hurt me. And I'd never want to hurt you.

I stalk out of my room and slam the door. I run to the kitchen and grab a dining chair, lodging it under the knob so wherever he's hiding, he can't escape. His name pops up as a FaceTime call and I answer, grinning because I know I've caught him.

"Sorry. You're going to be stuck in my room for a while." I hold up my middle finger. "But I'm not going to let you out until the police get here. It's what you deserve. What is *wrong* with you?"

"Let me out?" he asks, and I frown at the image on my screen. He's leaning against the exterior of a building, a leg kicked up behind him. The motorcycle helmet he's wearing hides his face, and my pulse jumps. "I'm not in your house, Max."

"You're not?"

"I was in your house. But I'm not anymore."

"It was you who did my laundry?" I whisper.

"Yes."

"And filled the fridge with food?"

"Mhm. Can't forget the new mattress I bought you."

"You…" I swallow and rub my forehead, anxiety clawing at the base of my spine. "You watched me get off. How *dare* you? I didn't consent to that, you fucking pervert."

"Didn't you?" He tips his head to the side. "You opened your curtains. You mentioned wanting me to watch you touch yourself. Guess what? I did."

I don't know if I want to scream or laugh. I don't know if his actions are predatory or sweet. My head hurts from trying to justify what he's done, but my body is hot from his words, the truth slipping out.

"I need to go," I say, and the disappointment in my voice surprises me. I should be ending this call and getting on the phone with law enforcement. Replacing my locks then finding a new place to live.

Hunter tries to say something else, but I hang up before he has the chance to defend himself.

I don't know why him not being here upsets me. Maybe it's because this is too much information all at once, a rush of realizations I wish I didn't learn. Maybe it's because deep down, I'm sick and twisted, someone who loves that he went out of his way to make sure I had food and took care of the chores that were piling up.

Maybe it's because I secretly like being watched without knowing. The dark and burning desire to have him push past my line of consent is intoxicating. It tells me who he really is, someone not quite as nice as the surface suggests, and I wonder what else he is capable of.

I exhale and make my way to the kitchen, needing a stiff drink. Sliding the knife back in its holder, I grip the counter, not surprised by the soft knock on the back door. The lock turns. The knob twists open. Heavy footsteps make their way down the hall, and when I glance over my shoulder, Hunter is there.

My mouth waters at the sight of him. The all-black outfit he's wearing is sexy, the dark riding pants clinging to his thighs like a second skin. The tank top does nothing to protect his arms but shows off his tattoos, a beautiful display of art and color.

"Max." He walks toward me, and my breathing hitches. "What's wrong?"

"Besides the fucking obvious? You *broke* into my *house*. I've known you for six seconds and you think you can act like that?"

"What else is wrong?" Hunter touches my cheek, his gloved hand offering me a soft caress. "You're upset."

"Can you blame me?"

"No." He hums and walks toward the living room, motioning for me to follow. I can't bring myself to hate him when he sits in the leather chair across from the couch and flips his visor up so his eyes meet mine. "Talk to me, angel."

"Is breaking into women's houses and folding their laundry a hobby of yours? How many cameras do you have set up in people's bedrooms, since I'm assuming that's how you've been keeping tabs on me?" I gulp down the bite of disgust. "I'd like to have a ballpark idea so I know what days I can expect your housekeeping services before you run off to someone else."

Hunter's lips twitch. "Maxine."

"Don't Maxine me," I snap, and there's a twinkle in his eye. "We hooked up. Big deal. Please tell me how many other people you're stalking so I know where I fall on the list."

"Come here," he says, taking off his helmet. It's low, commanding, liquid heat that slithers down my spine.

"Please," he adds, softer at the edges, and my shoulders sag.

My feet move of their own accord, crossing the room to him. He pats his lap, legs spread and arms open to make room for me. I hesitate, knowing the second I do this, the second I give in, I can't hold a grudge. It's acceptance. Agreement I'm okay with this behavior.

Hunter waits patiently.

He doesn't push or pry. He blinks up at me, an apology written across his face, and it nearly breaks me in two. I sit on his thighs, relaxing when he pulls me against his chest and runs his fingers down the shape of my jaw.

"I'm mad at you," I whisper. "Very mad at you."

"Is this our first fight, angel?"

"I'm close to throwing a book at your head."

"Make it a hardcover. I deserve to be punished."

"So?" I huff and lift my chin. "How many?"

"None."

"What do you mean, none?"

"You wanted to know how much laundry I fold. How many other cameras I have set up in bedrooms. The answer is none. I'm not sleeping with anyone else. I'm not following anyone else. I'm a loyal man, baby. When I'm attached to someone, I'm theirs. And it's pretty fucking obvious I'm obsessed with you."

I draw in a breath and touch his chest. His heart is beating fast, and I reach up and grab his necklace, giving it a tug. "Why the cameras?"

"Your ex," he says, and I rear back.

"*Brian?* Please don't tell me this is some dick measuring contest."

"No. I was worried about you after you mentioned he was hanging around. I installed one to your front door, one to your back door, and one in your room." Hunter rests his forehead against mine. "And I went overboard with watching you. It was supposed to be one time where I took care of some of your chores and left, but I've been back multiple times. I can't stay away."

"How many?" I demand.

"Six, I think? I watched you get off from your closet the other night."

"I *knew* there was someone there." I shove his chest, and he wraps his fingers around my wrist. "Apologize."

"I'm sorry." He kisses my nose, then my cheek. "I'm sorry, angel. You're under my skin, and I can't stop. No more stalking. If I'm there, you'll know I'm there."

"I should make you sleep outside."

"I'd do it willingly. But only after I give you the one hundred boxes of Earl Grey tea bags I bought for you."

"What are you talking about?"

"I know it's your favorite, and I drove around to every store in town finding the best brands. I also had some shipped in from England. You have a cup every night, and this was part of my apology plan." Hunter's hands roam up my back. "I'm sorry for scaring you and making you feel crazy. I'm pathetic when it comes to you," he murmurs.

"I'm so mad at you, but I'm also mad at you for making it hard to be mad at you." I grab a fistful of his shirt, bringing his mouth close to mine. "No more secrets. No more spying. Do you understand?"

There's a flash of reluctance that flints in his eyes, but he blinks it away. Gives me a wide grin and kisses me like the world is going to end tomorrow.

"I promise, angel," he says. "No more secrets."

TWENTY-ONE
HUNTER

I WAS twenty-five the first time I killed someone, and I threw up for days after.

I was never violent growing up. My mom called me a sensitive soul, a kid with big feelings who latched onto things he loved fiercely and didn't let go. *Hyperfixation,* my therapist told her. *But there's no cause for concern unless it progresses to erratic behavior.*

I wonder if pulling a knife from Darren Blimka's neck and staring down at the rapist bleeding out on the asphalt of a deserted parking lot would be classified as erratic behavior. I should probably give her a call and set up an appointment.

I give the fucker's shoulder a nudge with my boot. He twitches, covering his face.

Still alive, I guess. I sigh, knowing I'm going to be here longer than I want.

"I didn't mean to do it," he sobs. "My brain isn't right. I didn't see her as a child."

"She's *four.*" I squat, holding the knife in front of him. A drop of his own blood falls onto his nose, and he wails.

"When I chop your dick off and feed it to the alligators in the lake across the way, it's because my brain isn't right either."

"Please. Please. I'll do anything. Anything you want."

"Really?" I flip the knife and grin, catching it by the handle with ease. "Tell ya what. If you chop off your own dick, I promise I'll get you medical assistance. That wound on your neck won't kill you. Not yet."

"Y-you want me to…" His eyes widen and he starts to convulse. "No. No. I can't. I—"

"Punishment fits the crime, don't you think? You had no problem tormenting a child. It's only fair you're tormented too."

"It will never happen again. I swear. Please. I-I'll go back to the judge and ask them for a life sentence. I'll never touch another person. I've changed. You have to see that."

"The only thing I see is a coward too afraid to face the consequences of his actions." I don't listen to his whimper when I touch the knife to his cheek. "And someone who is going to make me late for my dinner plans because they won't shut the fuck up. Last chance, Blimka. If you want to live, you'll do what you have to do."

His eyes move from me to the knife. A drop of blood rolls down his neck, and his lip quivers.

Men always look so pathetic right before they die.

With a gasping breath, he snatches the weapon out of my hold. I expect him to try to stab me—that's what these assholes usually try and do—but he slowly brings his hand to his jeans and unzips the fly. He sniffs as he pulls out his small, unimpressive dick, another sob overtaking him.

There's a moment of hesitation, as if he thinks I'm going to laugh and say this is all a joke. A big prank to see how far he'd go to attempt to rid himself of his sins, but when I fold my arms over my chest, patience wearing thin, he brings the blade to his genitalia and starts to slice.

The scream he lets out isn't human. I grin as blood starts to spurt from the incision, each laceration bringing another shriek that's music to my ears. Darren's face goes chalk white, shock from the loss of blood setting in while the copper smell of torture and pain tickles my nose.

Watching his suffering brings me peace. I stand and step back, not an ounce of remorse in my veins as he reaches for me, begging with his last breaths to be helped, assistance I refuse to grant.

When he's on the cusp of mortality, toeing the fine line where lucidity starts to fade away and the body shuts down, I wrangle the knife out of his hand. I clean the blade with the hem of my shirt, scowling at the mess he made on the handle.

Lack of respect for other people's things always pisses me off.

"I'm going to tell you a secret, Darren," I whisper, crouching low so I'm the last thing he sees before his heart stops beating. "I was very mad at you for what you did before, but taking your sweet ass time to die after we both know your fate was inevitable means it's going to take longer to get to my girl than I wanted it to. Because of that —and because you're the foulest, ugliest, most disgusting specimen I've had the horror of being around—I think I should leave you with a parting gift. It's the least I can do."

Blimka's pupils dilate. He's less alert, the lack of recognition of his surroundings causing a blank, unfocused stare. I grab his wrist and the hand holding his penis, directing it to his face. I pry apart his jaw and shove the bloody, severed extremity to his mouth, wedging it between his lips.

"There." I pat his cheek and take my knife, stabbing his stomach. The lack of reaction to the blade sinking into his body tells me everything I need to know, and I turn the knife clockwise as his chest lifts one time, a final breath exhaled before he goes completely still. "Now everyone in hell will know how to welcome you when you arrive. I hope your soul stays stuck in purgatory until the end of time."

I wait, counting to two hundred before I carve the knife out of his flesh and stand, satisfied with another job done.

No one will miss this man. No one is going to come looking for him, but if they do, they won't tell anyone what they find. Disposing his body will be easy and so will the cleanup. The murky waters of a Florida pond on the other side of a low trafficked road is the perfect dumping ground for the evidence law enforcement won't care to search for.

I don't *like* killing people. Is there a rush when you stab someone who deserves to feel insurmountable pain? Fuck, yeah. Is it fun to watch a predator plead for mercy when they had none of their own to give to their victims? Undoubtedly. But I hate that any of this exists in the first place. I hate that there are humans out there who are so cruel, extreme measures must be taken to prevent them from ever hurting someone again. For as fucking cliché as it is, if it were up to me, my one wish would be world peace. A timeline where no one suffered, where everyone could exist without worry of feeling safe and protected.

I won't be able to get rid of every terrible shitbag like Darren Blimka, but tonight, the world can go to sleep knowing one less demon walks among them.

Stretching my back, I zip my jacket up to my neck. I slide my arms under Blimka's body, groaning at his heavy weight. I sway on my feet, grinding my teeth together as I cross the road and heave his body into the alligator-infested water.

A quick pour of bleach and scrub of the stained

asphalt later, I'm climbing in my car. I fire off a quick text to my boss to let him know the job is complete and he wires me the other half of my payment, a smirk pulling at the corners of my mouth when I think about what gift I'm going to buy Max with the large deposit.

There's a message from her waiting in my inbox, and I grin when I read her text.

MAX THE ANGEL

See you tonight. I'll bring over dinner!

ME

Can't wait, angel. Missed your adorable face.

The drive home is quick, and I wave to Leo sitting in the kitchen.

"Thought you might have had someone fight back a little too aggressively," he says, holding a glass of wine. He lifts the bottle my way, and I shake my head. "That one took you longer than usual."

"He needed some extra attention." I wash my hands, watching Blimka's blood disappear down the drain. "What are you doing tonight?"

"Some people from work are going to the bar." Leo yawns and jumps off his barstool. "I'd invite you to come, but I know you're busy with someone more important than me."

"So much more important than you. Call me if you need a DD?"

"Aye, aye, captain."

"And let Max in when she gets here? I'm going to rinse off."

"I live to serve you." He bows, and I throw the dish towel at his head, hustling down the hall.

I don't like running late for things. When my mom was alive, she was a ten-minutes-early kind of woman. I hated it as a kid, the first in the parking lot for sports and school, but the older I've gotten, the more I've appreciated her dedication to punctuality. Time is precious, especially when you spend it with people you care about, and I'm pissed Blimka put me behind schedule.

In my room, I play music from my phone, bopping along to an artist Max sent me to listen to. She's some pop star I haven't heard of before, but her music is good. A fun beat, and I'm too busy dancing and taking my knife from its holster to hear my door open behind me.

"Hi," Max sings out, and I spin, smiling at her. She freezes in the threshold of my bedroom, gaze darting to the weapon in my hand. Her eyes widen at the blood on the tip and she steps forward, grabs a paperback off my nightstand—one of hers, she'd be happy to know—and holds it above her head. "Why the fuck are you holding your knife? And why is it covered in blood?" She inhales sharply, dropping the bag of food she's holding. "Who the fuck are you, Hunter?"

"This thing? Whoops. Calm down, angel. I'm—"

The book hits me square in the forehead. I grin at her perfect shot.

"Do *not* tell me to calm down. I validated you breaking into my home. *Repeatedly.* I validated you watching me from cameras you installed. But a bloody knife? You're a psychopath."

"That's a little offensive. I'm in full control of my emotions and behavior. I'm well aware of what I'm doing. In fact, I'm making a conscious decision to do so."

"Then why the hell are you holding a knife covered in blood?" she almost screams, and I bite back a laugh.

She's so fucking adorable when she gets fired up about something.

"I haven't been totally honest with you."

I hold up my hands in surrender, then put the knife on my desk. Realizing it's going to make a mess, I strip off my jacket and shirt. I wrap the stained white cotton around the dirty blade, carefully setting it next to my laptop. When I face her, I don't miss the way her gaze roams down my body. How she admires my tattoos and muscles with lust.

"You think? Start talking," she demands.

"Hey. My eyes are up here, sweetheart."

Max scowls and throws another book my way. This one hits my shoulder, and I rub the small red mark it leaves behind.

"Hunter."

"Being a scare actor isn't the only job I have. I also dabble in extracurricular activities," I start with, watching her eyebrows wrinkle. "I have a friend who runs an underground organization. He's a former cop who hates how corrupt the force became, and he took matters into his own hands. He started getting rid of the horrible people who freely walked the streets after law enforcement didn't care about their crimes."

"Were *you* a cop?" she asks, another book poised and ready to toss my way.

"Fuck, no. Do I look like I'd be a cop?"

"I don't know anything about you! Is this the fucking *mob*? Am I going to be followed for sleeping with you?"

"I'm flattered you think I'm special." I flash her another smile and she flips me off. "I wasn't sure I was even going to join this group, but I started the process with them in case it all panned out. I took a weapons handling class. Learned how to use a knife, an ax, and a gun. Then I discovered all the ways I could kill a man—a very, very, bad man—with a towel, and I was hooked. I took out my first rapist six years ago, and I've done plenty more since."

"Hang on." Max slowly lowers the book. The color drains from her face, and her chest rises and falls. "You're… you're a serial killer?"

"That's offensive, Max."

She digs her phone out of her pocket, types something on the screen, then tosses it my way. I catch it midair, reading what she looked up on the internet and chuckling.

"*How to tell if the guy you're seeing is a serial killer?* Aw." I put a hand on my bare chest. "How sweet."

"Keep reading."

"Okay." I nod, because I'll do anything she asks. "I guess since the dictionary defines a serial killer as someone who's killed three or more people in a month, I technically am. But I'm a good serial killer. I promise."

"There are *good* serial killers?" she shouts, raising another book to throw at my head. It's alarming how much her feistiness turns me on.

"Of course there are, Max. We have tiers, sweetheart. The good ones get rid of the bad guys on the streets: murderers who have walked free after making a deal with someone in power. Rapists. Abusers. The bad ones kill without any reason because they like the thrill of it. They're vile and deserve to go straight to hell."

Max stares at me. Her eyes flick to the knife, then back to me. "How do I know I can trust you? How do I know you're not going to hurt me? We said no more secrets, and here you fucking are telling me you're a goddamn murderer."

"You *don't* know I'm not going to hurt you." I shrug and unwrap the knife from the shirt keeping it safe. I walk toward her, glad when she doesn't run away. "But if you want to hold onto this so you feel safer when I'm around, be my guest."

She blinks. Her fingers close around the handle and she weighs it, getting used to the heaviness. Keeping her gaze on me, she draws it back behind her head. "What if I threw it at you right now?"

"Well, your grip is all wrong. On the off chance you did stab me? I'd get the mark tattooed. I'd add a heart and write *property of Max* under it."

"You're insane," she mumbles.

"Not insane," I murmur, bringing my mouth to hers. The hitch in her breathing makes my cock throb in my jeans. "Thoroughly obsessed, remember? There's a big difference."

"Yeah?" She lifts her chin, defiance behind her eyes when her gaze meets mine. "And what's that?"

"If I were insane, you would've left by now. But here you are." I trace the line of her jaw, smiling when she shifts on her feet and squeezes her thighs together. "Practically panting and begging me to touch you." I dip my chin, pressing a kiss to her cheek and then her neck. Her soft moan is sultry, and I lick her throat. "Let me fuck you, baby. I'm all worked up, and only you can calm me down."

TWENTY-TWO

MAX

A BLOODY KNIFE?

A saner woman would be halfway home by now, but as I've learned over the last couple of weeks, I can't think rationally when it comes to Hunter.

I know he doesn't have an evil bone in his body. I've never felt like I'm in danger when he's around, and as I stare up at him, his eyes patient and kind, I know I'm going to give in.

From the moment I met him, I haven't stood a chance.

"How many people?" I whisper, and his fingers gently wrap around my hand. He takes the knife from my hold and tosses it out of the way, kissing the inside of my wrist. "How many people have you killed?"

"Eighty-seven over six years. I could tell you all of their stories if you want. The horrific things they did to their victims while they were still alive." His mouth ghosts over my knuckles, his breath warm on my skin. "But I don't want you to have to bear the weight of how evil this world can be. You're too perfect for that, Max."

"Did they all deserve to die?"

"Yes. Every last one of them." He guides me to the edge of his bed. My hands shake as he brushes a piece of hair out of my eyes. "I know you said I'm a serial killer. And, by definition, I guess I am. But I feel pain when I hurt someone I care about. I cry. I've never laid a finger on a woman out of anger, and I never will." Hunter rests his forehead against mine and sighs. "If you want me to stop, I will. I care more about you than the money this brings me."

"Wait." I pull away from him. There's a drop of blood on his forehead. Another on his earlobe. "You get *paid* to kill these people? How does no one report them missing?"

"I get paid generously. The guy who started the organization has investors. Rich people who need slates wiped clean. And no one reports anyone missing. That should tell you about the kinds of people I'm dealing with." Hunter stands and scratches his chest. "I'm going to shower. I don't like touching you when I have blood on me. I don't want you to get caught up in that part of my life."

"I've seen the knife. I'm pretty caught up in it."

"You're right." He bends and kisses the top of my head. "If you want to leave while I'm in there, I'll understand. If you want to stick around, I'll only be a few minutes. Forget fucking. I'll make you a cup of tea. We can watch a show and fall asleep. I know you have school in the morning." My throat bobs when he moves his mouth to mine, kissing me in a soft and easy way that could convince me he's never committed an act of violence in his life. "Whatever you decide, Max, I'll respect."

Hunter pulls away and gives me a smile, taking his bloody clothes to the bathroom. He shuts the door behind him, and I stare at the barrier, conflicted.

Could I fall asleep next to him every night knowing there's blood on his hands? Could I let him touch me and not flinch, a worry lingering in the back of my mind that he'd do the same to me?

Deep down in my heart, I believe he'd never do that. He's had the chance to overpower me multiple times, but he hasn't. He's been nothing but gentle. Even when I ask him to be forceful with me, begging for him to fuck me harder, there's hesitancy behind his actions. Concern he might break me, and that's the last thing he wants to do.

A deep breath centers me. A second long exhale relaxes my shoulders. By the third gulp of air, I've made my decision.

For as many shitty people as I've dated in my past—all the men who have ghosted me, who have cheated on me, who have ignored me and given me a half ass effort in our relationship—Hunter has constantly proven himself as one of the good ones.

Murder aside, of course.

I feel *safe* with him. I feel taken care of, *adored*, and I grab my phone, looking up something on the internet.

Hunter emerges from the bathroom ten minutes later, a wall of steam following behind him. A pink towel is wrapped around his waist, and water drips down his chest. He stops when he sees me on his bed, his whole face lighting up in a smile that's miles wide.

"You're still here," he says.

"To get the blood out of your clothes, you'll want to soak the stain in cold water as soon as possible," I tell him, and he hums.

"Yeah?" He takes a step toward me, mouth twitching. "What should I do after that?"

"You'll need to use hydrogen peroxide or bar soap. I'm assuming you have one of those?"

"Would you believe me if I said I have a big ass bottle of hydrogen peroxide under the sink for this very reason?"

"Once you do all of that, you can wash the clothes in warm water with bleach."

"It was only a tiny stain. I'm going to get rid of the jacket." Hunter climbs on the bed, crawling across the mattress. He positions himself between my legs, pushing open my knees. His blood-free hand runs up the length of my thigh, and I sigh at his touch. "You're still here," he says again, like he can't believe it.

"Against all my better judgment." I put a palm on his cheek, and he whines. "If you *ever* think of using a knife you used to kill someone on me, I will not be happy with you."

"I'd never do that. You have your own special knife, angel. The only action it gets is your pussy." He extends his arm, swiping something off his bedside table. "Do you want to use it tonight?"

"Among other things." I lean forward so I can take off my shirt, throwing it out of the way. Hunter tries to touch my breasts, but I put a hand on his chest to stop him. "I want you to tie me up. I want to feel like I can't escape you."

"Are you sure?" He takes both my wrists in his hold, lifting my arms above my head. I close my eyes, already wet. "We can just—"

"Tied up, Hunter," I say, and the mattress dips under his weight. I listen to him open a drawer and drop his towel, heavy footsteps moving back toward the bed. I smile when he kisses me, my eyelashes fluttering open to find him stroking his cock while his other hand touches the length of a rope. "And I want the knife too."

"My girl is greedy tonight," he muses. "Take your bra off. Let me see your tits, angel."

Obeying him doesn't take much effort. My body does it willingly, fingers twisting in the clasp of the bra and letting the material fall away. He sees me bare-chested and groans, arousal coursing through me at the sound of his excitement. No man has ever made me feel wanted like this before. There's always a visceral reaction from Hunter when I'm naked, and when I reach for the button of my jeans, he stops me.

"Is everything okay?" I ask.

He nods, eyes dark, and stands, looking down at me. "What you're asking for is called consent to not consent, Max, which I'm all for. But we need to establish a safe word, so if at any time you feel as if it's treading too far into no consent territory, we can end the scene."

"Okay," I whisper. The other times we've been together, he's given me a light system. He checks in frequently to see if my enthusiasm and willingness to participate drops from a green to yellow, unsure if I like something we're doing. "And if I say the safe word?"

"Everything stops. Immediately. Doesn't matter when you use it." He grabs my chin. Our gazes meet. His attention is sharp, unwavering. "I'll make you feel like you can't escape, but I'm also going to listen to you. I will not hurt you."

The moment is charged, but it's cloaked in adoration too. With Hunter's usual kindness, and I can't explain why my heart skips a beat. I can't explain why I break out into a smile and turn my cheek, kissing the center of his palm.

"I trust you," I tell him, and the grip on his cock tightens. "My safe word will be book, since I like to throw them at you."

"I like a woman with some fight in her." Hunter lets go of my chin and picks up a clean knife. I don't know where he got it from, and I'm wondering if he has a stash hidden somewhere in his room. "I'm serious, Max. Use that word anytime, okay?"

"Okay." I give him a gentle shove and throw my legs over the side of the bed. I gesture at my jeans and play with the top button. "Are you going to take these off, or am I?"

"Doesn't sound like someone who wants to escape." Hunter moves, standing right above me. He pulls down on my bottom lip, hinging my jaw open. I smile, ready to take his cock, but he traces my lips with the knife handle. I gasp when he presses the cold metal on my tongue and fills my mouth with the base of the weapon. "Get this nice and wet, angel. I'm going to fuck you with it."

I exhale through my nose, keeping my eyes on him. I tip my head to the side and lick from the handle all the way to the heel of the blade. I can see my reflection in the steel, the eagerness in my eyes, and Hunter's laugh is mirthless.

"Fucking slut who likes this, aren't you?"

"No," I challenge, even though we both know it's a lie.

His large hand rests on the back of my head, forcing my mouth to bob up and down. The danger of my tongue being so close to the blade is a rush of adrenaline, but before I can sink into a rhythm, he pulls the knife away. Hunter puts it on the mattress by my hip and grabs my ankles, dragging me across the sheets until my ass hangs over the edge of the bed.

"When I take your jeans off, I bet I'm going to find your pussy drenched for me."

He pulls on the zipper, tugging my pants off in one fluid motion. I shift on the bed, cool air against my skin a change from the heat radiating from Hunter's body. Lifting the knife, he cuts the waistband of my underwear on both sides, smiling when the small scrap of material exposes me to him.

"I'm not drenched for you." I close my legs, heart pounding with anticipation.

"Yeah fucking right."

I let Hunter lead the way. He grabs my knee. Shoves my thighs open, and I gasp at the forcefulness. His hand moves up my body, a torturous drag he takes his time with. When he gets to my hip, he presses a thumb against my clit. Rubs a slow circle and huffs out a dark laugh.

"I knew it. Spread your legs so I can get a good look at your cunt that's fucking weeping for me."

"No." I try to stand, leaning into this fantasy, but Hunter is stronger. Rough hands push me back to the bed. I scramble across the sheets to get away from him, a moan sneaking out when I see his cock thick and hard between his legs. "Please don't," I add, but there's nothing behind it except aching desire.

"You're so pretty when you beg." Hunter moves as fast as lightning. He pins my body to the mattress, the synthetic fibers of the rope pinching my skin when he ties my wrists together with a knot. I tremble, alight with pleasure in a way I've never been before. "Face the wall and lift yourself off the mattress."

"What are you going to do to me?" I try to ignore the liquid heat pooling in my belly, but it's impossible when he flips the knife in his hand, catching it by the handle.

"You're going to sit on my face. Right before you come, I'm going to use my knife to fuck you so I can taste you all over the handle. After, you're going to take every inch of my cock." He lifts me, moving me involuntarily. "And maybe something in your ass too."

"I've never—" I swallow, pushing up on my knees. "You'll have to be gentle with me. Please."

"Gentle? I'm never going to be gentle with you." Hunter chuckles again and lies on his back. He stabs the knife into the mattress, right by his head, and I jump at the motion. "Don't drop your hands, Max. If you move or struggle or make this difficult for me, you won't like what happens next. Better yet—" He grabs part of my discarded underwear and reaches up, shoving the pair in my mouth. "There. Now you're my toy. If you need to use your safe word, you tap me three times. Understand?"

Fuck.

I almost come from his words alone, each one punctuated by a slap to my ass, but I nod. Hunter's arms loop around my thighs. With surprising strength, he lowers me to his face. His tongue licks a hot swipe over my entrance, and I squirm, having nowhere to go but lower, sinking further onto his mouth as his tongue parts my pussy lips.

"Did I say hover?" Hunter practically growls, fingers digging into my flesh. I cry out, the sound muffled by the ripped lace in my mouth. "Sit on my fucking face, Max. Suffocate me, angel. I'm not letting you move until I taste your come, baby, so you might as well admit you love this as much as I do."

TWENTY-THREE

HUNTER

I'VE DONE the CNC route before. It's one of my favorite things in the bedroom, but it's even better with Max. She tries to fight her way off me, and her effort is adorable. It's even more adorable she thinks I'm the one with the power. One word from her, and I'd fold. I'd stop all of this and pull her tight to my chest. I'd rock her to sleep, dreaming of her as I drifted off too.

Hell.

I'm so turned on. My dick throbs as I lick her, savoring her taste. I can't help but moan when she squeezes her legs together, thighs pressed against my ears. I give her a light pinch, wanting her to look at me, and she rocks forward. She dips her chin, looking down at me. I keep my eyes on her, my tongue buried inside her, a silent question behind my attention.

Are you okay, baby?

Max gives me a small nod, the hook of a tiny smile, and I grin with renewed enthusiasm.

"Lift your hips," I say, holding up three fingers. "Ride

my hand, angel. Show me how you're going to fuck that knife, then my cock."

She tries to groan but it's muffled. A distracted sound she covers up by lowering herself onto my hand, her pussy stretching around me. I reach up, my palm wrapping around her neck, and Max arches her back.

"That's my girl. Taking my fingers so well." I kiss her thigh then follow it up with a bite, teeth nipping at her skin. "You said you wanted me to stop, but look at you. You're going to come, aren't you? My beautiful slut can't resist being filled, can she? God, angel. You're exquisite to watch."

Max drops her head back, her pace quickening. I tighten the palm around her neck, watching her nipples harden. She's dripping on my hand, and her legs convulse when I surprise her with a fourth finger.

"There you go. You're doing so well," I whisper. "You're going to get three orgasms tonight, angel, and after, I want you to thank me for each one."

She nods and I reward her by playing with her clit, pinching and licking and marveling at how her body reacts to me. Her movements turn frantic, desperate, and I know she's close. Max lifts her hips, raising herself all the way off my hand before sinking back down on my fingers. She doesn't stop, her body a coil coming undone, and she tries to let out a scream. She claws at the wall, unable to get any traction because of her bound wrists, riding the wave of pleasure that slams into her with full force.

I told her I wasn't going to be gentle, and I'm not. I don't let her recover, wrenching the knife out of the mattress and holding it up so she can see. She shakes her head, a plea behind her gaze.

"Is there something you want to say to me?" I tap her chin, proud when she opens her mouth. I take the underwear and trace her lips with the wet lace. "You know what my answer is going to be."

"Please don't. I can't—it's going to hurt and—"

"I'm not hearing any safe words. What I *am* hearing is a lot of begging. Do not let your hips drop, Max." I scoot out from under her thighs and bring her hands to the curve of the headboard. Her body shakes and I kiss her shoulder, moving the hair away from her neck. I sit next to her, using the pre-cum on my cock to wet my length. "You're going to do this, and you're going to like it, angel. You've been asking for it, and it's too late to take it back. Don't pretend like you haven't wanted this."

"I have," she whispers. "Since the moment I first saw you."

I almost come on the spot. It's nearly impossible to focus, but I do, not wanting to hurt her. My thumb and index finger form a pinch grip, grasping the handle just above the blade. I spin the weapon in my hold then stab it in the mattress again, right under her pussy. I put a hand on her hip, lowering her slightly so she's an inch above the handle.

"Ready for round two, baby?" I ask, giving her the reins. She's in charge now, and when she nods, I smile. "Legs open a little wider for me. That's it. *Fuck*, Max. You're perfect."

I put two fingers on her clit and lean forward to take her nipple between my teeth, distracting her. She closes the distance between herself and the knife, the first part of the handle disappearing in her pussy. Max's startled moan echoes around us when I guide her down the knife, stopping near the blade, and her breath catches.

"I'm sorry." Max bites her bottom lip and shakes her head. "You might need to gag me again. This—*ah*." She rolls her hips, chasing another high. "It feels better than anything I could've ever imagined."

"Scream, baby. This is just like that dream of yours, right?" I murmur. "Putting on a show. Pretend there a dozen people here watching you."

"No. *No.* I don't want anyone to see me. I don't want them to know I like this. I don't. I hate it."

"You're staining my sheets, angel. You don't hate a fucking thing about this."

"This is all your fault. You've made me like things I've never liked before." She sighs. I don't know if it's with relief or gratitude or acceptance, but whatever it is, it flips a switch. Her movements turn sultry, intoxicating. I can't stop looking at her, especially when she bats her eyes and smirks. "You like it too."

"Of course I do. I like everything about you, Max." My palm dances up to the back of her head, bringing her mouth to mine. I kiss her, swallowing down the moan she makes when my tongue brushes against hers. "Take what you need, baby. Let me watch, then I'll worship you after."

"Dirty boy," she murmurs, finding a rhythm.

I touch myself, matching her tempo. Every time she works the knife another inch deeper inside her, my fist reaches the base of my cock. I want to come more than I've ever wanted anything else in life, but fucking her after this is all I can think about. She's going to be so wet and ready for me, and I groan in anticipation.

"Are you close?" I ask, and she nods.

"Touch my clit," she begs, and I shake my head.

"No. The knife only, sweetheart. You can get creative."

Frustration flashes across her face. "Can I move my hands?"

"As long as you don't touch yourself."

Max adjusts her position, wincing as the knife slips out

of her. I keep my hold on it, wondering what her plan is. Surprising me, she kneels on the mattress. Her forearms rest against the pillows, putting her on all fours, and she slowly rubs her clit against the handle. A long, low groan works out of her, and she closes her eyes.

"Perfect," she whispers. "So perfect."

"Open your eyes, Max. Look at the mess you've made." Reluctantly, she blinks and glances down. Her cheeks turn bright pink at the sight of the handle and the damp spot on the sheets. "You could never not want this."

I let her do what she wants, awestruck as she brings herself close to the edge again. Her breathing changes, tits heaving and chasing the high I know she craves.

"Hunter," she pants, and I can tell fatigue is setting in. Determination glints behind her eyes and she throws her head back, sinking into the raw indulgence of getting what she wants. I watch her like a hawk, ready to haul her out of harm's way if her legs give out. "I'm going to come."

"Good, angel. Then it's my turn," I say, kissing her. She gasps, the full-body experience sweeping over her. I'm there to catch her, gathering her in my arms and replacing the knife with my fingers, the aftershock catching her by surprise. "Such a pretty cunt. I've got you."

Max swallows down another gasp as I slow my fingers. I kiss her forehead and smile when she wiggles in my hold, lifting her wrists.

"Let me go," she says. "I want to touch you."

"There's an offer I can't say no to." I use the knife to cut the ropes, freeing her hands. She puts her palms on my cheeks then my chest, kissing me. "Are you doing okay?"

"I'm great." Her lazy smile tells me she's transcended to the blissed-out spot of subspace: glassy eyes. Brain fog, complete calm. "That was all very intense. Lovely."

"Do you need a breather?" I check her wrists, kissing

the pink skin rubbed slightly raw by the rope. "Some water?"

"No. You mentioned something about my ass. Don't go easy on me now, Hunter."

"Are you sure?"

"Yes." Max straddles me, and I rest my hands on her hips. "Are you going to fill me up, or do I need to find someone else who can?"

I growl at the idea of someone else touching her and flip her off me. I put her on her stomach, dragging her knees back. Ass in the air, face in the pillows, I wrap her hair around my wrist and tug, gleeful when she cries out.

"Stop being a brat just because you got off." I reach into the bedside table drawer, pulling out the new butt plug I ordered just for her. I grab a bottle of lube too, and rest back on my heels. My thumb traces along the line of her crack, and I smile. "Has anyone touched you here?"

"No." She shivers and rocks into my touch. "You'd be the first."

"Good. We'll do my finger first, then the plug."

"Is it going to hurt?"

"Probably, but the same rules apply." I cover my fingers with the lube and kiss her shoulder. "You say your word, we stop."

"You're not going to use your dick, are you?"

"No, angel. Not yet. You know I'm too big."

"God. At least you're humble." Max grunts when I ease my finger into her ass, a hand on her lower back to reassure her. "*Fuck*. Okay. That feels—"

"Give it a minute." I fold my body over hers, kissing the space between her shoulders and her neck. "Relax."

"Says the guy who doesn't have a finger up his ass."

"You can put one in mine if you want. I'm not opposed." Her laugh is soft, following it up with a quiet "*oh*" when I push all the way to my second knuckle. "That's it. I can already feel you stretching out. Almost there, then we use the toy."

I'm patient, working off her cues and carefully adding another finger when she tells me it's okay. Max is quiet at first, and then there's a sigh. A groan and a nod. She reaches behind her, a hand on my thigh, and I squeeze her ass cheek with my other hand.

"I like that," she whispers, a secret she's afraid to admit. "With your cock and the toy, I'm going to feel unbelievably full."

"That's how you should always feel with me." I'm careful when I take out my fingers. I wet the plug with my mouth then with the lube, bringing it to her hole. "It's going to feel more intense than my finger, but it's not much bigger."

"Your fingers are *thick*."

"Compliment after compliment from you, angel. I'm going to make sure to fuck you nice and hard after this to thank you for your flattery. Deep breath for me, Max? Thatta girl," I say, the head of the toy disappearing in her ass. "Halfway, and you're doing so well."

"Halfway? You're shitting me. Oh, my god. *Shitting.* Please don't tell me I'm going to—"

"You're not. And if you do, that's what the shower and towels are for." I move behind her. Looping my arm around her front, I reach for her breast. I twist her nipple at the same time I insert the rest of the plug, proud when her body doesn't protest. "*Perfect.*"

"*Shit*, Hunter. Why does this feel so *good?*"

"Because it's always good when we're together." I don't give her any warning before I push my cock inside her pussy, all the way to the hilt. "You're the best I've ever had, baby."

"It's too much." Max's hand reaches for the head-board, her palm flat against the mahogany. "I can't—"

"You can, and you will." With my palm on the back of her neck, I thrust forward, groaning at how wet she is. "Trust me, this isn't going to take long. Watching you fuck yourself multiple times? I'm a goner, sweetheart."

She blows out a breath, her hips snapping against mine. It's incredible how well we fit together, and I'd be happy if the world ended tonight. How can I complain when her hand reaches behind her, urging me to move faster? How does it get better than this, our sweaty bodies joined, not knowing where one starts and the other ends?

"Goddamn. Your fucking cunt, Max. My favorite fucking pussy. I swear I see stars when I'm inside you," I say.

"You're so cheesy." She laughs, rocking back into me so hard, I almost keel over. "You make me feel so full. There's no one I'd rather do this with than with you."

"Now who's cheesy?" My balls tighten, and I groan. "No judgment on how quick I'm going to finish, angel. And don't move when I come. Every drop that lands on the sheets instead of in your pussy is a spanking."

"I'm not sure that's the threat you think it is." Max does something with her hips that has me spiraling. I'm holding onto her so tightly, I know my fingerprints will linger on her skin long into the night. "God. I can't wait until you fill me all the way up. Let me be your slut, Hunter."

Possessiveness rips through like a thunderbolt. I yell her name, spurts of cum coating the inside of her pussy like a fucking tattoo. I want to be ingrained in every part of her like she's imprinted herself on me. Permanently, and someone I'm never going to forget. I'm indebted to her,

her body my salvation, and I don't stop marking her until my legs give out.

"Shit." I bring her onto the mattress with me, our limbs intertwined. I ease the plug out of her, making sure I'm gentle. "Sorry. That rocked me like a fucking hurricane."

"Maybe you're just old." She giggles when I touch her ribs, tickling her. "Hey! Careful! I don't want to waste anything."

"Fuck. Hearing you say that shouldn't make me hard again." I bury my face in her hair, trying to control my breathing. "You must be a witch who has too much power over me."

"It is almost Halloween."

"I knew you weren't human. An angel is right."

Max smiles and rests her cheek on my chest, a content sigh leaving her. "Dinner is definitely ruined."

"What? Why?"

"I left the bag of food over there." She gestures vaguely to the other side of my room. "Everything is going to be cold."

"I'll order us something new as soon as my heart stops feeling like I'm going to go into cardiac arrest."

"It must suck to grow up."

"The absolute worst." I yawn and stroke her hair, careful with the knots I find. "Stay the night?"

"Sure. But only if you do something for me."

"Whatever it is, the answer is yes."

"You don't know what I'm going to say!"

"Don't have to. I'd do anything for you."

"Such a sap." Max pushes up on her elbow and taps my nose. "I want you to meet Skyler. I've met Leo, and I don't like lying to my best friend about where I've been. Plus, you're… you're starting to be important to me. And for as much as I like being with you in the bedroom, I think I'd like to do more than that. Outside the bedroom. If… if that's something you want too."

"Max Walters." I roll on top of her, my hips pressing into hers. "Are you asking me to be your boyfriend?"

"*No.* You told me you murder people, so it seems like this has gotten pretty serious."

"Should I get a little piece of paper that says *check yes or no?*"

"You're exhausting." She touches my cheek, but she can't stop smiling. "But, hypothetically, how would you answer?"

Baby, I'd put a ring on your finger tomorrow if it wouldn't scare you off. What cake flavor should we go with? Do you want two kids or four?

"I'd say fuck yes. I can't wait to meet your best friend. If she's important to you, she's important to me."

"I'm going to tell her about the serial killer part."

"When you do, will you remember to mention the *good* serial killer part? I don't want to be confused with the people that slash throats for shits and giggles."

"Yeah, yeah." Max kisses me, and I smirk. "Whatever you say."

I hold her tight to my chest, not sure how anything gets better than this.

"IS IT NOVEMBER YET?" Skyler groans and rests her head on the arm of the couch. "I feel like I'm a zombie six seconds away from death."

"Oddly specific." I sit next to her and drape a blanket over our legs. "I'm glad you got the night off. You needed it."

"My manager forced me to sit out tonight. If I get anyone sick the last week of performances, she's going to be pissed."

"I bet Dominic is missing you," I tease, and she snorts.

"Fuck him. He texted me and said he heard I was under the weather. He followed it up by letting me know he was going to put laxatives in my water bottle if he catches a cold."

"What a gem." I rest my hand on her forehead and hum. "You don't feel too warm. Do you want me to get you anything? Some water? Hot soup? A milkshake?"

"I'm fine. Thank you for being such a good friend, Max." She smiles. "And since I've been such a shitty friend who is busy as hell, I need you to catch me up on what's going on in your life. I feel like I haven't seen you in days. Do you have a secret boyfriend I don't know about? Did you join one of those MLM groups? I swear to god if you try and sell me hair care products or makeup, I'm going to be pissed."

"I've successfully avoided another round of messages from Jessica, the former high school prom queen, trying to recruit me for some girl boss group I don't want to be a part of."

"Don't make me vomit."

"I do kind of have something I want to talk to you about. But I don't want you to freak out."

"Freak out?" Skyler's face falls. "Oh, shit. Did you find out who broke into the house? Do you have a stalker? Men are out of their fucking minds these days."

"No, I don't have a stalker. Well. I guess I kind of do?" I take a deep breath and laugh. "I met someone. Someone I really like."

"*What?*" She squeals and leans over to wrap me in a hug. "Details, please! What's his name? Where did you meet? Is he cute?"

"He's an actor at Fright Nights, actually."

"He is? Did you meet him at a bar? Oh! Is that where you disappeared to the night of the sinners and devils party?"

"I met him when we went to Fright Nights together. Remember when I got lost in line and ended up backstage? He's the one who... *rescued* sounds silly. He helped me, and we talked. I thought he was cute. So much so, I couldn't stop thinking about him. I went back to see him and we... oh, *god.*" I bury my face in my hands. My cheeks are on fire and I shake my head. "Brace yourself."

"Hey." Skyler peels my hands away and studies me. Her eyebrows pinch together, and I know it's her serious face. The one she only uses when she's really worried about someone, and I can't help but smile. "Is he hurting you?"

"No. *No*. Nothing like that. The opposite. We... we hooked up the second time I saw him. And we've been hooking up pretty regularly since. He's also kind of, um, a serial killer? And a stalker? But I'm not sure if he's technically a stalker, because he's only stalked me?" I add, because why leave anything out? "Semantics, I guess."

"A serial killer?" Skyler drops her head back and bursts out laughing. "Right. Okay, Max."

"I'm serious. He set up a camera in my bedroom. He hid in my closet one morning and watched me get off. He's the one who's been sneaking into the house and leaving me notes. As for the serial killer part—" I roll my lips together. "He's one of the good ones, and he wanted me to tell you that."

"One of the *good ones*? Jesus, sweetie. Is he brain-washing you? I mean—a camera in your bedroom? That's sick."

"He also put one outside our front door after I mentioned the possibility of Brian hanging around. I don't know, Sky. He's the one who broke in and folded my laun-dry. He texts me and asks about my day. He bought dozens of boxes of my favorite tea."

"So he does the bare minimum?" Skyler scoffs.

"You were okay with it when he was in our house before. The serial killer part is the line?"

"Yeah, because that's not normal!"

"I know his hobbies are... intense, but he's nice. He's... mostly honest and tells me what I want to hear without giving me a roundabout answer that ends up being bullshit down the road."

"You're justifying him killing people by saying he's a *nice guy*? Max. That's—"

"Trust me. I know how it sounds. If you told me you were seeing a guy who killed people for money, I'd be so concerned on your behalf."

"He does it for *money*? Oh, my god. This can't be real. What happens when he gets caught and you're implicated for being an accessory to murder?"

"An accessory? It's not like I'm out there doing it with him!"

"But you know about it." She wrings her hands together. "Do you promise he's never hurt you? Or implied that he would hurt you if you didn't listen to him?"

"I swear. If he did, I would leave without looking back. The only time he's anything but gentle with me is in the bedroom. The sex? Skyler. It's the best I've ever had."

"*Really*?"

"That's putting it lightly. He's so sexually open-minded. There's no judgment when I share a fantasy or an idea with him. Everything I ask for is met with enthusiasm, and he takes care of me."

The majority of my relationship with Hunter has consisted of hooking up, but I know if I took the sex away, I'd still be attracted to him. He makes me feel special. He listens, he's respectful. I've dated men who treat me horribly, and I'd rather take the serial killer with a good heart over someone who dumps me in a text message and forgets my birthday.

There's a *very* good chance I have daddy issues.

"Can we talk about the serial killer thing again?" she asks, and I wince.

"When he told me that, I freaked out. I don't like weapons. I don't like conflict. He shared who he kills, and... saying it makes sense isn't right, because I can't comprehend it, but I understand *why* they're on the receiving end of his violence. It's not innocent people he's going after, Sky. He's taking down horrible, wretched humans who shouldn't have a place in society. He didn't give me too many details because I'm not sure I'd be able to stomach knowing, but their death is an equal punishment for the crimes they've committed."

"This is a lot to process." She takes my hand in hers, looking me straight in the eye. "You're an adult. You can make your own decisions, and you know what works and what doesn't work for you. As your friend who loves you, I have to know two things."

"I'll tell you anything."

"Are you safe?"

"Yes," I say without hesitation. "I am."

"Are you happy?"

"Yeah." A grin breaks free, and I giggle. I've never experienced something like this before. Sometimes when we're in bed, I'll catch Hunter looking at me out of the corner of my eye. He has this dopey smile on his face, and it makes me feel like I'm on top of the world. "I'm so happy."

"I've never seen you this giddy, which means I need to meet him immediately and give him my seal of approval. Or disproval if he's not worthy."

"Want to meet him right now?"

"He's *here*?"

"He might be waiting in my room."

"Bring him out. I need to judge him for myself."

I climb off the couch and practically skip down the hall. When I get to my bedroom, I slip inside and close the door behind me.

Hunter is sprawled out on my bed, a book open in his lap and an arm tucked behind his head. His eyes flick away from the page he's reading to me, lighting up. He shuts the book and opens his arms, letting me curl up in his hold.

"Hi, angel." He kisses the top of my head. "You look excited about something."

"I told Skyler about you, and I feel so much better. I don't want to keep this from her. Not when I'm…" I trail off and look up at him. "When I'm really enjoying spending time with you."

"Yeah?" Hunter loops an arm around my waist and pulls me closer. "I'm really enjoying spending time with you too. What's the verdict on Skyler?"

"You're going to have to pass her test."

"Uh oh. What does that entail?"

"Guess you'll find out." I rest my hand on his cheek, and he sighs. "How do you think you're going to do?"

"If it means winning your affection, I'm going to do my damn best." He gestures to his backpack on the other side of the bed. "I brought the ingredients to make soup since you said she's not feeling well. There's also a gift card to a ballet store in downtown Orlando in there because you mentioned she liked to dance."

"You did all of that without having met her?" I gape at him, flabbergasted. Brian couldn't even get Skyler's name right. The guy before him kept trying to hit on her. "Why?"

"I told you: she's important to you, so she's important to me." Hunter's grin is sly. "I also really want her blessing."

"You are…" I laugh and shake my head, disbelieving. My heart somersaults in my chest. "Very wonderful."

"Glad you think so." He kisses me and I sigh against his mouth, happy. "Come on. Let me meet the love of your life. I usually don't like to be in second place, but I'm willing to make an exception."

"She knows about the serial killer thing, by the way." I pat his chest and jump off the bed, fixing my shirt. "You might have an uphill battle."

"I'm fully prepared for whatever is thrown my way." Hunter picks up his backpack and holds my hand. "Lead the way, baby."

"You've been here plenty of times. You know where to go."

"Who says I don't? I just want to look at your ass."

I laugh and tug him down the hall, finding Skyler on the couch where I left her. "Sky? This is Hunter."

"*Hunter?*" She looks him up and down. "You're sleeping with Hunter Wilder, the famous scare actor?"

"Okay, famous is a bit of a stretch." He rubs the back of his neck. "Hi, Skyler."

"Hang on. You two know each other?" I ask.

"We've interacted briefly in passing," he says. "And by interacted, I mean I said hello to her backstage on Sunday."

"I saw you in the cafeteria on Friday. I had no idea you were the one breaking into my house and terrorizing my best friend. I also had no idea you were a mass murderer." Skyler eyes the bag he's holding. "Any bodies in there?"

"Nope. I like to reserve mutilations for Mondays and Tuesdays. Plus, I like this shirt." He touches his collar and smiles. "Blood wouldn't make it look as nice."

"Who do you love the most in this world?" Skyler questions.

"My mother. But not in an Oedipus way. It's a normal, healthy amount."

"Have you ever killed an animal?"

"I ran over a squirrel with my bike when I was ten, and I'm still distraught. I had a funeral for it and everything." Hunter rubs his jaw. "I'm allergic to dogs, otherwise my roommate and I would have a plethora of canines in our house. There's talk of a cat, though. But, no. No animal killings. I like them more than people."

"Are you a coffee drinker?"

"I don't trust people who aren't."

"Hey. I don't drink coffee," I interject, and he kisses my cheek.

"It's your one and only flaw, angel."

Skyler glances at me, subtly mouthing *I like him*, then turns her attention back to Hunter. "How do you feel about pole dancing?"

"I've watched some videos, and it requires strength I don't have. I support the women—and men—who enjoy it." Hunter drums his fingers against my waist and looks my way. "Do you know how to pole dance, angel?"

"Very poorly." I laugh. "Skyler teaches classes when Fright Nights isn't going on, and for as many times as she's given me pointers, I can't figure out the logistics behind moving my body that way."

"Don't listen to her. She's good," Skyler says.

"I heard you were a dancer, so I brought you something." Hunter unzips his backpack and holds a small box her way. "I hope you like it."

"Is it an ex-boyfriend's middle finger?" she jokes, laughing when Hunter shrugs.

"Open it and find out."

She pulls on the ribbon holding the box together, gasping when she sees what's inside. "A gift card?"

"To a ballet shop in Orlando. Max told me you do all sorts of dancing." Hunter smiles. "I haven't had a chance to see your show at Fright Nights, but I hear it's incredible."

"This is... wow. Thank you, Hunter." Skyler clutches

the box to her chest. "Totally unnecessary, but very much appreciated."

"Good." He looks down at me. "I'm going to get started on the soup. I'll be back in a few. Be nice when you two talk about me."

With a kiss to my temple, he heads for the kitchen. When he disappears around a corner, Skyler grabs a pillow off the couch and screams into it.

"Oh, my god. Are you okay?" I ask.

"That man is in *love* with you. Let me literally kick my feet at the way he looks at you."

"He is *not.*"

"He so is, Max my darling, and what a wonderful thing because he's *great.*"

"You've known him for minutes!"

"And my gut is always right. People at Fright Nights love him. Like, they are obsessed. He's a legend, and I've never heard anyone talk poorly about him."

"Really?" I sit beside her, feeling like we're back in high school talking about our crushes. "I get butterflies when he's around."

"I'm not going to lie and say I'm totally onboard with the murderer gig, but it's also not my decision to make. You're my best friend. If you're okay with it, eventually, I will be too. But if he hurts you? I'll have *no* problem retaliating."

"I know you wouldn't." I hug her and laugh. "I never used to believe this when people said it, but I think it might be true: I could absolutely fall in love with him. Not tomorrow or next week. But somewhere down the road, I know it's going to happen. I just hope he doesn't break my heart. I'm not sure I could take it."

"He won't. That's a *man*, Max. And men know how to treat their women right."

"My nose itches, which tells me you two are talking about me," Hunter calls out. "I hope you're being nice."

"All compliments," I call back, and his chuckle echoes down the hall. "I really am happy, Sky."

"You deserve it. And I better be your maid of honor."

"We're not there yet. If we *do* get there, I promise you will be."

"Good. I'm so happy for you, sweetie."

"Me too," I say, feeling like my heart could burst.

MAX IS ALWAYS GORGEOUS, but seeing her get excited about the old school video games at the arcade bar I brought her to is next level. She lights up when she sees the pool tables and Skee-Ball lanes, boldly telling me she's going to kick my ass.

I'm letting her shit talk me because it's my first time being out in public with her, and I'm nervous as hell. I want this to go well and I want to do this *right*. If that means letting her beat me at a couple games so she keeps smiling, so be it.

God.

She's so beautiful when she's happy.

"I see two seats at the bar," she practically yells over the '90s music playing from the speakers on the wall. "Gosh. It's busy in here, isn't it?"

"I'm not a fan of crowds, but I am going to be a fan of watching you bend over the pool table. I'm going to imagine I'm fucking you from behind."

"Are you ever *not* thinking about fucking me?" Max laces our fingers together and guides me over to the high-top counter. "I'm starting to think you're only with me because of my ass."

"It's a very nice ass, baby, but only one thing on the long list of reasons why I like spending time with you."

"Yeah? What's at the top of this list?"

"How wonderful you are." I tug the belt loop on her jeans, pulling her toward me. "How happy you make me. Leo told me this morning he doesn't know if he's ever seen me smile so much. That's because of you, angel."

"You're being a sap." She puts a hand on my chest, grinning. "It's making me want you to bend me over the pool table."

"So scandalous, Max."

"Only so I can show you off. Half the women in here haven't stopped looking at you since we walked in."

"Like I care about that. I only have eyes for you. You make me go out of my mind. I'm a mess when you're around."

"When you say things like that, you make me think…" Max trails off, and I lift her chin so she looks up at me. "That this could be something serious."

"Do you want it to be something serious?" I ask, and I could throw up waiting for her to answer.

"Yeah." She stands on her toes, kissing my cheek. I want to pump my fist in the air and cheer. "I do. I don't want to rush anything, but I like you, Hunter Wilder. I like you a lot."

"What a surprise." I slide my hands into her back packets and give her ass a squeeze. "I like you a lot too, Max Walters."

"I figured that was the case after you *stalked* me."

"Can't wait to tell the kids how we met."

She laughs but stops abruptly. "Fuck my life." She

glances over my shoulder, a frown pulling at her mouth. "You've got to be kidding me."

"What's wrong?" I look around us, confused. "Are you okay?"

"My ex is here." Max hesitates, pinching the bridge of her nose. "He also… I didn't want to tell you this, but Skyler said she saw him drive by the house over the weekend. Three times."

"She did?" My blood runs cold. I touch the knife attached to my hip on instinct. I can't believe I didn't position the camera on her porch to face the road and missed this happening. *Stupid fucking mistake.* "Have you talked to him?"

"No. Maybe it was a coincidence."

"A coincidence that he shows up at your school and repeatedly drives past your house? That's intentional, Max." I survey the bar, pretending like I don't know exactly what this douchebag looks like. "Which one is he?"

"The blond in the corner with a group of friends. Striped shirt. Khaki shorts."

Of *course* this shithead wears fucking khaki shorts.

"Has he seen you?" I ask.

"I hope not. I don't want—I don't understand why he's doing this. He didn't… he never told me he loved me. Ten months together, and he never said the words." Max shakes her head, blowing out a sigh. "And, I'm glad he didn't, because it made getting over him so easy, but I just don't get why he *cares.* Why now?"

What a fucking idiot.

I'm fighting not to tell her how I feel *weeks* after meeting her. I can't imagine going months without letting her know I'm crazy about her.

"Men are stupid creatures. There's no rhyme or reason

to a lot of what we do," I tell her. "If you makes you uncomfortable tonight, I'll take care of him."

"Are you going to protect me, Hunter?"

"Yeah, angel." I tilt my neck, brushing my lips over hers. If this guy is watching, I want to give him a show. "I'll always protect you."

"My hero." She giggles and puts her hand on the back of my head so she can kiss me. I taste the whiskey she drank at my place earlier on her tongue, happily walking her backward until her shoulders press against a wall. Max smiles against my mouth, letting out a gasp when I nip at her bottom lip. "*Oh.*"

"You're mine." I move my mouth to her neck, sucking on her skin and leaving behind a little mark. "I'm going to take care of you."

"Call me yours again." Her fingers slip into the waistband of my jeans, and I roll my hips into hers. "I like hearing it."

"You're mine, angel. My girl. My obsession."

I pull away, and movement catches my attention. Brian —*Connor*—is leaving his friend group and making his way down the hall to what I assume leads to the bathroom. Now's my chance to get him alone, and as much as I don't want to leave the gorgeous girl slipping a warm palm under my shirt, I need to take care of this piece of shit once and for all.

"I'm going to use the bathroom." I kiss Max's cheek, stepping back. "I'll meet you at the Skee-Ball lane when I'm finished so we can put all your showboating to the test."

"Deal." She smirks. "I can't wait to kick your ass, Hunter."

I toss her a smile and sidestep past a group of women walking to the bar for a round of drinks. I follow Brian, whistling as I push open the door to the restroom and let it slam shut behind me.

He's standing at one of the urinals with his dick out, and I feel so sad for what Max had to deal with before me.

"You look familiar." I stand next to him, breaking every urinal rule, and pull out my own dick. "Do I know you?"

"Huh?" He turns my way, frowning. "I don't think so."

"You sure? I could've sworn I've seen you before."

"I don't know. Maybe. I have one of those faces, you know?" He flashes me a grin, and I'd really like to punch his skull in. Or cut out his eyes and feed them to the birds. "What's your name?"

"Hunter." I finish peeing and tuck my dick back in my pants. "You?"

"Brian."

"Really? Or is that what you tell your girlfriends so they don't find out about your arrest record?"

He narrows his eyes and zips up his pants. "I don't know what you're talking about."

"I've never liked liars."

"I'm not lying about anything."

"Except to poor women who think they're meeting someone else." I grin and wash my hands. "You're lucky I don't use it against you."

"How would you use it against me?"

"Oh, I don't know. Like, if you don't stay the fuck away from Max, I'll plaster your information all over social media, *Connor*. I will ruin you."

"Max? You're dating that bitch? She's boring, isn't she?" He snorts and turns away from me, but I grab his shoulder. I shove him against the wall and pin my arm against his neck. "Jesus Christ, dude. What the fuck is your problem?"

"My problem is I don't appreciate when people go

after what's mine. Max and I have been spending time together, but I hear *you've* been hanging around places where she might be. And she doesn't like it."

"It's not private property, man." He tries to shove my chest, but I don't move an inch. "I'm allowed to drive wherever I want."

"You mean by her house, *man*?" I push my arm harder into him. "If I catch you doing it again, we're going to have a problem."

"Oh yeah? What's a tattooed pretty boy like you going to do?"

Well.

That wasn't very nice.

I step back and release him from my hold. Brian touches his neck, but instead of letting him go, I pull out my pocketknife and open it. His eye widen, and he tries to move past me.

"Pretty boy, huh?"

"Look, dude. I didn't mean anything by it. She thought I was cheating and broke up with me. I didn't do shit."

"So you didn't have your dick in someone else while you were seeing her?" I toss the knife in the air and catch it by the handle, grinning when he inhales a sharp breath. "That's not what I heard."

"We weren't that serious."

"Is that what you said to all the girls you've roughed up? It wasn't *that serious*?" I laugh. "You're a piece of shit. I'll say it one more time: stay the fuck away from her, or we're going to have a problem. Understand?"

"Yes, you fucking psychopath."

That's much better than pretty boy.

"Great. Pleasure doing business with you," I say.

With a salute, I put my knife away and make my way back out to the bar, happy to find Max at the Skee-Ball game. She's swaying to the music, totally unbothered, and she grins when she spots me.

"There you are." Max taps her wrist. "Took you long enough."

"Sorry, sweetheart. There was a line." I see Brian heading for the exit. He's practically twitching when he looks over his shoulder, and my grin is smug. "Is it ass kicking time?"

"It is. And I thought we could make it interesting."

"You have my attention, angel."

"We can each come up with something we want the other to do if we win."

"Like, if you lose, you have to ride on my motorcycle with me?" I ask, and she groans.

"Ugh. I'm scared, Hunter. I don't want to go fast."

"We won't go fast. Just around the neighborhood. I bought you a pink helmet I think you're going to like."

That perks her up. She smiles, dark eyelashes blinking open then closed. "You did?"

"Yup. And a protective jacket that will keep you safe."

"Okay." Max gives me a slow nod. "Fine. If you win, I'll go on your motorcycle with you."

"This is the best night of my life." I scoop her in my arms and spin her around. "Not that it's going to happen, but what do you want if you win?"

"Um." She buries her face in my chest. "I'm embarrassed to say."

"That means it's going to be good. Whisper it in my ear, angel, so no one else can hear."

"If I win… I was hoping you'd fuck me with your Ghostface mask on," she says softly. "And after, I want you to chase me."

"Chase you," I repeat. "Like, through the woods?"

"Behind your house, yeah. And you only get to have me if you catch me."

"Oh, sweetheart." My adrenaline is pumping. Fuck the motorcycle, I'm going to lose on purpose. "We both know I'm going to catch you."

"That's why I want you to do it."

"Guess we better get to work." I set her down and motion at the game. "Do you want me to go first?"

"Yes, so I know what score I need to get to beat you."

"What happens if I throw the game? Chasing you sounds like the best consolation prize."

"I'll be very mad at you, because I want to win fair and square." Max puts her hands on her hips, and the way she sticks her bottom lip out in a pout is adorable. "Please, Hunter."

"Who am I to say no when you ask so nicely?" I put a couple quarters in the game and roll up my sleeves. "I'll give it my best shot."

Except my best shot sucks. Each of my throws is too aggressive, and I groan when my score only totals 100.

"If that was really your full effort, it was terrible." Max giggles and nudges me out of the way. "You should stick to scare acting and killing people."

"Thanks, baby. Your support means a lot," I draw out. "I'm sorry I can't be the Skee-Ball man of your dreams."

"I'll survive."

Max, on the other hand, is brilliant at Skee-Ball. She sinks three balls in the one-hundred-point hole off the bat, laughing when I gape at her skills. Her final score totals 570, and I can't believe I got my ass handed to me so supremely.

"That was impressive. Where the hell did you learn to play like that?" I ask, and she flips her hair over her shoulder.

"One summer, Skyler's parents rented a beach house up in New Hampshire for the week, and I tagged along. It rained every single day, so we put in *a lot* of hours at the arcade. I got pretty good at this and the Whac-a-Mole game."

"I'll say. Forget teaching. You need to start entering in some leagues, angel."

She collects her winning tickets and smiles, dangling them in front of my face. "Maybe when I retire."

"What are you going to get with all your earnings? A pencil with a cool eraser? A miniature slinky?"

"I was hoping I could cash them in and see how long it takes you to chase me down." Max slips the tickets in my front pocket, and I hum. "Want to play, Hunter?"

"That's a game you're not going to win, sweetheart. But fuck, I can't wait to see you try."

TWENTY-SIX

HUNTER

I DESERVE a goddamn medal for keeping my hands to myself on the drive back to the house. I want to reach over and touch Max, but I know if I do, I'm going to crash this car.

She's practically squirming in the passenger seat. Every few minutes she clears her throat, and I glance at her when we pull up to a red light.

"Are you doing okay, angel?" I ask, and she huffs.

"That's one way to put it."

"Having second thoughts?"

"Not at all. I'm excited. Nervous." Max laughs. "I also can't believe I found a guy who wants to try all of these things with me. I doubt it would be easy to meet someone for a cup of coffee and let it slip I want them to stalk me through dark and deserted woods. They'd look at me like I was crazy."

"You're the furthest thing from crazy." I test my self-restraint by touching her leg. I rub my thumb up her thigh and continue driving when the light turns green. "I hope it's clear by now I'll try whatever you want, angel."

"What are some of your fantasies?"

"Anything involving you," I say, turning onto my road, and she laughs again.

"I've spilled my guts to you! You have to give me *something*, Hunter."

"Fine. My most recent fantasy is fingering you so hard, you squirt. I want you to drench my bed, my face, I don't care. I just want to watch, because I think it's one of the hottest things in the world."

Max sucks in a sharp breath. "I've never—I don't know how I would—"

"I do. We'll try tonight and see what happens."

"I don't want to ruin your sheets." Max unbuckles her seatbelt when I park in the driveway. "I *like* your sheets."

"Baby, you can ruin anything you want."

"We can try, but don't get your hopes up. I've never been close to experiencing that before. I doubt I'll be able to."

"Sometimes the journey is even better than the destination." I grin when she reaches over and flicks my ear. "Let's go. We have things to do."

"Is Leo home tonight?"

"Why? Do you want him to join us?"

"No." She blushes a furious shade of red and practically leaps out of the car. "I was just curious."

"Do you want two people to chase you through the woods, Max?"

"I'm not sure I can handle one." Max looks at the land behind my house and shivers. "It's even darker than I thought it would be. I'm not going to be able to see a thing, am I?"

"Nope." I grin and climb out of the car, locking it behind us. I wrap my arms around her waist, nudging her toward the porch. "But I will. Working in haunted houses for years has given me very good night vision."

"That's unfair. I'm at a disadvantage."

"You were always going to be at a disadvantage, baby. But that's what you want, isn't it? You don't want to think you're going to outrun me. You want to know you're going to be caught."

"I'm scared," she whispers.

"I'm going to fuck you with the mask on first so you can relax. After I get you off, I'm going to find you in the woods. When I do, I'm not going to be nice."

She shivers against me, her head dropping into the crook of my shoulder. Her eyes flutter closed when I pinch her nipple over her shirt, a soft sigh escaping when I move to the other side.

"Is that promise?" she asks, grinding her hips against me. I'm already hard, my cock straining against my pants, and I groan when she drags her ass down my length. "I'd hate to be disappointed."

"When have I ever disappointed you?" I practically kick open the front door and tug her inside. Not wanting to waste time, I lift her off the ground, throwing her over my shoulder. She squeals and I give her backside a hard smack, smiling when she whines on the walk to my room. "You've never complained."

"I never will."

I drop her carefully on my mattress and look down at her. Her eyes are wide, her lipstick is slightly smudged. Her skin is flushed, and I'm so turned on just by the sight of her.

"I'm going to put the mask on outside the room to play into the illusion of you not knowing who I might be," I say. "Is that okay with you?"

"Yes," she says, scooting back to the pillows. "That will make this so much hotter."

"Do you remember your safe word?"

"Book."

"Good girl." I bend and kiss her, the last bit of gentleness I'll show her until after we finish. "Take off your shirt and your pants. I want you to touch yourself until I get back."

Max is quick to listen, and I stare at her black lingerie greedily. I can't believe I get to have her like this: vulnerable. Willing. She's my perfect girl, and I'm mesmerized when she runs her hands up her body. When she pulls down the cups of her bra so she can pinch her nipples.

"Go," she breathes out, gasping as she twists her fingers. "I'm already so wet, Hunter."

I make a pit stop in my closet, grabbing the mask I bought for Halloween a couple years back. I blow her a kiss, and she giggles, her fingers dipping into her underwear when I slip out of the room.

Patiently waiting is almost fucking impossible, but I tug the mask on over my hair and fix it so my eyes are lined up with the holes cut out for viewing. I resist the urge to shove my hand down my jeans and fist my cock, knowing her cunt is going to be even better.

I count to one hundred and move back to the door, opening it quietly. Max has her legs spread, thighs tipped wide, and I watch her pump her fingers in and out of her pussy. Her eyes are closed. She hasn't realized I'm here, and I lean against the wall, watching her.

Her moans are soft, breathy little gulps of air when she touches her clit under the lace. She sighs, pleased, and I take a step toward her.

"Sit up," I say, and her eyes fly open. Her mouth parts in fear, in lust, I don't know, but she complies, arching her back off the pillows. "Get to the end of the bed and spread your legs." Max stares at me, gaze raking over my body. She lingers on the mask, her chest heaving when I cross my arms and look down at her. "Now, or I'll move you myself."

The warning kicks her into high gear. She scrambles across the mattress, her feet resting on the floor. I hum my approval and position myself in front of her, grabbing her chin.

"I said spread your legs," I say, and her knees open. I shove them farther apart. "There we go. Hold your underwear to the side. I want to see how wet you are for a guy you don't know."

Max's fingers shake as she hooks them around the fabric of her underwear. She pulls the lace to the side, whining when I drop to my knees.

"Drenched. I'm not surprised." I run a finger along her slit then drag it across her chest. "Do you get wet for everyone, Max? Or is it only the mask that does it for you?"

"I like the mask," she whispers, like she's embarrassed to admit it.

"What was that?" I shove two fingers in her pussy, sliding my hand over her mouth when she cries out. "When I ask you a question, you need to speak up."

"I like the mask," she says louder against my palm. Her hips swivel, chasing the friction I know she's craving, but I don't give it to her. "*Please.*"

"Please what?" I climb onto the bed behind her, my legs framing hers. I rest a hand on her stomach, the other tangling in her hair, tilting her head to the side so I have access to her neck. "Please give you more? Please fill you up? Please make you come? You're going to have to be specific, Max."

"All of the above." She relaxes her back against my chest. Her palms sit on my thighs, and I lift my hips, letting my cock rub her ass. "I want you, whoever you are, to make me come."

"That wasn't difficult, was it?" I yank her underwear to the side, ripping it in the process, and touch her clit. "What makes you a whore for masked men, Max? Is it because you can pretend it's someone you shouldn't?"

"I like feeling like I'm doing something bad. It could be anyone under there." Her gasp is sharp when I push three fingers inside her, my palm facing up. "The possibilities are endless."

"Lean back a little, baby," I whisper, and she does. "And spread those legs as wide as you can. Like you're showing off your pussy to the world. It's such a good pussy, too. Pink. Wet." I increase my pace, nodding when she lets out a loud cry. "That's the spot, isn't it? That's so good, Max. Don't think about it. Just enjoy it."

"Your fingers are so big. I always feel so full, even when you're not fucking me." Her legs open wider, and she whimpers. "I need you to touch my—"

"I've got you." I press on her clit with my thumb. She reacts instantly, her body jolting as her hips buck off the bed. "*Fuck*. So responsive. Stay still, Max. I promise I'm going to give it to you."

"I need more," she begs. "I can take more. I want to come. I *need* to come."

"Loop your arms around my neck. That's perfect."

I know she's looking forward to what happens in the woods, but I want to make sure she enjoys this too. Her pleasure is the most important thing in the world to me, and I could spend the rest of my night touching her like this.

The squirting would be an added bonus, not something I need, but I'm still going to try.

I fall into a rhythm, listening to every sound she makes.

Max sighs. Moans. Trembles, her fingers digging into my hair.

"Wait. Hunter. Stop. Please. It feels—"

"That's normal, I promise."

"I'm going to—"

"You're not. It's different." I pull my fingers out of her and circle her clit with quick strokes. I glance up at the mirror in front of us, the one on my dresser, watching as she gasps, unable to sit still. "That's it. *Fuck*, Max. You're doing it, baby."

She sobs, giving in as she drenches the sheets. My cock throbs at the sight, the wet spot under her thighs and the way she stares between her legs, mouth open.

I keep my fingers against her clit, the pressure rough and fast. She tries to break out of my hold, but I don't let her, giving her a second orgasm that makes her collapse against me in a rush of another round of release.

"Book. Book," she cries out, and I stop immediately. I pull my hands away from her and move off the bed, kneeling in front of her. "No. *No*. Come back."

"I'm here. I'm right here." I take off the mask and kiss her knee. "I didn't go anywhere."

"I need a second." Max lies on her back, trying to control her breathing. I rub her foot, helping her decompress, and she lets out a giggle. "What the hell happened to me? That was... *intense* is putting it lightly. Jesus *Christ*."

"Don't bring him into this. He'd be appalled." I smile and sit up on my knees, leaning over her. "Hi, angel."

"I... I made a mess. I thought I was peeing and—"

"I can't speak from experience myself, but apparently that's how it's supposed to be. Did you like it?"

"I don't know? I didn't like feeling like I was about to pee on your bed, but I didn't hate it? It's not something I want you to do to me every time we're together, but I wouldn't mind it occasionally." She sits up on her elbows. "Did *you* like it?"

"I almost came in my pants watching you. It was unbelievably hot."

"Oh my god." Max covers her face, and I laugh. "It's everywhere. Your poor sheets."

"Stop being embarrassed. That's what the washing machine is for. You remember I have no problem doing laundry, right?" I take her hand, running my fingers over her knuckles. "Do you want to call it a night?"

"No." Her eyes meet mine. "I told you I wanted you to chase me, Hunter. I still do."

"Catch your breath." I grin. "Then I'm going to try and catch you."

TWENTY-SEVEN

MAX

AN HOUR AND A SNACK LATER, Hunter leads me to the back porch. I put my hands on the patio railing, looking out at the woods. There are no lights, only a forest of dense trees. I take a deep breath, trying to figure out how this is going to go.

"Are there any rules?" Hunter asks, kissing my neck. "What is off-limits?"

"I don't want to get hurt. If I trip and fall or feel unsafe, I want to stop," I say.

"If you're in pain, we'll stop right away."

"I don't want you to wear your mask. I want to know it's you."

"Done." He tosses it on the table to his right. "How much of a head start do you want? Five minutes? Ten?"

I clearly didn't think of logistics when I shared this fantasy. The land is unfamiliar to me, but it's something he sees every day. A head start sounds like a good idea. I need all the help I can get, and it will help ease my nerves.

"Um. Five minutes? I guess? But you can't look at where I'm going."

"I won't. The edge of the property is completely fenced."

"What if I get lost?"

"Turn around and walk straight. You'll end up back at the house." Hunter pulls something from his pocket and hands it my way. I stare at the small package, then glance up at him, confused. "And use this. It's a glow stick. Open it, crack it, and I'll be able to find you."

"How are you this prepared for everything?" My laugh is hesitant, on the edge of excited. "How many women have you chased out here?"

"None. This is a first for me, but I've told you I'm always going to keep you safe." He taps my wrist and smiles. "If I see the glow stick, the game is over. Fair?"

"Fair." I tuck the glow stick away. "I think I'm ready."

"Okay. Before you go, there's one more thing I have for you."

"My very own knife?" I joke.

"No. But we can get you one if you want." Hunter cups my cheeks and kisses me. It's slow, indulgent, and I sigh against his mouth. "I miss you already."

"I miss you too."

"Go on, angel." He gives my ass a tap and steps away from me. "I'll see you soon."

"Don't be so sure about that." I fix my ponytail and start for the stairs that lead to the ground. "I'm a former athlete. I have some speed in me."

"If you make it all the way to the far end and back without being caught, you're the winner. I can be a very sore loser, though, and this is a game I want to win."

He's hard to make out under the cloudy night sky. I don't know if he's already started the clock or if he's giving me a second to gather myself, but when my feet hit the grass, I take off.

I run until my lungs burn. Until my calves feel like they're on fire, an ache settling in my thighs. Until I reach the fence he mentioned on the outskirts of their land before I turn around. I pump my arms, a stitch in my side when I reach a large tree.

My heart is beating so fast, I'm afraid it might fall out of my chest.

I've never been so terrified in my life.

Or so turned on.

I know exactly what I asked for when I brought this up to him. The thrill of what's waiting for me if I lose is so hot, I almost don't even want to try. But a larger, more insane part of me knows this will be more fun if I struggle. If I give it my best effort and think I'm going to get away when there's absolutely no way I will.

Pausing to catch my breath, I listen for any signs he might be close. The air is still. There's no breeze, no noise. Even the leaves refuse to rustle, and I expect him to be moving like a shadow, seeing me while I can't see him.

A stick snaps, and I jump. I gather my courage and spot another tree up ahead, off the main path that leads to his house. That's my next target, my moment of refuge I have to get to before I let myself rest again.

I just have to hope he doesn't catch me first.

I brush my hair out of my face and take off again, sprinting like my life depends on it. I jump over a small stump. I step on a pile of leaves that tickle my calves. When I make it to the checkpoint without being spotted, I start to believe maybe I can outsmart him.

He's a stealthy serial killer who's never been caught committing any crimes?

So what?

Men aren't shit.

I'm a badass who can hold my own.

The outline of his house comes into focus off in the distance, and I smile.

Four more trees, then I'll reach safety.

Four more trees, then I win.

I glance over my shoulder, eyes darting to every possible place he could be hiding: behind the small bench under a large oak. Blending in with the tall hedges on the property line. There's nothing there but dark night, and I start to relax.

I would know if he was close. I would be able to feel him nearby, his gaze heavy and impenetrable, and I can't. It's my sign to move forward and I dart out from behind the trunk of the tree, my destination set out before me.

A large branch almost makes me trip, but I right myself and continue ahead. The house grows closer. I can see the patio furniture on the back deck, my car in the driveway. I'm so close to safety, victory within reach, when large arms loop around my waist. A hand slides over my mouth, muffling my screams, and exhilaration races through me.

"Did you really think you could outrun me?" His voice is deep and dark like the night. I struggle against him, thrashing in his hold, and his laugh makes me shiver. "Don't fight it, baby. We both know this is exactly what you want."

I try my best to pretend I *don't* want this, clawing at his arms and kicking his shins, but Hunter leads me to a tree. He spins me so my back is pressed against the bark and yanks down the zipper on my jeans. He ripped my underwear earlier, and the cool air against my warm, bare skin heightens everything around me.

Shoving my thighs apart, Hunter wastes no time pushing two fingers inside me, groaning when he finds out how wet I am.

"Already dripping. You love this, don't you?"

"No." I try to move, inadvertently riding his fingers. The bark bites at the back of my thighs. A stick pokes my ass, and I can't help but moan at the overwhelming sensations. "I don't."

"Such a fucking liar." He digs my discarded underwear out of his pocket and shoves them in my mouth. My eyes go wide but he stares at me, a silent question hanging between us.

The moment is electrified, seeping with lust, and my silly little heart stumbles over itself at his check-in. At the softness behind his gaze, so different from the forcefulness in his movements.

God.

I like him so much.

Hunter waits for me to give him an answer, and my subtle nod makes him grin. It makes him lift my arms above my head and spin me, my front pressing into the tree.

"I can't wait to take what's mine, sweetheart. I've been waiting a long time to feel your cunt around me."

It's barely been an hour, but when he grips my neck and hitches one of my legs up, my ass canting back as he does, it feels like maybe it's been years. I'm panting against my underwear, tasting my arousal from earlier on the fabric, and I try not to cry out when he slides his fingers back inside me.

"You can take them," he murmurs, and I sink into the exquisite bliss he brings me. Facing this way, I can't see him, but I can *feel* him; the hard press of his cock against my ass. His teeth leaving marks on my neck. "Should we try four?"

I shake my head, but my body betrays me. My legs open wider. I'm getting wetter, more turned on as the seconds pass, and I jolt forward at the addition of two more fingers.

"Need to get you stretched out for my cock."

His tempo is quick, matching the pace from earlier in his bedroom, and I try. I try so goddamn hard to not ride his hand, but I can't help myself. Not when he holds my throat so tight, I start to see stars.

The tree bark is rough under my hands, scratching up my palms as I fidget and swivel my hips in time with his movements.

The only thing that would make this better is if I was completely naked, my whole body exposed and belonging to him as he had his way with me.

Hunter lets go of my neck, and I hear the zipper on his jeans. His pants hit the ground and he spins me again, a gasp escaping when my back connects with the tree. Hoisting me up from under my thighs, he lifts me, determination in his eyes.

"I'm going to fuck you, Max. And when I finish, I'm going to come inside your tight pussy. If you let any of my cum slip out of you, you're going to get on your hands and knees and lick it off the ground. Because that's what needy sluts do, isn't it?" He grunts and lifts his hips, the head of his cock pressing against my entrance. I groan at the stretch, at the thickness of his length compared to his fingers. "They listen, and they don't argue."

I nod, tears springing to my eyes at the brief burst of pain before it melts to pleasure. I'm sore from earlier, but that doesn't stop him from thrusting into me. The first half of his shaft disappears in my pussy, and I try to yell, but no noise comes out.

I scratch at his shoulders, his neck, anything I can reach. Each time I do, he rocks his hips, harder and harder until he's buried fully inside me. It's far from the first time we've done this, but it feels different out here in the open. Like he's claiming me, once and for all, and I melt into the glorious sensation of being full. Of wanting this. Loving every single second, ecstasy behind the way our bodies fuse together.

"Hell. I can never last long with you, Max. Your cunt is too amazing. I want to stay in here forever. I'll wake you up like this every day." Hunter closes his eyes. A bead of sweat rolls down his cheek, and he groans when I rock my hips against him. When I squeeze my thighs together. "*Fuck.* Keep doing that and you're going to make me come, angel."

I want him to come more than *I* want to come. I want to know I had a part in it. I move with him, thrust for thrust, exhilarated. I feel sexy. *Invincible,* and he puts a hand on the tree, right next to my head. He leans in close, mouth inches away from mine, and I smile.

"You drive me wild." Another grunt from Hunter, followed by a whimper when I lift my shirt and press my breasts together. His eyes flash with desire and his cock swells inside me, thickening to the point of deliriousness. "Is it okay if I come?"

I nod, frantic for it, but he doesn't make the moment just about him. He includes me too, a thumb on my clit at the same time he drives into me with a force strong enough to shake the whole tree. I screw my eyes closed. I explode into a world of color as he plucks me apart, again and again until his cock twitches. Until he roars and buries his face in my shoulder, warm spurts of his release filling me up.

We stay there, frozen in time for what could be hours. Slowly, with languid movements and delayed reaction, Hunter leans away from me. He blinks, eyes glassy, and smiles my way.

"I think I need to call you Earthquake Max, because you rock my fucking world." His fingers touch my chin then my lips, opening my mouth. He pulls out my underwear and balls it in his fist, humming at how wet it is. "Repeatedly."

"Every time is always so good," I pant, glad to be able to breathe normally. "But that was double the workout."

"And you didn't have to use your glow stick." Hunter winces when he pulls out of me and slowly lowers me to the ground. "You have some speed in you, angel."

"So do you. Did you see me right away?" I ask, reaching for my jeans. "Please tell me you had to work for that."

"I was searching very hard," he says, but I know he's appeasing me. He had his eyes on me the entire time. "We'll have to play again soon."

"I can see why you're a serial killer. I didn't even see you coming." I fasten my jeans and put my arms around his neck. "You're good at your job."

"Shucks, baby. An unbelievable orgasm and your flattery? I'm a lucky asshole." He grins. "I'm taking you inside and cleaning you up."

"Is there any cum on the ground?" I ask, and Hunter glances at the leaves and sticks under our feet.

"I don't see any. Nicely done, Max. I'm proud of you for not wasting a drop."

I beam at the praise. "I'd never waste anything from you."

He leads me to the house, and I groan, knowing I was so close to winning. A hundred feet and I would've made it, but when he keeps his hand in mine and looks over at me with a wide smile, I decide I'm the happiest loser there's ever been.

TWENTY-EIGHT
HUNTER

ME

Do I get to see you today?

MAX THE ANGEL

As soon as I'm finished with a few things around the house. Any second I can get with you will be nice. Your next five days are going to be so busy, you'll barely have time to answer my text messages. Almost Halloween!

ME

I'll always have time for your text messages, angel. I clearly care more you more than my job, if finger fucking you in the haunted house tells you anything.

MAX THE ANGEL

Always so depraved.

Thank you for the flowers, by the way.

Attachment: 1 image

I STARE at the picture that comes through and frown at the bouquet sitting on her kitchen table. I didn't send her flowers, but someone else did, and I don't like that one fucking bit.

Was it a secret admirer?

A colleague congratulating her on an accomplishment at work?

Skyler being a nice friend and wanting to make her smile?

I decide to call her, doing a lap around the living room while I wait for her to answer.

"Hey," Max says, out of breath when she picks up. "Sorry. I'm changing laundry over. If you ever feel like washing my dirty clothes and folding them for me again, I wouldn't be upset."

"Noted. I love doing chores. Listen, sweetheart. I hate to be the bearer of bad news, but I didn't send you those flowers. Was there a note?"

"You didn't? Hang on." There's a muffled noise on her end. "Let's see. There's a card that says *I miss you*. Are you sure it wasn't you?"

"Positive, but now I'm going to make up for it with an even bigger bouquet. Who do you think they're from?"

"I'm not sure. There's—hang on. What the fuck?"

"What's wrong?" My spine straightens. I'm already reaching for my knife and moving toward the door, ready to head to her house. "Max?"

"Sorry." She laughs and I relax, setting the knife on the coffee table. "They're from Brian. I wonder if it's an old delivery that got lost in the system."

"He sent you *I miss you* flowers?" I pick up my knife again, disappointed this motherfucker hasn't gotten the hint. I guess I didn't make myself clear during our bathroom run-in. "When did the delivery come?"

"They were waiting on my porch when I got home from school. They're beautiful. I feel bad throwing them away, but I don't want to look at something someone I don't like sent me." Max sighs. "Is there a flower burial ground anywhere?"

"You don't want them?"

"God, no. Any suggestions?"

"Yeah, actually. I'll pick you up in fifteen. You're taking the bike for the first time, sweetheart."

"I get to be a backpack?" she asks, and I put her on speakerphone so I can flip over to the camera in her bedroom. I smile when I see her sitting on her bed, a hand over her chest.

"You know what a backpack is? I'm impressed."

"Only because I've been watching videos in anticipation of this moment. You've helped me with things I want to try. I want to try things for you too." She heaves a deep breath. "Hunter Wilder. I will ride on the back of your motorcycle."

"*Fuck*, baby. I'm so excited. I promise I'll go slow. We'll take the backroads, and I'll keep you safe."

"I know you will. Are you going to tell me where we're going?"

"It's a surprise, but I think it's time for you to meet the most important person in my life."

"Oh, no. Am I the other woman? You have a wife and kids, don't you?"

"The only person I want to knock up is you," I say, watching her roll onto her stomach and cradle her chin in her palm. "If you want kids, of course."

"I'm open to the discussion of children." Max grins. "I'll see you soon, biker boy."

"I can't wait, angel."

LATER THAT AFTERNOON, Max sits behind me on the bike, her arms wrapped around my waist. Her laugh is loud in the headset I installed in our helmets so she can communicate with me.

"Doing okay?" I ask, and I feel her nod against my back.

"This is so invigorating. I feel *free*. Like I could fly!"

"That was my exact reaction the first time I got on a bike. It's dangerous. Soon you'll want one of your own, and we'll spend every weekend riding across the state."

"I'm so onboard. I thought having my head confined would make me feel claustrophobic, but being able to talk to you helps. Seriously, Hunter. This is so much fun."

"I'll take you on another ride again soon."

I squeeze her thigh and pull into the entrance to our destination. Shifting the speed, I slow my bike to a crawl, passing rows of graves until I find one near the back and kill the ignition. I throw the kickstand down and jump off, holding out a hand for Max. When her feet are firmly planted on the ground, I unbuckle her helmet and slide it over her head.

"You're going to have to explain why we're in a cemetery," she says. "This feels like the start of a horror movie."

"In broad daylight? Really?" I reach behind her, grabbing the flowers from the storage pack attached to the bike. "We're visiting my mom."

"What?" Max whispers, tugging on my arm. "Your mom is—"

"She died when I was twenty-five. At the hands of my abusive father."

"Oh, Hunter." She stands on her toes and kisses my cheek. "I'm so sorry."

"I've made peace with it, but I try to get out here to see her. Haven't had the chance lately with Fright Nights being so busy, so I wanted to make the trip today."

"Will you tell me about her?"

I smile and take off my helmet, resting it on the back seat of the bike. I reach for Max's hand and slide our fingers together. "She was my best friend. We did everything together. She was the one who taught me how to ride. Bought me my first motorcycle." I smile when I think about the present in the driveway on Christmas Day with the big red bow on it. The drives we'd take out to the beach for the afternoon, sitting in the sand and watching the ocean waves. "She had this vivacious energy about her. Never backed down from a fight. Always found the good in people. It's why she kept letting my dad back in. She believed him when he said he changed."

The first time she kicked him out, I was eleven. He hit her during an argument about money, and when I intervened, he threw me against the wall. That sent him packing with a ticket to rehab and signed divorce papers. Six months later, after he said he was clean, he was living with us again.

For a while, it was fine. There were birthdays and Christmases we all celebrated together, the picture of a perfect family.

But the thing about abusers is you can't fix them. They can't stay perfect forever, and eventually, they break. They crave the high that hurting someone smaller than them brings, and I saw the bruises on my mom's arm. I heard them fighting from my bedroom, the yelling I tried to block out with headphones but never could.

The back and forth went on for years. He'd leave, then reappear. Mom reassured me that *this time* would be different. It never was. It's why I stuck around the house for so long, putting up with the jokes from my friends at work who told me I was too old to be living at home.

I did everything I could to protect her, but in the end, I couldn't.

Not when he set the fucking house on fire with her inside.

He was the first person I murdered.

A baseball bat to the skull in the middle of the night, and I made sure he knew it was me who did it.

There are times I wish I hadn't killed him so I could keep him alive years later, torturing him like he tortured my mom until her last breath.

"That must have been hard for you," Max says, and I blink. I let out a rage-filled breath, relaxing when she rests her head on my arm. "To see that unfolding and not be able to do anything about it."

"It was the hardest part of my life. I'd do anything to bring her back." I pause, leading her over to her headstone. "It's why I started doing what I do."

"Killing?" she whispers, like someone is listening to us, and I chuckle.

"Yeah, angel. Killing. My father paid for what he did, but so many pieces of shit get away with things they shouldn't. After seeing what Mom endured, I vowed to protect all the women out there who haven't found justice. They shouldn't have to live in fear while these fuckers live freely."

"I get it now. You don't kill because you're dark and evil. You kill to get rid of the dark and the evil. To bring good to the world. You're the light people need, Hunter."

"I'd never harm someone who was innocent. And I recognize we all make mistakes. But people who continue to intentionally harm others? That's not worthy of forgiveness."

"Do you mind if…" Max trails off, gesturing between the flowers and my mom's grave.

"Please." I hand her the flowers and give her elbow a gentle tap. "Thank you."

She steps forward and brushes the leaves off the head-stone before kneeling in the grass. Max gets rid of the twine holding the stems together and tucks it in her pocket. Propping the flowers up, she traces each letter in Mom's name before sitting back on her heels.

"It's so nice to meet you, Katherine. I'm Maxine. Max for short. I've been spending time with Hunter, and I want you to know you have a wonderful son."

My heart skips a beat when she says that, and there's no doubt in my mind I'm going to marry this woman. There will be a ring on her finger sooner rather than later, and I can't wait to give her my last name.

Or take hers, if that's what she wants.

"Mom would've liked you because you can put me in my place," I say, and Max grins at me over her shoulder. "She loved headstrong women. Women who could do things by themselves, but had no problem asking for help if they needed it. That's you."

"I'm sure I would love her." She fixes the flower arrangement and nods her approval at the tulips and sunflowers. "I'm sorry you're getting secondhand flowers from a shitty douchebag, Katherine. Next time, I'll bring something I picked out."

"She would've loved them anyway."

We stay there for a while, listening to the wind. Every few minutes I'll tell a story about Mom and Max will light up, hanging on to my every word. She bursts out laughing when I mention the time Mom caught me streaking after a truth or dare game went wrong. She wipes under her eyes after learning my mom was a teacher too, at a school near hers. She takes my hand when I let Mom know this is my last Fright Nights, a surprising tear escaping me at how much I'm going to miss it.

It's perfect. Exactly how I imagined the two of them meeting would go. Max doesn't rush me, even giving me a couple minutes alone with Mom. I spend that time talking about Leo and Max, a weight lifting off my chest when I kiss the headstone and stand.

"Thank you," I say. "For coming with me."

"Thank you so much for inviting me." Max loops her arm around my waist. "Is there anyone else you want to visit while we're here?"

"Nope. Mom is the only resident I know. Unless you feel like poking around and trying to summon the Grim Reaper?"

"Absolutely not. I don't want to disturb the spirits. They're sleeping peacefully, and I don't need to pull the Grim Reaper from her very busy schedule."

"Her, huh?" I pluck a leaf from her hair. "She's a woman?"

"Please. You think *a man* is organized enough to handle all the souls in the world? She's definitely a woman."

"Whatever you say, angel." I press a kiss to her forehead. "Ready to head out?"

"If you are. When you come back, can I join you?"

"Of course you can." We walk to the bike hand in hand. Peace like I've never experienced settles over me, and I know it's because she's by my side. "Have I told you today how much I like you, baby?"

"No." She smiles and shields her eyes from the sun, looking up at me. "You should remedy that. Immediately."

"I like you very much." I cup her cheeks with my palms, staring into her eyes. "I don't want there to be any doubt."

"There never is with you. I like you very much too, Hunter. Some days I think I…" Max blushes. "One day."

"Me too, angel." I lift her by her hips and set her on the back of the bike, putting her helmet back on. "Me too."

I OPEN my bedroom door after finishing Fright Nights and find Max curled up in my bed. The lamp on the end table is on. The sheets are tucked under her chin. Her head is buried in the pillows, and she looks so peaceful, I almost don't want to disturb her.

But I missed her so fucking much. I spent the majority of tonight's shift in the spot where I met her the first time, and it made me want to speed home to be with her. I smile and crack the door behind me, kicking off my shoes. Peeling off my shirt and jeans, I sit on the mattress next to her.

"Hunter?" Max yawns and turns on her side, blinking up at me. She sits up, brushing her hair out of her face. "What time is it?"

"Three. Sorry. I didn't mean to wake you."

"That's okay." She yawns again and reaches for her water glass, taking a long sip. "How was work?"

"Long, but tolerable. No one tried to punch me, so that's always a plus."

"I missed you." She peels back the sheets so I can crawl

under them with her and throws a calf over my leg. "It's been lonely here without you."

"Has it?" I run my hand down her bare thigh, glad to find her naked. "What did you do while I was gone?"

"Graded some worksheets. Stole your leftovers for dinner. Touched myself to the thought of you." Max gives me a coy smile. "I might've come in your bed twice."

"Where?" I kiss down her body. "Here?"

"Yeah." She hums, tangling her fingers in my hair. "Right there."

"Dirty girl." I put my hand down my briefs, stroking my cock. "Would three times be too many? Or should I—"

"You're already down there. Might as well do the work."

I laugh and kiss the inside of her thigh, watching her spread her pussy open with her thumbs. "When the lighting is better, I want to record myself going down on you." I lick over her entrance, putting a hand on her stomach to keep her still. "So you can watch it back whenever you miss me."

"Guess I'll be watching it a lot, because I miss the hell out of you when you're gone."

"We'll also make a video when I'm fucking you." I grind my hips into the mattress for relief, groaning when her thighs nudge wider. "I want to see you when—"

My bedroom door swings open.

"Hey, Hunt. Are you—*fuck*. Shit. Sorry, man. I didn't know you had company," Leo says from behind me.

Max squeals and covers her chest. I whip around and look at him over my shoulder, finding him standing in the doorway.

"What do you want?" I almost growl.

"I was going to ask if you wanted me to make you a grilled cheese, but I can see you're busy." He flashes me a sheepish grin, eyes flicking to Max's legs and then back to me. "Carry on."

Max arches her back off the bed and tries not to moan. I turn my attention to her, finding flushed cheeks and a hand over her eyes.

"Something you want to share with me, baby?" I ask, kissing her calf. "Is there a reason why you're squirming while my roommate could see you?"

"I'm just…" She pushes up on her elbows and stares at Leo over my shoulder. "It would be mean to ask him to leave, wouldn't it?"

Understanding dawns, and I push two fingers inside her pussy. She moans and drops her head back, hands fisting the sheets with a tight grip. "You want him to watch you come?" I ask.

"Yes. I don't think I want him to fuck me," Max whispers. "But m-maybe touching me while you fucked me? Holding me down or…" She swallows, mouth parting on an exhale. "I'd like that. I want to try it."

I move back up her body and kiss her. She answers me greedily, tongue brushing against mine and teeth nipping at my bottom lip.

"I'm going to let him stay. Leo knows not to touch what isn't his unless he's given permission to," I say.

"Have you two done this before? Have you two—"

"No. Nothing with each other. But he'd love to watch. And I'd bet he'd love to help."

"I'd be okay with that." She pulls back and licks her lips. "But only if I get to come."

"Oh, sweetheart. I think more than once sounds good, don't you?"

She grins, giving me the confirmation I need. I turn to look at Leo again. He's still in the doorway, and I don't miss the subtle way he brushes his hand over the front of his jeans. How he shifts on his feet and blows out a breath.

"Take a seat, man," I say, lifting my chin to the chair at my desk.

"Yeah?" he asks.

"Yeah. It's her first time having someone else watch her, so we're going to be gentle with her."

"I can be gentle." Leo practically sprints for the chair. He sits down and leans forward, elbows on his thighs. "I promise I won't touch."

"I think she's going to want you to." I rub Max's knee. "You trust me, angel?"

"Yes," she breathes out, and it's my turn to smile. "I trust you more than anyone in this world, Hunter."

"Good." I move away from her, no longer blocking her body. "I want you to get off the bed and stand near Leo so he can see you."

Max only hesitates for a second. Soon, she dips her chin and slowly climbs off the mattress. She shuffles across the floor until she's in front of Leo. I sit on the edge of the bed, just like I did the other night when I put the mask on for her.

"If you want to stop, say your magic word," I tell her. "And all of this will end."

"No." She shakes her head. "This is… I'm so wet, Hunter."

There's something special about seeing Max so vulnerable. Watching her learn her boundaries is incredibly hot, and I tug on her arm until she's sitting in front of me, her back against my chest. I move so there's room for her to put her feet on the mattress and kiss her cheek.

"She's wet," I tell Leo, and he groans.

"Fuck. She looks like she has a pretty cunt."

"Best I've ever had, man. Tight. Sweet. She takes me

so well. Makes these sweet little noises when I get nice and deep. Do you want to see?"

"Only if she's okay with it. I don't want her to do something she's not comfortable with."

"This is your call, baby." I kiss her neck, smiling when she drops her head against my shoulder. "Do you want to show Leo how lucky I am?"

"Yes," she whispers. "I need to come, Hunter, and I don't care who sees."

"Bring the chair closer so she can put her feet on your thighs," I tell Leo, and he moves until his knees press against the bed. I relax back on an elbow, taking Max with me. "You can touch her ankles. Set them on your legs and spread her open."

Max tries to squirm when his fingers wrap around her feet, but I drape my arm over her chest, not letting her move. Her cheeks are pink, looking between her legs, then up at Leo. When she tries to glance away, I grab her chin and turn her head back his way.

"I want you to look at him." I move my fingers down her stomach, sliding one inside her. "So he can see how much you like being a good little slut for me."

Leo's eyes meet mine and I nod, letting him know he can move his palm onto her thigh. He strokes her skin, and she whines. "Jesus. Look at that pussy. Can she take all of you?"

"Easily." I kiss Max's forehead, the hand on her chest moving to her neck. "I wonder how she would do with two cocks. One in her cunt, one in her ass. Or her mouth." I add a second finger, smiling when she pulses around me. She must like that idea too. "God. She does these little pussy flutters that are the hottest thing."

"You're so pretty, Max," Leo whispers. "Thank you for letting me see you like this."

"I could come from this alone," she says, keeping her eyes on my best friend.

"You need to keep still, angel. If not, I'm going to make Leo hold you down while I fuck you," I say, and when I feel her tighten, I hum. "It's not just the watching, is it? You want to be consumed. Teased and touched and fucking worshiped."

"Yes," she says, and it comes out almost like a sob. "Do whatever you want to me. I-I'll say my word if I don't like it, but this is…" Max tilts her head back, eyes on me. "This is better than anything from my dreams."

Fucking hell. I need to make a decision and fast. She's fueled by adrenaline, the heat of the moment spurring her on, and I look at Leo.

"Rules," I say. "You can't fuck her. She likes it rough, but if she says the word *book*, you stop. Immediately. If you don't, I will hurt you. You do not kiss her. If at any point she only wants me with her, you can watch, but I will not let you continue to touch her. This is about her, not about you. Your clothes stay on. Do I make myself clear?"

"Crystal." Leo nods vigorously. "I understand."

"Good. Let's move her up to the pillows and tease her for a minute."

"He's bossy," Leo mumbles, and Max giggles.

"So bossy. But so hot," she says.

"Move up there, sweetheart," I say, and Max complies. "Legs open. Wider. There you go. That's it."

"Wow." Leo lets out a soft laugh. "I've heard you two before. I never thought I'd get to see it firsthand."

"Touch her clit while I finger her. That won't take long to get her off. After, I'm going to fuck her."

"Asking me to perform under pressure is *cruel*, Hunter." Leo puts a hand on Max's stomach. He rubs his palm over her bare skin and drops his fingers lower, brushing against her clit. "She *is* wet. Shit."

"And so pretty." I watch her reaction to make sure she's not overstimulated or overwhelmed. When her eyes flutter closed and she sighs, content, I add three fingers to her pussy. "We're not that loud, are we?"

"Dude. The walls fucking shake when you two are together. Now shut the fuck up. This isn't about you," Leo says.

I hold back a chuckle, but he's right. It's not about me. It's about *her*, and I take her hand with my free one.

"Doing okay, sweetheart?" I ask, kissing her palm.

She nods, a slow smile taking over her face. "So much better than okay. You two are being way too gentle with me. What happened to the guy who chased me in the woods?"

"You chased her in the *woods*?" Leo reaches over and knocks my arm. "You could share some of the love with us pathetic folks, you know."

"Nah. This is more fun." I let go of her hand and tug off my briefs so I'm naked, not caring that Leo sees me like this. I've never been modest about my body, especially when Max's pleasure is the focus. "You want me to be rough? Open your mouth, angel, and suck my cock while my roommate and I get you off."

THIRTY

MAX

IF THIS EXPERIENCE is what sends me to hell, I can't be bothered to care.

How can I, when two men are touching me? When they're stroking me, *teasing me*, a filthy fantasy of mine brought to life.

Hunter rubs the head of his shaft against my lips and my mouth parts, delighted when he rests his heavy length on my tongue. I taste his saltiness, closing my lips around him and sucking him to the back of my throat at the same time Leo kisses my hip. The two competing sensations are dizzying, my body not sure which to react to first.

My feet drag across the sheets, desperate to open my legs wider. Aching for them to get deeper, imagining what it's going to feel like when Leo holds me down while Hunter buries his cock somewhere else.

I didn't know how the logistics would work in a threesome with the number of limbs and hands and body parts, but these two make it effortless. Hunter slides in and out of my mouth, saliva hanging from my lips. Every sense is electrified when Leo draws slow, steady circles over my clit. He pulls his hand away for a fraction of a second, his touch returning with wet fingers and more intensity.

It's like they're toying with me. Competing against each other, almost, to see who can bring me the most pleasure, and I'm the luckiest girl in the world.

I put one hand on Hunter's thigh, tracing up his leg. The other reaches for Leo, my palm resting flat on his chest, and I can feel his heart racing.

I've gone most of my life without being worshipped by one man, let alone two, but here I am: spread out on the bed like I'm their favorite meal, waiting to be devoured.

"Enough." Hunter pulls out of my mouth. I blink, looking up at him. "Any more and you're going to make me come, angel."

"Would that be so bad?" I ask with a sly smile, and he pinches my nipple.

"When I want to fuck you? Yeah, it would be." He looks at where Leo is touching me and lets out a low, pleased hum. "Is he good at that, baby?"

My cheeks heat. I don't want to compare the two of them because they're so different: Hunter is sure of himself. A couple flicks of his wrist and I'd fall apart, a wet and weary mess. Leo is more timid, a little shy, but I like it. I like how he's watching me, learning which pattern I like the most. When he finds one I enjoy, he works my clit with determined, eager circles. He brings me to the precipice of ecstasy then pulls away, making me groan, frustrated and wanting more.

"Yes," I grit out. "But he's teasing me when all I want to do is come."

"That's not very nice, is it?"

"No. He's—*ah*." I gasp when Leo gives my clit a hard slap. "*Shit*."

"He said you like it rough," Leo says, pinching me, and

my body revolts. My skin is splotchy. My breathing picks up, and I'm close. I'm so close, seconds away from splintering into a million pieces, but he pulls his hand away again, and I almost scream. "It's not fair you two get to have all the fun."

"I think we should let Leo have a taste, don't you, Max?" Hunter kisses my cheek and lifts me off the mattress so he can slide behind me. With both hands on my knees, he spreads me open, He hooks his legs over my thighs so I can't move, trapped in his hold. "Eat her out until she comes, man. You can probably get her twice. I'll hold her down."

The anticipation alone could make me finish. Both of their big, strong bodies are in control, *owning* me. I'm entirely at their mercy. Theirs to use, theirs to play with, and Leo gives me a wide grin before he positions himself on his stomach between my legs.

He spits on my clit and uses his fingers to spread the saliva around, only stopping to push three fingers inside me. I moan, surprised, and my hips buck off the bed.

"Holy shit, Hunter. You weren't kidding. I can feel her pulsing like you said. And she's unbelievably tight," Leo says.

"So hot, right? Keep going. She can take four."

Leo adds another finger, and I swear I'm levitating off the bed. I'm transcending to some place far beyond here, because it's magical. Absolutely heavenly when he alternates the gentle thrusts of his hand with the flick of his tongue.

I'm being greedy. I'm trying to move as much as I can, but Hunter doesn't give me an inch. My orgasm starts at the base of my spine then spreads to the rest of my body. It grips me, suddenly, urgently, refusing to let go when Leo slaps my clit again and sends me free-falling, blinding pleasure ripping through me.

I cry out and try to close my legs, certain I can't take anymore, but I'm overpowered and outnumbered. Rendered useless when Hunter covers my mouth with his big hand and says, "*Another one. She'll give it to you.*"

And I do. The second orgasm hits me faster than the first, Leo's tongue parting my pussy and lapping at me like I'm the key to his salvation. He pins me down too, arm over my stomach, the other cupping my ass, and when his thumb brushes against my hole, I forget my name.

"Switch places with me," Hunter says, and his body is replaced with something new. Less broad, but just as nice. I blink up at Leo's face, and he grins at me, lips wet from his hard work.

"You're really good at that," I whisper, and he blushes.

"You think so?"

"Yeah. You're patient. Women like that."

"Thanks, Max." He carefully peels a piece of sweat-soaked hair away from my eyes. "I think Hunter is jealous of the attention I was giving you."

"He's always jealous. This is about me, remember?" I give him a sated smile and look at Hunter between my legs. He's stroking his cock, fist jerking up and down with his gaze on me. "It's your turn."

"Did you like that, angel?" Hunter asks. "Not too much?"

"No. Just right."

"Good." He pulls down on my bottom lip. "Are you ready for my cock?"

"I've been ready since you left earlier this afternoon."

"I'm going to tell my boss I can't come to work anymore." He laughs and holds his body over mine, lining himself up with my entrance. His hand rests next to me on the mattress. "I have a very needy, very hot woman in my bed who needs my attention."

"As you should. I—" I gasp, his shaft sliding inside me. "*Fuck*. That's a good spot."

He grunts and drives into me, each of his movements rougher than the last. Leo struggles to hold me down, and I can feel him hard against the curve of my ass. I whimper, a thrill rushing through me when Hunter hooks one of my legs around his waist. The angle lets him get deeper. His thrusts turn frantic, like he doesn't think he can hold on much longer. As if every minute he's in me, he's going out of his mind, and I smile, squeezing tight around him.

We stay like that, our tempo perfected, and knowing each other's bodies. He's not gentle but I welcome it, glad he gives me exactly what I want.

"*Goddammit*, Max." Hunter groans, fingers pressing into my knee. "You're exquisite, angel."

"I think you're pretty great too." My voice hitches, breath catching when he grabs my other leg and wraps it around his waist. This position is even better, and he lets out an honest to god whimper when Leo touches my chest. "I can't wait until you fill me up, Hunter."

"You always know the right things to say." He straightens his spine and closes his eyes. Again and again his cock disappears in my pussy, and I never want him to have anyone else like this. I want it to be me, and only me, and when he looks down at me, I know he's thinking it too. "I'm going to come, baby."

And he does. Loudly, messily and bordering on unhinged until he finally slows the thrust of his hips, still inside me.

Minutes pass. The room quiets as we all settle down. The three of us are breathing hard, sweaty and exhausted, and Leo is the first to break the silence.

"Well. Talk about a turn of events," he says. "That's not what I thought would happen when we got home."

I giggle and smile up at him. "Hopefully you're not disappointed."

"Far from it." Leo is careful when he moves out from behind me and rests my head on the pillows. "Thank you for letting me join y'all."

"Max is the only one you should thank." Hunter pulls out of me, and I wince at the loss of contact. He gathers me in his arms, dropping a kiss on my forehead. "She's in charge."

"I hope all this power doesn't go to my head." I sigh, relaxing in his hold. "Are you okay, old man? Sounds like I did a number on you there."

"Watch your tone," he growls, but there's no bite behind it. Not when he hangs his head and laughs. "You've murdered me, Max."

"I'll make sure the Grim Reaper sends your soul somewhere nice." I look down at my body and huff. "Gosh. I need a shower before I go to school. I smell and look horrible."

"No, you don't," Hunter and Leo say in unison, and I blush.

"You look as beautiful as ever. But I'll get you cleaned up, and we'll take a nap before you have to start the day." Hunter's eyes dart over to his best friend. "This won't be a regular thing, but I think Max enjoyed herself."

"Very much." I smile shyly at Leo. "Promise not to make things weird between us?"

"Never." Leo ruffles my hair and climbs off the bed. His erection presses against his jeans, and he clears his throat. "I'm going to, ah, turn in. I'm getting tired. You two enjoy the rest of your night. Morning. Whatever the hell it is."

He practically sprints from Hunter's room, and I laugh. "Did he have that bad of a time?" I ask.

"The opposite. Poor guy needs some relief. Hey. Be honest with me, angel. Are you okay? I feel like we went from zero to one hundred there and—"

"I enjoyed every second." I tug him onto the sheets, lying on my side. "You're right about it not becoming a regular thing, though. I had a great time, but I like things with you the most."

"I'm glad I won't have to fight my best friend over you."

"Never. You're who I want." I sigh and close my eyes. "Thank you for indulging me, Hunter."

"I'll give you anything you want, baby. Which includes a shower before you get ready for work."

"I want to sleep all day. I'm so tired." I put a pillow over my face to block out the light. "Will you rinse off with me?"

"Cleaning you up is one of my favorite things." Hunter scoops me into his arms, and I giggle when he nuzzles his cheek against mine. "Bath or shower?"

"Shower. If I get in the bath, I'll never get out." I hide my smile in his chest. "You'd never be able to get rid of me."

"That would be okay. Getting rid of you is the last thing I want to do."

Hunter rinses me off in the shower and wraps me in a fluffy towel. We fall asleep for another hour before I get up, groggy and sore and so satisfied. He stands on the front porch when I leave for work, waving at me as I pull out of the driveway, and I already can't wait to see him again.

THIRTY-ONE
MAX

HUNTER

How's school, angel?

ME

Busy, but good.

HUNTER

Glad to hear it. Come over tonight?

Better yet, be in my bed when I get home from work. I haven't seen you in 24 hours, and I'm going out of my goddamn mind.

ME

So needy. I guess I can make that happen.

HUNTER

I miss you and your pussy more than I've ever missed anything in my life.

ME

You're a modern day Shakespeare.

HUNTER

Romeo, Romeo, wherefore art thou,
Romeo?

ME

Romeo and Juliet? Really? We're doomed.

HUNTER

Doomed with you? Can't wait ;)

I TURN my phone over and shuffle through the vocabulary homework my students turned in this morning. My goal was to get everything graded by the time they got back from lunch, but Hunter is too distracting. Putting my phone down and ignoring him feels impossible, but for the sake of my job, I have to.

I laugh and uncap a red pen, ready to see how many of my stellar students spelled *applause* right. The knock on my classroom door is another distraction, and I'm surprised to find Principal Sheehan standing there. Panic rushes through me at the thought of a missed meeting, and I give her a cautious smile.

"Hi, Dr. Sheehan." I stand, walking her way. "Is everything okay? Oh, no. Did someone start a food fight in the cafeteria?"

"The sloppy joes are tempting to use as ammunition, aren't they?" She smiles and gestures over her shoulder. "You have a visitor at the front desk. A gentleman."

"Really?" I blush and dip my chin. I didn't expect Hunter to stop by on his way to work, but it's a nice surprise. "That's exciting. I'll follow you to the office."

"He said something about not being able to get a hold of you because of a dead cell phone. I told him it's probably the lack of service in these old buildings. One day they'll upgrade our 5G network so we can communicate with the outside world."

"Dead cell phone? I was getting text messages earlier." I fall in step beside her. "Maybe it's a problem on his end."

"It's important enough to track you down. It's nice when men are determined, isn't it?" She winks and holds the door to the office open for me. I stop in my tracks when I spot Brian sitting in one of the small leather chairs against the wall. "I'll be in the back if you need me."

A quick glance around tells me the room is empty. Janet, our secretary, is away from her desk, and I curl my hands into fists.

"What are you doing here?" I ask, keeping my voice low. The last thing I want is for someone to overhear me and think there's a problem, even if I want to smash his face in. "I don't want to see you."

"Max." He stands and puts his hand on my shoulder. I knock his arm away and he winces, hanging his head. "You weren't answering my texts."

"Because I blocked you."

"I need to talk to you. Your new boyfriend threatened me at the bar, and I think he's bad news. He pulled a *knife* on me. Are you safe with him?"

"What are you talking about?"

"He told me if I talked to you again, he'd kill me, which I think he'd follow through on. I'm taking a risk being here and seeing you."

"*Hunter?* He's protective. If he threatened you, you probably deserved it, but you don't have to worry about me." I fight off a smile. It sounds exactly like something Hunter would do. "And you and I don't have anything to talk about."

"I have some clothes I need to give back to you. That sweater you love? And a pair of jeans."

I groan. I know exactly what sweater he's talking about: light blue, warm. It's my favorite thing to wear when the weather dips below seventy degrees in Florida.

My brain is screaming at me to walk away, but getting those things back will end any and all ties I have to Brian. He won't be able to hold it over my head. He won't have an excuse for coming around. It will be *done* and over.

I'm so happy with Hunter. With Fright Nights ending in a few days, I'm excited to see what happens next. If this is how good things can be right now, what's it going to be like in December when we exchange Christmas gifts? When we drive around town looking for the best decorations?

So fucking good, I tell myself.

"Fine. Where should I meet you?" I ask, and Brian lights up.

"How about my place? Don't give me that look," he adds when I narrow my eyes. "You can do a final walk through to make sure there isn't anything else of yours."

"I'm not staying long. I have plans tonight, and I don't want to spend half the evening at your house. In and out."

"Twenty minutes. That's all," he says, and I sigh.

"I have a parent teacher conference so it might be closer to five, but I'll be there."

"Perfect." Brian offers me a tentative smile. "Thanks, Max. I know I did some shitty things, but I hope one day we can be friends. You're a great girl, and I'm the asshole who screwed up."

I know his words should hold some weight, but they don't. They're empty, easily forgettable. It sounds like something he's rehearsed a hundred times, and I'm so glad no part of me wants a friendship with him. This is my chance to wipe my hands clean and never have to deal with him again.

"We can forgive and forget," I say. "Move on to better things, you know? I'm sure the right person is out there for you. You need to learn to keep your dick in your pants and your hands to yourself first, but I bet you'll find her. Hey. Maybe she's down for an open relationship."

"Trust me, I've learned my lesson." Brian laughs. "I'll let you get back to your day. Sorry for barging in unannounced."

"I'll see you later this afternoon."

"Can't wait."

I walk back to my classroom, knowing I should tell Hunter what I'm doing. He won't like it, but he doesn't like anything about the guy. The last thing I want to do is have our first real fight. Not after we had such a good time visiting his mom's grave together.

Something shifted between us when he brought me there. I feel like I really know him now. Deeply, emotionally. I don't think he tells just anyone about his mom, and to be part of the lucky ones is an honor I don't take lightly.

He means so much to me, but I'm still my own person. I'm allowed to make my own decisions, even if he won't like them. Brian isn't dangerous. He never harmed me when we were together, and he's not going to start now.

It's a quick trip to his house, then he can leave me alone.

Easy enough.

I LOCK my car and walk up the path to Brian's porch. There's a fall wreath on the front door, and I touch the fake leaves on it. I knock and the door flies open, revealing a nervous looking Brian.

"Hey," he says, scanning the street behind me.

I spin, frowning at the empty road. "Is something wrong?"

"No, no. Everything is fine. Just glad to see you." He offers me a one-armed hug I awkwardly return, then closes the door and locks it behind me. "How was the rest of your day?"

"I had a kid barf all over the reading area rug after lunch, so that was fun to clean up. Other than that, no drama."

"Do you want something to drink?"

"Sure. Water is great." Brian leads me down the hall to the kitchen, and I listen to the quiet house. "Where's your roommate this weekend?"

"Hm? Oh. Away. Visiting his parents or something." He grabs a glass from the cabinet and smiles at me. "Tap or filtered water?"

"Born and raised on tap. I can handle another glass."

He laughs and turns for the sink, busying himself with the faucet. "It's what makes us invincible, right?"

"I'd say so." I accept the glass and take a sip. "Where are my things?"

"Give me a second." Brian points at the table, and I sit. He takes the seat across from me and sighs. "First, I want to apologize. I'm sorry for how our relationship ended and how immature I was. I've been going to therapy the last couple of weeks, and I'm learning I was an asshole to you. You didn't deserve that kind of behavior from me, and I'm sorry."

"Sleeping with someone else while we were seeing each other was pretty shitty," I agree. I drink another gulp of the water and set down the glass. "But, in a way, I'm glad you did. It's clear the two of us weren't compatible in the long term, and because we broke up, I met Hunter. And he's *wonderful*."

A dark look flickers across Brian's face, but he schools his features quickly. He leans back in his chair and nods. "Are you two serious?"

"It's only been a few weeks, but we're headed that way, yeah. He's so different from anyone else I've dated." I smile. "And I'm excited to see where things go."

"That's good. Minus the knife thing, he seems like an okay guy."

"Like I said, he's protective. I told him I had seen you in the school parking lot and on my street a few times, and he assumed the worst."

"Which is what?"

"I don't know." I rub my eyes and blink. The lights above the table look like they're glowing, the bulbs turning hazy and blurry. "That you still had feelings for me?"

"Are you okay?" Brian asks.

"I think so?" I reach for my glass, knocking it over. "I'm so tired all of a sudden."

"Maybe you should lie down."

"No. I should go." I try to stand, but I fall back in the chair. I gulp down a breath, starting to panic. "What's happening to me?"

"Rohypnol." Brian checks his watch and smiles. "Took less time than the guy said it would. I thought we'd have to sit here and have a heart to heart for half an hour."

"What?" The word comes out slurred. My tongue is heavy in my mouth. "You roofied me?"

"I had to. It's the only way I'll get that asshole off my tail. He knows about my past and who I really am. I'm going to have to kill him before he kills me, and the only way to do that is to use you as a pawn."

I don't know what's going on. I don't know what he's talking about when he mentions his past, and it's impossible to sit upright. My head hurts. So do my limbs, and the room feels like it's spinning.

"Why?" I whisper. "I haven't done anything."

"You're the piece I need." Brian stands and grabs the glass I've been drinking from the table, moving it to the sink. He rinses it out with soap and water before setting it in the dishwasher. "Close your eyes, Max, and go to sleep."

THIRTY-TWO

MAX

THE ROOM I'm in is dark, but I'm sitting on something soft.

A bed, maybe.

Or a comfy couch.

Is it my couch?

No. Definitely a bed. A bed that's not my bed, and that's alarming.

I open my eyes to take in my surroundings, but pain radiates in my head. I wince. It's like someone is hammering my skull and bashing it in repeatedly. When I try to sit up, I realize my hands are tied together.

I can't move. I'm bound, held against my will, and panic claws at me. I do my best to piece together what's happening. I dig into my memories, trying to pull the last couple of hours free, but I can't. There's nothing there, an empty void I can't figure out, and my eyes prick with tears.

Think, Max.

There's school. Vocabulary words and talking to Principal Sheehan.

But after that?

Not a single fucking thing.

Noise from outside a door makes the panic even more nerve-racking. My shoulders shake. My breath comes out rough and ragged, and taking a deep breath feels like I'm swallowing knives.

Knives.

Hunter?

No. This isn't his room. I don't smell him. I don't feel him. I don't *hear* him, the sounds of his movements something I've started to memorize.

This is somewhere I don't want to be, and I tell myself to calm down. To rationalize what's going so I can have a clear head, but it's impossible.

Footsteps approach. Heavy, determined. A flicker of light appears under the sliver of the door. The handle turns, bathing the room in bright colors as Brian steps inside.

Brian?

"Good. You're up." He walks toward me, and I flinch. There's a flash, a grainy recollection of a glass of water. Feeling very tired. He laughs when I try to get away from him and rips a piece of tape away from my mouth. I try to scream, but my throat is dry. "Why so jumpy, Max? It's just me."

He reaches behind me. Now that I can breathe better, I can think clearer. My hands are tied to the headboard, but my feet...

My feet are free.

I am not fucking dying today.

I have too much to live for: my job. The kids I teach. Skyler and her warm and wonderful hugs.

Hunter.

The only way I get out of here is by fighting, and I

need to prepare myself for what could happen in this struggle.

Injury.

Severe pain.

Torture.

All are better than the alternative, and I let out a slow exhale.

One second at a time.

"Why are you doing this?" I croak. "I was nothing but good to you."

"I told you. Your boyfriend is poking into places he shouldn't be poking." Brian positions himself over me, his large body caging me in, and checks the security of my wrists with a grin. "You can blame him."

"We're not even really together. I said that to make you jealous," I blurt, running with the only idea in my head. *Distraction. Diversion.* Anything to stay alive. Brian freezes for a fraction of a second, and I wonder if I might be able to get out of here unharmed. "It's just sex. That's it. Nothing important."

"It's too late. He's digging up things from my past. The only way I walk away from this is if I kill him. And I will, to keep my secrets safe."

"What secrets?" I cry out. "Who the hell are you?"

"Since you're not surviving tonight, I'll tell you. Seeing people's reactions is one of my favorite parts. My name isn't Brian. It's Connor."

"Connor is a nice name. Is Brian your middle name?" A tear rolls down my cheek and hangs on the tip of my nose. "I could've called you Connor."

"I go by Brian because the women I've dated have been hell-bent on ruining my life. Filing false claims against me. Saying I pushed them around and hurt them. Is it against the law if they *deserve* it? Fucking whores who spend my money," he snarls. "Who claim they like me, then two weeks later, move onto something 'better.' I always give them a black eye as a parting gift. The arrests are worth it to keep them in their place. I'd kill them if I thought I could get away with it." His eyes drag over to me. "But you. You I *can* get away with. A boyfriend who threatened me? It's the perfect setup. An easy plant. This will be *his* fault. And no one will know."

"Br—Connor. Just let me go. I can bring him to you. I can *help* you," I beg. "I promise."

"Shut up, bitch," he yells, surprising me by slapping me across the face. My cheek stings, a burning pain slicing through me, and I can't hold back my wail. "From now on, you're only going to talk when I give you permission to."

"Please. Whatever you're going to do to me, just do it." I sniff, looking at him straight on. His gaze is soulless, blank. Devoid of any human emotion, and I know he's beyond help. My fate is sealed. The grave is dug. I have to accept and bear it. "Don't make me wait."

"I want to do a lot of things to you." He reaches down. Yanks my skirt up to my waist, and I squeeze my eyes shut. If I don't look, it's not really happening. I can pretend it's a nightmare. Something I'm watching from above, not actively a part of. "And I know what's going to hurt him the most. Torturing him before killing him is going to be so much fun, and touching what's his is the perfect way to do that."

I should've told Hunter where I was going.

I should've shared my location or not trusted someone so blindly, and both of us might die because of it.

How fucking *stupid* of me.

There's no time to wallow. Not when Brian is running his hand up my leg. Leaning in close, his mouth on my neck, and moaning when he touches my underwear.

It's now or never.

This is my chance.

When he pauses to undo his belt buckle, I draw my leg back. I open one eye so I can see my target, ramming my knee into his stomach as hard as I can.

"Fucking bitch," he spits out on impact, keeling over. When he tries to reach for me again, I flail my lower body, aiming my feet wherever I can land a blow: his ribs. His shoulder when he tries to grab my ankles. I don't stop moving, but Brian launches himself at me. He forces me into the mattress, rendering me useless with his body-weight, and I know this is it. "Stay fucking still," he whispers, and my shoulders shake with a sob. "Cry all you want. Struggling makes it more fun."

I take a deep breath, letting my mind disappear to anywhere but here.

I wonder what Skyler is doing. Would she assume I'm spending time with Hunter and not think to ask him where I am? Fright Nights has to have started by now. She won't have time to check her phone.

And Hunter.

The pain is coming, but I smile anyway.

I've had the best month of my life with him, and I wish I could've told him how much he means to me. I wish I could've told him how easily I would've fallen in love with him, if I had a little more time. How I'm already on my way there, not caring if it's too soon.

I wish, I wish, I *wish*, but the wishes mean nothing now.

Not when Brian grabs my knee and digs his fingers into my skin. Not when he yanks his pants down and sneers, a drop of saliva dripping on my forehead.

I brace myself, waiting for what comes next.

Pain.

Loneliness.

So much ache.

"Max?"

I'm so far gone, I'm hearing things that aren't here. Pretending I know someone I care about is nearby, when really, I'm all alone.

"Max? Where are you angel?"

My name echoes down the hall, and it's *real*. It's real and I let out a choked laugh, joy radiating over me.

"Right on time." Brian smirks.

Footsteps—lighter, *urgent*—race down the hall. They match the beat of my sputtering heart. I blink and the door is flying open. Hunter is there, his eyes on mine, and I want to scream *I love you. I love you, please keep me safe*, but no words come out. His attention moves to Brian, a look I've never seen from a human flashing across his face.

In two steps, he's covering the length of the room. He's hauling Brian off of me and shoving him against a wall, lifting him as if he's made of feathers, not a pathetic excuse for a man.

"I warned you," Hunter says, a knife pressed against his throat. It's the same one he held the night I found out about the other parts of his life. "I told you to stay away from her, but you couldn't resist, could you?"

Brian tries to fight back. He kicks and he swings his arms, but his attack is pointless. Hunter keeps him there, feet off the ground. Struggling and cutting off his air supply.

"You're going to be very sorry you ever touched her," Hunter adds, then he bashes his head with the handle of the knife.

Brian falls to the floor, a crumpled body against the hardwood. Hunter kicks him in the ribs, and when he doesn't move, he rushes toward me. He brings the knife to my hands, cutting my wrists free from the ropes binding them together. Gathers me in his hold and wraps his arms around me, a shield from the evil in this world.

"You're here," I sob. My shoulders shake with exhaustion and fear. I can't stop trembling. "I can't believe you're here. I thought I was going to die."

"I've got you, sweetheart." Hunter's voice cracks, pain lacing the words. He hugs me tight to his chest, stroking my hair. "You're safe. You're okay. He can't hurt you anymore."

"I should've told you where I was going. I didn't think he would act like this, but then he roofied my drink. The next thing I knew, I was waking up with my hands tied to the bed and—this is all my fault." I sob again. I'm so cold, so tired. "I'm sorry. I'm so sorry. I didn't—"

"Baby. It's not your fault. Do you hear me? You did *nothing* wrong. I should've taken care of him when I had the chance, but I didn't." He kisses my forehead, my cheek. "This is my fault."

"How did you know where I was?" I wipe under my eyes, pausing when I see the raw skin around my wrists, a mark from my struggle. "I never shared my location with you."

"You don't think I put a tracking device on your car the minute you mentioned that dirtbag was hanging around?" he says, and a laugh rattles out of me.

"You're insane. Of course you did."

"When you didn't answer my texts before Fright Nights, I tracked your car through GPS. I realized it was his place and snuck in through the back door after doing recon to make sure this piece of shit doesn't have an arsenal of weapons."

"He said he wanted to kill you and use me to do it. He said you were poking into his life. Is that true? Why didn't you tell me who he really was? I never—" I stop to gulp down another breath. It feels like I'm being held underwater. "I wouldn't have come here had I known."

"I'm sorry. I'm so sorry. I should've. I thought I could protect you by not letting you know what he was capable of, but I was so, so wrong."

"How many women has he hurt?" I whisper.

"Too many. At least five, but I'm sure there are more that have been unreported because of threats."

"Oh my god." I bury my face in my hands. "It could've been me. It *should've* been me."

"But it's not. It's not ever going to be you, because I'm going to take care of him."

"You're going to kill him, aren't you?"

"Yes," Hunter says without any hesitation. "Unless you tell me not to."

I look over at Brian's body and think of the women he's terrorized. How *afraid* they must have been, knowing no one was going to come and help them. There was no escape, no heroes.

Only fear.

"He's not worthy of being saved," I say. "He deserves whatever happens to him."

"Then that's what I'll do." Hunter stands, holding me. "We're going to my place so you don't have to be alone. I texted Skyler, but she hasn't replied to me yet. Leo is coming home. He can sit with you while I—" His grip on me tightens, like he's afraid I'm going to disappear. "While I handle Connor."

"Can I take a shower when I get there? To get the memory of him off of me?"

"Anything you want, angel. God, Max." He rests his forehead against mine, and I see the tears in his eyes. The pale cheeks and fear still written on his face. "I thought I lost you, baby. I thought I lost you, and I wanted to die. I would've. Life wouldn't be worth living if you weren't in it."

"I did too. I thought that was it for me. And all I could think about was you."

"Me?"

"Yes. I guess I'm just as obsessed with you as you are with me."

His laugh is the sweetest thing I've ever heard. Sun after days of rain. A warm blanket on the coldest night. Light in so much darkness, and it makes me cry again. He doesn't say anything else when he buckles me in the passenger seat. When he disappears back in the house and carries Brian to the trunk over his shoulder, but I can feel it when he sits next to me. As he takes my hand in his, kissing each knuckle.

A reminder that I'm here. That I'm still fighting.

Love.

Brilliant, blinding love.

THIRTY-THREE

HUNTER

MAX CAN'T STOP TREMBLING in the front seat, and I can't stop seeing red.

Vicious, murderous red.

I'm trying to stay calm. I'm trying to be rational on the drive to my house, but I'm seconds away from pulling off the road and slicing up Connor's fucking neck until he bleeds out in the median.

Then I'd throw him into oncoming traffic so his body splattered across someone's windshield.

I want to reach over and touch my girl. I want to take her somewhere far away where she's safe, where she feels protected, because I'm afraid what I'm doing isn't enough. She's jumpy. Shaken up and not saying anything to me, and I could kill myself for not getting to her sooner.

It can't take more than twenty minutes to get home, but it's like hours pass. Pulling into the driveway with her unscathed and Connor still breathing in the trunk is my greatest fucking accomplishment, and I drop my head back when I shut off the engine.

"I'll keep trying Skyler," I say.

"Okay."

"Do you want a shower? Or does a bath sound better?"

"A shower. I-I want to scrub my skin until I feel clean." Max pauses and glances at me from across the car. She smiles weakly, and my heart rips in fucking two. "Will you shower with me?"

"Would that make you uncomfortable?"

"No. I-I don't want you to be far away. I want you to hold me."

"I'll hold you for as long as you want," I say.

Forever, I want to add. *Please let me hold you forever.*

The last two hours have been the scariest of my life. When Max didn't answer my texts, I thought the world was ending. I broke every speed limit to get to her. I ran red lights. I skipped stop signs. *Nothing* mattered but her, and I've never experienced fear like that. I would've lit fire to everything in this goddamn world, gladly watching it burn to ash if it meant finding her.

I would cross every end of the universe to keep her safe.

I would cut myself open and give her my blood if she needed it.

I would kill a thousand people—a *million fucking people*— if it meant she never had to live in fear again.

I've known it since the first night I met her: I'm in love with this woman. My soul fucking *aches* when she's not around, and I'll tie myself to her from now until eternity if she's willing.

And if she's not?

I'll wait.

For months. For years.

It doesn't matter.

When she's ready, I'll be there, ready to kiss the ground she walks on and bend to her every beck and call.

I hop out of the car and jog to her side so I can open her door. She smiles at me again when I offer her my hand, her fingers slotting into mine. Her eyes flick to the trunk and I shake my head. Connor is staying there until I'm ready for him. Waking up disoriented, bound and gagged is going to be the best part of his night, and it would be rude of me to rush to the next part without letting him panic for a few minutes.

"Can you turn the water as hot as it will go?" Max asks in my bathroom.

"Sure thing, angel. One shower in the throes of hell coming right up." I adjust the temperature and put my wrist under the running water, making sure it's warm enough. Satisfied, I peel off my shirt and toss it on the floor, holding out my arms to her. "Come here, baby."

Max walks toward me, undoing her top as she moves. She pulls off the blouse and drops it next to my shirt, putting a hand on her chest.

"He hit me," she whispers.

I freeze. "Excuse me?"

"Bri—Connor. Whoever the hell he is. I-I tried to fight back. He slapped me across the face."

Rage like I've never experienced before blooms behind my vision. I close my eyes and squeeze my hands into fists. The urge to pummel that sack of shit until he's nothing but a pulp on my floor is nearly overwhelming. That's the easy way out, though. It would be too fucking generous of me, and he's not worthy of it.

Not when I'm going to make him suffer like I've never made anyone else suffer.

"He will pay for his sins." I keep my eyes on her and the small pink mark on her cheek. "I promise you that."

"I'm so glad you're here," she whispers, and I tip her

chin up to kiss her. Soft, sweet. A vow that I'll always be here. "I'm so glad I have you."

"You are the most important thing to me, and I will keep you safe until the end of my days."

I love you, I almost shout.

I love you so fucking much. Take my bleeding heart and keep it in a jar, because I'm never giving it to anyone else.

"Thank you." She kisses my chest, lips warm on my skin. "Thank you for being my most wonderful surprise."

We take off the rest of our clothes. I help her into the shower, the water hot and steam rising around us. I reach for the bottle of her favorite shampoo, lather it in her hair, and massage her scalp until she relaxes against me. Pliant muscles, mouth half open. She looks serene. Finally at ease, all while I'm thinking about the ways I'm going to torture Connor when I get him out of my trunk.

"Okay?" I ask into the curve of her neck. She nods and I detach the shower head, bringing it to her head. I take my time rinsing out the shampoo before I switch it for conditioner, careful as I run my fingers through the long strands. "How's the water temperature?"

"Like I'm melting, so it's perfect." Max sniffs, a new wave of tears filling her eyes. "Everything is as perfect as it can be. *You* are perfect, and I'm not sure I'll ever get over how wonderful I think you are."

"And to think. A couple weeks ago you threw a book at my head," I murmur, and her laugh is the shot of serotonin I didn't know I needed.

"You have charm, I guess." Max runs her hands down my back, but I step away from her. "What's wrong?"

"I want to clean you up." I brush my fingers over the curve of her cheek. "I want to get the smell of him off you. The feel of him off you. Would that be okay with you?"

"Yes." Her bottom lip wobbles. "I just… I don't want to…. I'm sorry, but I'm not ready to—"

"I would never." I grab her body wash and squirt a generous portion of it onto her loofah. It smells like flowers and vanilla and good things in the world. "Your body, your choice, and right now? Right now, all I can think about is taking care of you. All I can think about is making sure you're okay." I drop to my knees, the water running down my back. I carefully hook my fingers around her ankle and rest her foot on my shoulder. "I just want you by my side, angel. I don't need anything else."

Max is crying, but I let her have the moment to herself. I don't try to comfort her. I don't tell her what she should be feeling. I don't say a word, taking my time to clean her thighs, her stomach, her arms. I'm gentle when I wash her chest, keeping my touch light and unrestrictive when she tenses under me.

I stay on the shower floor for what could be hours, until the water turns cold and Max's tears dry. I swallow down my own emotion, a war raging in my head while my hands shake. When I stand and rinse off my palms, fingers pruny and wrinkled, I know I'd do it all again.

"Thank you," she tells me, and I kiss her cheek.

"Let's get you into some warm clothes," I say, wrapping her in a towel.

In my room, I grab a sweatshirt and sweatpants for her to put on. Pulling back the covers, I wait until she climbs on the bed before I bring the sheets up to her chin. Downstairs, the front door opens and closes, and Max freezes.

"Hunt?" Leo calls out, and she relaxes. "Where are you?"

"Bedroom," I answer, turning back to her. "I'm going to have him stay with you while I handle Connor. I'll come back and check on you soon."

"I'd like that," she says.

Leo knocks and waits for me to throw on some jeans and a shirt before he pokes his head in my room. His eyes bounce between Max and me, unaware of how severe the situation is. I didn't have time to explain it to him in the breakroom, pleading with him to clock out early and meet me back at the house.

And he did, because he's such a good fucking friend.

"Hey. Is everything okay?" he asks.

"No." I grab my favorite knife from my desk drawer and spin it. "I need to take care of something in the basement. Can you stay with Max? I don't want her to be alone."

"Sure. Yeah. Of course." Leo nods and kicks off his shoes. "Is it okay if I—"

"You can come up here," Max says softly, patting the space next to her. Leo looks at me for confirmation, and I give him a nod.

He might've watched me fuck her, but I know he doesn't have feelings for her. Not like that. I'm not jealous when he climbs on the mattress and lets Max rest her cheek on his chest. I don't feel angry when he strokes his hand up and down her arm and gives me a concerned look.

"Later," I tell him, moving to the side of the bed where Max is. I kiss her cheek and rest my forehead against hers. "I won't be long."

"Are you still going to—"

"Yes. And I have to be honest with you, Max. This is only the second time in my life I'm going to enjoy doing it."

"I know." She tugs on my necklace and sighs. "Make it hurt, Hunter. Make him suffer."

"I'll make sure he begs for forgiveness from you before I end him." I grin and tuck her hair behind her ear. "Welcome to my world, angel."

THIRTY-FOUR
HUNTER

I PAID good fucking money to put a basement in my Florida home. The waterproof walls, the drainage systems and sump pumps were all worth it for this moment as I walk around Connor's body hanging from the shackles attached to my ceiling. I grin, doing another lap just because I can.

There's nowhere for him to move. Nowhere for him to go, and it's nice to see someone who thinks they're invincible struggle.

"You're a monster," he spits out. Blood spills from his mouth and splatters across the floor, and I'm mad about the extra clean up I'm going to have to do. I fucking hate the smell of bleach. "Fuck you."

"That's pretty rich coming from the guy who stalked, drugged, and harassed someone important to me. And we can't forget about all the shit you've done in the past."

Connor regained consciousness about thirty minutes ago, howling in pain when I cuffed his wrists and ankles. He's been dangling in the air, and I wonder how I want to torture him first.

A knife to the throat?

Too quick. The pain would be brief, and I told Max I would make him suffer.

Slicing out one of his organs?

His kidney was my first thought. If he wouldn't go into shock from the pain and being unmedicated, I'd do it, but I want him fully lucid. Aware of every way I'm going to mutilate and maim him, laughing when he begs me for death.

"Those bitches in my past asked for it. I didn't do anything wrong." Connor glares at me, and it's cute he thinks he's getting out of here alive.

"Tsk, tsk, Connor. We don't talk about women like that." I bring my knife to his stomach, slicing a small sliver of skin where his appendix is. His flesh hits the plastic tarp covering the ground while his screams echo in the sound-proof room around us. "You're such a fucking baby. Why don't you learn to take it like a man? That's what you said to those women you hurt, isn't it? *Just take it.*"

"That's not who I am today." Connor yanks on the chains, wailing when I dig my knife further into his flesh. I'm toying with him now, but it's so *fun* when he starts to cry. "I'm different. I've changed."

"If following Max, shoving her into a dark room, and keeping her there for hours is you *changed*, I don't want to know how sick and twisted you were before." I turn the blade, smirking when blood trickles out from his stomach. "Do you think anyone is going to miss you, Con? If there was a funeral, who would come?"

"I only wanted to scare her. To get her to pay attention to me."

"Now you have *my* attention, and that doesn't bode well for you, my friend." I sigh and spin the knife. "I stopped having sympathy for you the second you put your hands on her. No. The second you breathed the same air as her. Like you think you're worthy." I stop in my tracks, an idea coming to me. "Ah. An eye for an eye. That's what we'll do."

"I'm sorry. I'm sorry! I'll apologize! I'll make it up to you."

"To *me*? You don't need to say shit to me. It's *her* you need to get on your knees for, but I'm never going to give you that chance."

"Just put me out of my misery." Connor hangs his head, and I wonder what he would look like with this knife between his eyes. Maybe I'll use a hammer instead. "Please."

"I don't think so, pal." I pat his cheek and walk toward the door. "I need to take some tea up to my girl. I'll be back in a few, then we'll have some real fun."

Connor tries to say something else, but I flick off the light, plunging the room into darkness. I climb the stairs out of the basement two at a time and stretch my arms. I lock the door behind me, finding Leo in the kitchen.

"She wanted tea," he says, and I smile.

"I was just coming up to make some for her."

"Here." He sets down a mug and gestures to it. "I don't want to overstep."

"You're not. My hands are messy. I'd be grateful if you could finish it for me."

Leo hums and checks the kettle, leaning against the counter. "Are you going to tell me what's going on?"

"That's her ex. He hurt her." I turn on the sink and wash the flecks of blood off my hands. "He lured her to his home. Roofied her. Tied her to the bed and tried to—" Bile creeps up my throat, and I grip the porcelain to steady myself. "Tried to touch her."

"You're fucking joking."

"No." I blow out a breath and look out the window at the woods behind the house. I'll bury him out there, in a spot no one will ever find. "He slapped her too."

"That piece of fucking shit. I'm going to go down there—"

"No. Your heart is too good, Leo. Don't tarnish it. I'm handling it, okay? Can you just… keep an eye on my girl, will you? I want to be up there with her, but I need—"

"I've got her. I promise." Leo clasps my shoulder. "And with no ulterior motive than caring about her because you care about her."

"What did I do to deserve a friend like you?" I smile. "Make sure you put in a little bit of milk and a touch of sugar. She likes her tea sweet."

"You'll tell me if you need me?"

"Yeah. Thanks. I'll be up when I can. And I'll make sure there's no trace of him when I'm finished. I brought him here, and the last thing I want is for you to get involved in case anyone starts asking questions."

"Like that will happen." He snorts. "Take your time. I'll text you if she needs you."

"Appreciate you." I jog downstairs and turn on the light, laughing when Connor winces and shuts his eyes. "Nap time is over, motherfucker."

"Thought you'd be gone longer, but then I remembered Max is a quick fuck."

I know he's baiting me, and it takes all my willpower to walk past him and not drill a nail into his skull.

"Funny. With a dick that small, I'm surprised you could fuck at all," I toss back, and he scowls.

"I've had no complaints."

"You sure? Because she screams my name when I'm with her. I doubt she even whispered yours." I open my toolbox and weigh a wrench in my hand. "Did someone hit you growing up?"

"What?" Connor frowns at the change in question.

"I'm curious why you started abusing women. Were you a violent kid?"

There's a long pause and I look over my shoulder to make sure he's still awake.

"My father. He…" Connor shakes his head. "He did fucked up shit to me. It made me think that—" Another pause. "That that was how I was supposed to act too. I've tried to break the cycle but I… I can't. I like it too much."

I want to feel sympathy for him. I want to share that my dad did the same thing, that we're similar in more ways than he knows, but that's where our paths no longer overlap. I *did* break the cycle. I will never have the urges he does, and I can't feel an ounce of remorse toward a man who knowingly harms women because he fucking can.

"The first person I killed was my father." I trade out the wrench for a cleaver and walk toward him. "He abused my mother. Me too, occasionally, but not as much as her. I bashed his skull in. Staged it to look like a suicide, and no one dug into his death because no one cared about him. I've killed eighty-seven people since then, but you? I'm going to enjoy killing you the most."

"We've been here for almost an hour and you haven't done shit. I'm starting to think you're all talk." Connor laughs. "You really just a fucking pretty boy, aren't you?"

"Maybe we should change that." I drop the knife I'm holding and adjust the shackle around his right wrist. I move the chains up his arm, to his elbow, and flash the cleaver. "Want to count to three for me?"

"What are you doing?" His eyes widen with horror when I touch the weapon to his skin. "You can't—I'm not—"

"One."

"Please. *Please.* What about my foot? Or my ear?"

"Two."

"I'll do anything you want. *Anything.* Just let me——"

I don't get to three. I bring the cleaver up then back down, slicing through his flesh and bone. His screams fill the room as his severed hand falls on the tarp with a thump. Blood pours out of him in spurts, and I pick up his discarded limb by the finger, holding it in front of him. Making a tourniquet is useless. I don't want to save the fucker. Letting him see what I've taken from him is more fun.

"There are consequences when you touch things that don't belong to you, Connor. Not only did you touch Max, but you *hit* her too. I have to take the other one."

Connor blinks, his cheeks turning pale. "The other one?"

This time, I don't count down. I bring the cleaver to his left wrist, this cut cleaner than the first. Connor's body tilts forward, his head lolling as the chains tighten with his movement. He gags, projectile vomit spewing halfway across the basement floor, and I sigh.

More fucking cleanup.

We've reached the point of no return, his shock setting in as his organs start to shut down. I let go of both limbs and kick them out of the way, proud of myself. This is the most dismembering I've ever done. The most restraint I've ever shown too, because I could've ended this in six seconds like I do with most of the people on my hit list.

"How are you doing, Connor?" I ask, grabbing my knife again. I touch the blade to his nose, then his cheek, testing his reflexes. There's nothing there but clammy skin. Shallow breathing and disorientation. "Wow. I thought you would've held on longer than that. Guess you can't take it, huh?" He mumbles something incoherent, a trickle of blood running down the corner of his mouth. I move the knife under his neck, lifting his chin. "Sorry. I didn't hear you. Say that one more time?"

"I'm sorry," he whispers. "I'm sorry. If I could take it all back—" He coughs, gasping for air. "She didn't deserve it."

"No, she didn't. But you know what the good news is? She'll never have to see you again. You'll be burning in hell."

I stab his stomach, twisting my knife. Hitting his aortic artery is easy after years of target practice, and his body goes limp. I wait, watching his chest, and when it rises for the last time with his final breath, I stare up at the ceiling.

Finally.

The knife and cleaver hit the ground, and I almost sprint upstairs. I stop to wash my hands, scrubbing under my fingernails and up my arms until I feel clean. When I do, I make my way down the hall, reaching my bedroom. The second I see Max on my bed, fast asleep with Leo reading a book next to her, it's like I can breathe for the first time in days.

He locks eyes with me and scoots off the mattress. He collects her mug and moves my way, knocking my shoulder with his.

"She fell asleep ten minutes ago," he whispers.

"How is she doing?"

"Better, I think. Still skittish, so I left the light on."

"Thank you. I'll take it from here."

"Anything I can do?"

"Yeah. Don't go in the basement." I take off my shoes, heading for the bed. "That's tomorrow's project, and I don't need you and your squeamish stomach making more of a mess."

"The fucker's dead?"

"The fucker is dead."

"Good." Leo nods and slides out of my room. "You know where I'll be."

He closes the door behind him, and I'm careful when I sit on the edge of the mattress. Max jolts awake, her eyes scanning the room before they settle on me.

"Hunter." She blows out a breath and draws the sheets to her chin. "It's you."

"Sorry it took me so long to get here, angel."

"Is everything okay?"

"Everything is great. Did Leo keep you company while I was gone?"

"Yeah." She smiles. "You know I like him very much, but you're my favorite."

"Good news: you're my favorite too, and I'm not planning on going anywhere anytime soon. Did Skyler ever text you back?" I ask.

"She's going to stop by in the morning, if that's okay."

"Of course it's okay." I'm gentle when I peel back the covers and take my side of the mattress. "Do you want to sleep alone tonight? I can take the spare—"

"No." Max is quick to wrap her arms around my waist, her cheek resting on my chest. "I need you here. Please."

"Then this is where I'll be." I kiss the top of her head and turn off the light, relaxing when she snuggles into my hold. "I've got you, angel."

Tonight. Tomorrow. For as long as you'll have me, I think, forcing myself to stay awake all night, just in case she needs me.

THIRTY-FIVE

MAX

I WAKE up to sunlight and warmth. I open an eye and find Hunter's arm draped across my body, his tattooed hand resting on my stomach. I smile and spin in his hold, not surprised to find him awake.

His hair is messy. There's a drop of dried blood on his neck, right below his ear, and he's looking down at me, a dozen questions on the tip of his tongue.

"Good morning." I yawn and stretch my arms, glancing out the window. "What time is it?"

"Seven."

"Thank god I'm off from school today. If not, I would've been late."

"I would've called in sick for you so you didn't get in trouble. How did you sleep?" he asks, his fingers working out a knot in my hair. "Any nightmares?"

"No. I felt safe with you next to me. And, you know, the stash of knives you have hiding in here."

"I'm glad." Hunter gives me a lazy grin. "You're right about the stash. I have plenty of knives."

"I don't ever want to see them. You can keep that secret to yourself."

"I'll never tell where they're hiding. Skyler will be here soon. What are we thinking for breakfast? Pancakes or waffles?"

"Pancakes, obviously." I pause, a wave of emotion hitting me as I think about where I was twelve hours ago. How different the outcome could've been if Hunter hadn't been at the right place at the right time. "Can we talk about what happened?"

"What do you want to talk about?" He sits up, the sheets pooling around his waist. "If you think you owe me details about last night, you don't. The last thing I want to do is make you relive all of that, and I—"

"I know I don't, and the last thing I want to do is remember…" I shudder, doing my best to wipe the thought of Connor's hands on me from my memory. "I want to talk about you. About us."

"Is this about the tracking device I put on your car?"

"No." My lips twitch. "Not yet. We're going to argue about that in a minute."

"I'm looking forward to it, angel."

"You… you killed someone for me," I whisper, and Hunter nods.

"And I'd do it again."

"Did he say anything?"

"Nothing worth repeating." Hunter hesitates. "He told me his dad abused him, and that's why he acted violently toward women. It made me wonder if that's how my brain is supposed to be programmed too. If because my father was a piece of fucking trash, I'm destined to be the same. Am I going to wake up one day and have the urge to hit someone?"

"No. *No*, Hunter. You two are nothing alike." I crawl into his lap, relieved when his arms fold around me. "When I woke up yesterday and saw Connor, I felt… It was paralyzing fear, Hunter. I believed I was going to die. I believed he was going to hurt me. The moment I saw you… I've never experienced relief like that. The weight of the world lifted off my shoulders, and you were my savior. Never, not for one second, have I ever felt like you would harm me. Your soul is so *good*."

"I'd hurt myself before I ever hurt you." He rests his chin on my shoulder and touches my cheek. "But I need you to do me a favor, Max."

"What is it?"

"If you see me exhibiting any signs that scare you, I need you to tell me. Okay? I don't want to turn out like that. Not with anyone, but especially not with you. I know a lot of what we're feeling for each other is from physical attraction, but I'm almost done with Fright Nights. When I have hours to sit around and have long dinner conversations with a glass of wine, I want to learn everything about you. I want to know your favorite color and your biggest dreams. You don't need me as your savior, Max, but I want to be by your side, holding your hand, for as long as you'll let me."

His words hold weight, and after what I went through, their magnitude is not lost on me.

This is a man I want to keep around. Someone who will be there to help, but will also let me try to handle things on my own. Our lives and personalities are different. Down the road, I know we're going to argue about something stupid, but that *excites* me. I'm giddy thinking about what I could get him for Christmas. I'm excited he's going to be around to celebrate my birthday and daydreaming of the adventures we're going to go on together.

I never knew what my dream partner looked like, but

with Hunter in front of me, I know it's him. My heart could explode with happiness for about what's to come. I throw my arms around his neck, hugging him tight. I kiss him, and he kisses me back, but it's not the sensual kind I'm used to with him. It's a promise. Tender. A glimpse into what our lives could look like down the road, and it's everything I want it to be and more.

I don't care if it's too fast or if I don't know enough about him yet.

People always say *when you know, you know*, and with him, I'm certain.

"Yes," I whisper against his mouth. "That's what I want too."

The doorbell rings, and my phone buzzes. Hunter runs his hand up my spine, squeezing my shoulder. "Skyler is here," he says. "Why don't you two hang out in the living room, and I'll get breakfast going?"

"Okay." I kiss him one more time because I can, laughing when his fingers press into my ribs. "What did you do with Connor?"

"Nothing yet. That's this afternoon's project." Hunter helps me climb off of him and grabs a sweatshirt to pull on. "It's not your problem to worry about, and I'll let you know when I'm finished."

"Okay." I smile and stand, heading for the door. "Hey, Hunter?"

"Yeah, angel?"

"I like my pancakes with a lot of syrup. Since you want to know everything about me."

His grin is slow, magnificent. "Coming right up, baby."

"OH, MY GOD, MAX." Skyler wipes a tear away from her cheek and looks me up and down. "I'm so sorry that happened to you. I'm so sorry I wasn't there right away to help and—"

"There's nothing you could've done." I take her hand in mine. "And you're here now. That's what matters."

"I can't believe he *roofied* you. What was his plan? To keep you locked away for the rest of your life?"

"He wanted to kill Hunter, and, in turn, kill me. I don't know if he would've gone through with it, and I'll never find out. Hunter..." I swallow. "Connor is no longer going to be an issue."

"He was using a fake name because of his arrest records? The fucking asshole. I swear to god men are pieces of shit. Someone needs to design an app for women that creates a database of men and their personal history. Have they been in jail? Are they divorced? Are they still married even though they claim they are separated? Men hurt us just because we *exist*, and it's not fucking fair."

"I wish I had a way to tell the women from his past he got what he deserved." I bring my knees to my chest and sigh. "They can go to sleep tonight knowing their demons are gone."

"And yours too." Skyler sniffs and fights back tears. "You're so strong, Max."

"I didn't feel strong in that moment. I felt so weak, even when I tried to fight back. I knew what he was capable of. I knew what was coming, and I just... I accepted it, you know? Through disassociation. But Hunter found me and I... Now I'm here."

"Ladies. I hate to interrupt, but the food is almost ready," Leo says, gesturing to the kitchen. "If you'd like to join us. Or, if you'd prefer a man-free space, I can deliver your plates here."

Skyler assesses Leo. "You look familiar."

"Leo Reynolds, at your service," he answers. "I work at Fright Nights too."

"Do we like him?" she whispers, leaning in, and I giggle.

"Yes. We do. He's safe to be around. We'll come join you for breakfast," I say, tugging Sky to her feet. "This is Skyler, by the way."

"Oh, I know. I've seen her backstage."

"I feel very left out not being part of Fright Nights," I say.

"Maybe you'll come work with us next year so you can have fun." Leo grins. "There's OJ on the table and the world's biggest bottle of syrup for Max, an apparent sugar lover." He points to the place mats and glasses. "Coffee too, if anyone needs it."

"Yes please." Skyler takes a mug, and I settle in a chair. "Do you need help, Hunter?"

"Nope. We're almost ready. You two relax." There's an apron tied around his waist, and he flips a pancake with an easy flick of his wrist. His phone lights up on the counter and when his eyes bounce over to it, he groans. "*Shit.*"

"What?" My spine straightens. "Is it the police?"

"No. It's Janey."

"Who is Janey?" I ask.

"Our best friend and haunted house supervisor. She pretends like we aren't friends during Fright Nights season, but we all know me and Hunter are her favorites," Leo says with a grin. "I can't wait for you to meet her. She's so badass, and she's constantly putting Hunter in his place."

"Is she?" I laugh. "I have a feeling I'm going to love her."

"You gonna answer it, Hunt?"

"If I don't, she's going to keep calling." He groans and

taps the screen, putting the call on speakerphone. "Hey, J. What's up?"

"What's up? What's *up*? What's up is both you *and* Leo cut out of work early last night, and now I hear you're not going to be there tonight? It's October twenty-ninth, Hunter. One of the biggest nights of the year. We're down two actors. I just found out I have a whole fucking hockey team from DC booked for VIP tours that are going to slow our line down multiple times this evening. I need you there."

"I'm sorry. I really am, but I need another night at home." Hunter runs his hand through his hair. "You know I care about Fright Nights, but I care about this situation more. I wouldn't ask if it wasn't important to me. Please, J. This is…" He flips another pancake, and I watch his shoulders curl in. "This is up there with Mom."

The silence on the other end of the line is broken by a heavy sigh, and Janey must know about his past.

"It's that serious?" she asks.

"Yes," Hunter says without a second thought. "It's that serious."

"Okay. I can give you the night off only if you swear on our friendship you'll be there tomorrow."

"I will. I'll be early. I'll stay late. I will scare the shit out of people like I've never scared before. I'll give the best Fright Nights performance Adventure Oasis has ever seen."

"Fine, but I need Leo tonight. I can't cover for both of you."

"He'll be there. Thank you, Janey. Really. You're the best."

"I know I am."

They exchange a round of goodbyes, and Hunter's shoulders sag with relief. He doles out the food onto plates, adding slices of bacon to accompany the pancakes. He takes the seat next to me and touches my knee under the table with a smile.

"You don't need to skip work for me," I say.

"I want to. When I tell Janey what happened, she'll understand."

"Does she know about your… *side hustle*?"

"You're making it sound like I belong to a pyramid scheme, angel." Hunter douses his pancakes in syrup and laughs. "But, no. She doesn't know about my side hustle. She does know I'm protective of the people I care about, so it won't come as a surprise I needed to spend a few extra hours with you."

"Wait. Do I need to pay you for killing Connor?" I ask, keeping my voice low. "You normally get compensated for that kind of thing, right?"

"Yeah, but your money is no good here." He smiles at me. "How about dinner on November first?"

"I think my calendar is free." My smile matches his, and butterflies swarm in my stomach. "It's a date."

I BURY Connor and his hands in the back corner of my property, as far away from the house as I can get. I don't want Max to be able to find any trace of him, so I bury the tarp, the cleaver, and knife too. There's relief when I toss the last shovel full of dirt over his body. I don't care about my calloused palms or the sunburn on the back of my neck.

He's gone, and I'm on top of the fucking world.

I whistle on my way to the back porch, knowing I need to get ready to head to work soon. Spending the last twenty-four hours with Max has been exactly what I needed. We stayed in our pajamas after Skyler and Leo left for Fright Nights, curled up on the couch watching shitty television shows.

She woke up in the middle of the night after a nightmare scared the shit out of her. I turned on the light and held her until she fell back asleep, her head on my chest and my heart in her hands.

I'll do that every night if she needs me to.

I toss the shovel under the steps and dust off my hands, glad that's done. There's a glass of cold water waiting for me in the kitchen and a smiley face doodled on a ripped paper towel. I grin and walk down the hall, finding Max on my bed, a book in her lap.

"Did you steal my romance books?" she asks, not looking up from the page she's reading.

"You're just now realizing that? Sweetheart. I took them weeks ago."

"Of course you did." Max uses her fingers to hold her spot and sticks out her tongue. "Do you plan on returning them?"

"Nope. Why bother transporting them back to your house when you can read them here?" I take off my shirt and head for the bathroom. "It also gives you a reason to stick around."

"Kidnapping my books is a heinous crime, Hunter." She appears in the doorway, smiling at me in the mirror. "How are you going to apologize?"

"By building you a library and filling it with all the books you have at your place. And more. You'll have multiple copies of your favorite stories, so technically it's not kidnapping anymore."

"You're going to build me a library?"

"Yup. How do you feel about a ladder?"

"I would love a ladder."

"Good. I'm also going to clean out a drawer in my dresser so you can keep some clothes here. There will be space in my closet for you too, and a desk where you can grade worksheets and vocabulary lists. Anything you could ever want, I'll give you."

Max blinks, and I see the tears in her eyes. "That's very domesticated of you."

"I can be a house husband, baby. I'm a man who wears many hats."

"Is there anything I can do to help with Connor?"

"All taken care of." I unzip my pants but leave my briefs on, facing her. "Want to wait for me in the living room? I'm going to finish getting ready, and I'll be out in a few."

"I'm taking my book you stole and a blanket." She pauses. Her smile is soft. "You're a good man, Hunter Wilder."

"You make me a good man, angel."

She blows me a kiss and disappears, and I know I'd trudge through hell and back just to see her smile like that again.

"SECOND TO LAST Fright Nights shift. How are you feeling?" Leo tosses me a rubber knife and grabs his mask. "Wishing you were home with Max?"

"Yup." I zip up my jumpsuit and shove the knife in my pocket. "It's only eight hours, then I can see her."

"That's not long at all. Hey. I've been meaning to ask you about Connor."

"What about him?"

"All of your killings are usually planned, but you went rogue with him. What did you do with his cell phone?"

"I tossed it in a dumpster that's been taken to an incinerator. Lucky for me, he doesn't have any cameras outside his home. Neither do his neighbors, so there's no footage of him being loaded into my car. Guess he changed names and towns again."

"Smart." Leo grins. "I'm proud of you, man. I know

that's the most attached you've been to a… client before, but you got the job done."

"Yeah, after he made a goddamn mess. My back is still sore from cleaning the basement floor. Maybe downstairs will flood with the next hurricane, and all the evidence will disappear."

"Those meteorologists I listen to said hurricane season goes until the end of November. That's a whole month for the weather gods to work in our favor."

"Wouldn't that be nice?" I stifle a yawn and silence my phone. "Ready to go? I want to be out there before Janey comes by. I'm trying to stay on her good side."

"So *that's* why you brought her a coffee the size of her head when we clocked in today. Because you're sucking up."

"Obviously." I hold the breakroom door open, gesturing for him to go down the stairs first. "When have I ever not sucked up?"

"Never. What position do you want to start with?"

"I'll take the middle of the house. It's my favorite spot, and come next year, I'm sure I'll miss it. Gotta soak up all the time I can."

"Look who's feeling nostalgic just in time to retire." Leo knocks his shoulder against mine and waves to the crowd standing in line. "Ready?"

"Yup. I'll see you on break. Hey! Want to play haunted house bingo to keep tonight interesting?" I call out when we split off to head in different directions. "Last one to get five in a row is on dish duty."

"Deal." Leo gives me a salute and veers left. "I'm going to kick your ass, Wilder."

I chuckle and find my spot in the house, shucking off my robe. The technicians said the air conditioning has been acting up today, and I groan at the oppressive heat that greets me. I'm already sweating, and with an hour to go before our first rotation, I'm going to be miserable by the time break rolls around.

The house lights shut off, signaling the five-minute warning before the guests start coming through the line. I test everything at my station, making sure the sound cues are synced up, then take a swig from my water bottle.

"Two minutes," Janey calls out, making her final walk through. "Good to see you, Hunt."

"You too, J. Thanks again for being so understanding."

"I do have a heart, you know. No fighting tonight. I'd like to close out the season without any more paperwork, so if you could keep your hands to yourself, that would be great."

"Tell that to the people shotgunning two beers in line," I yell after her, laughing when she flips me off.

The first forty-five minutes of a scare shift always pass in a blur. The adrenaline is high. The guests aren't belligerent. I have all my energy, and when there's a brief lull in the line because someone is too scared to move forward in the previous room, I chug the rest of my water so I don't pass out.

"Excuse me," I hear from behind me.

"This is a backstage area. Guests aren't supposed to be —" I whip around, freezing when I spot Max standing there in a leather skirt and orange top. It's the same outfit she wore the night we met, and I gape at her. "What are you doing here, baby?"

"I'm lost." She glances around, her hands on her hips. I grin behind my mask, taking two steps toward her. "Could you help me find my way?"

"That depends. What are you looking for?"

"I'm not sure yet. But I like this." Max motions at my outfit with a coy smile. "Especially the mask and knife."

"This is a nice surprise." I sweep her off her feet, holding her in my arms. She giggles and pushes my mask to my hair, touching my face. "The best part of my night."

"Really? Because it's the worst part of mine," she teases, and I pinch her ass. "I wanted to say hi. So. Hi."

"Hi, angel. Everything okay at home?"

"Yeah. I missed you. Oh! I also brought you a little gift."

"Is it a pair of your underwear I can keep in my pocket the rest of the night?"

"You have *no* manners." Max swats at my chest and I set her down. She reaches into her purse, pulling out a small box. "This is for you."

"Are we celebrating something?" I ask, ripping off the tape. "If so, I need to get you a gift."

"No. We had a Halloween festival at school recently, and when I saw this, I thought of you."

I lift an eyebrow, intrigued, and open the box. Inside is a small Michael Myers figurine, complete with a mask and knife that matches mine. I laugh and rub my thumb over the paint, bringing it next to my face. "What do you think? Do you see the resemblance?"

"Without a doubt." She grins. "Okay. I should go. Skyler's show starts soon, and she's the real reason I dragged myself through all this scary shit again."

"Hey." I take her hand and kiss the inside of her wrist. "Thank you for coming by."

"See you later, Michael. And happy almost Halloween." With a wink, Max saunters back to the line, but she turns to look at me over her shoulder. "Oh. By the way. Is that a knife in your pocket, or are you just happy to see me?"

I burst out laughing and hold up my hands, making a

heart in her direction. "You, Max Walters, are the best thing to ever happen to me."

"Right back at you, biker boy."

She disappears back into the crowd, leaving me alone. She might be gone, but I can still feel her everywhere. In my hands, in my heart.

"I love you," I say, and I swear I hear her say it back.

EPILOGUE

**One year later
Max**

"HAPPY HALLOWEEN!" I bound into the kitchen, frowning when I see Hunter standing by the sink, not dressed in the costume he said he was going to wear. "Why aren't you ready? We're supposed to go trick or treating. Bailey is going to be very disappointed if you don't come dressed as her favorite Barbie."

"Change of plans. We're making a slight detour, then I promise I'll put my costume on. I'm going to rock the shit out of workout Barbie, and Janey's daughter won't know the difference about our tardiness." He grins and bends to kiss me. "It won't take long."

"Okay, but when Janey kicks your ass for missing the bobbing for apples game, I'm going to say I told you so."

"And you'll get pleasure out of doing it, I know. Your ability to give me shit is one of the many reasons why I love you, angel."

I laugh and stand on my toes, draping my arms around

his neck. His skin is warm from spending the last hour outside. I watched him out of the living room window while he put the finishing touches on the Halloween displays. He also set up a cooler of candy at the end of our long driveway for the neighborhood kids so the chocolate doesn't melt in the Florida heat.

"I love you too," I say, squealing when he scoops me off the ground and tosses me over his shoulder. "Where are you taking me?"

"Somewhere with all my love and affection." Hunter pulls something from his pocket and hands it my way. "Can you put this on for me, baby?"

"A blindfold? Didn't we use this last night?"

"Yes, but this is for a very different reason."

"So, you're not bending me over the kitchen table and fucking me with the curtains open? Darn."

"Nope. If you would be so kind to slip that on, that would be great."

"Does this have anything to do with the detour we're making?" I slide the blindfold over my eyes, relaxing at the silky smooth fabric.

"It does. You trust me, right?"

I can't help but smile at the question he knows the answer to.

One year with him, and I trust him with everything I have. Every day is the best day of my life, and I keep wondering how things get better than *this*. I already have so much. I don't see a world out there where I ask for more.

Leo moved out of Hunter's place six months ago, and I moved in. Our groups of friends have all become friends, a family that does barbeques and dinners and holidays together. There are movie nights and swimming in the pool. Babysitting Bailey and taking her shopping with Skyler.

I'm still teaching. Hunter, after claiming he was done with scaring people at theme parks forever, took a job as Assistant Director of Fright Nights. He's busier now than when he was working in the haunted house, having a hand in the set design process every step of the way. He uses his expertise to offer input on what guests want the most when they step through the gates of the park, ready to be terrified.

"Of course I trust you," I say, and he places me in the car. His arm reaches across my body, buckling my seatbelt. "I just don't do well with surprises."

It might stem from my encounter with Connor. The memory has been hard to shake. I still have the occasional nightmare that wakes me up, afraid I'm back in his room with his body over mine. Therapy helps, and so does having Hunter around. He's quick to reassure me I'm okay. He never argues when I keep him awake for an hour or two, finally relaxing to sleep with his face buried in my hair.

"I know you don't, which is why this will be quick. I promise."

"As long as I get to see you in your workout Barbie outfit after, I'll be happy."

"My calves look great in legwarmers, angel. Prepare to have your world rocked."

I laugh, the car jolting forward as we take off in the direction of wherever we're heading. "Leo told me he might be bringing someone special to Thanksgiving this year. Has he mentioned anything to you?"

"No, the bastard. Is it that girl in Skyler's show? He thinks she's cute."

"Nope. It's the girl who worked in the haunted house next to yours last year. I guess they've been talking on social media, and when she mentioned she's not visiting her parents for Thanksgiving because they'll be out of the country, Leo invited her to our place."

"How the hell do you know all of this? I'm his best friend," Hunter says. "I don't like being left out."

"Because you don't do face masks and watch rom-coms with us. You're too busy being a manly old man with your cleaver and ax and whatever hell other weapons you use to mutilate people."

"It makes me happy to know you listen when I talk, angel." Hunter rests a hand on my knee, giving my leg a squeeze. "Permission to join the next skin care and movie night?"

"Permission considered. I'll consult with the rest of the participating parties and get back to you," I say, squealing when his hand moves to my ribs and tickles me. "Hey! Both hands on the wheel! You have precious cargo here."

"You're right." I hear the smile in his voice, the deep adoration he has for me like I have for him. "I do."

Twenty minutes later, he's helping me out of the car, the blindfold still in place. I listen to the noises around me, trying to piece together where I am, but there are too many competing sounds. I hear music and conversations and someone yelling about cinnamon sugar pretzels, and I'm even more confused.

"Just another minute, baby," Hunter murmurs in my ear, a palm on my hip. "And I want you to remember you trust me."

"Oh, god. Now I'm scared about what this could be. If this involves bodily harm or blood, I'm going to be so mad at you."

"Well, it doesn't involve *real* blood."

"*Hunter.*"

"*Max.*" His hand is at the back of my head, easing the

blindfold off. I squint at the change in lighting and turn my chin, spotting a sign up ahead. "Tada."

"You brought me to Fright Nights? Are you out of your mind?" I stare at the entrance to Adventure Oasis with dread. Fog billows through the iron gate. The trees lining the path into the park are decorated with pumpkins and spiderwebs, and I burst out laughing. "Absolutely not. I'm not going in there."

"Baby." Hunter leads me to a smaller gate away from the large crowd. He nods hello to a security guard and takes my hand. "We missed our one-year anniversary. What better way to celebrate it than by going back to the place where we first met?"

"That requires being terrorized, and I'm not mentally prepared for this. I was expecting marshmallows decorated as ghosts and spiders made out of chocolate and pretzels, not complete and utter fear."

"There are still going to be marshmallows and spiders. Just not yet."

"How long do we have to stay?" I ask.

"Ten minutes. We'll be in and then out, I swear."

"A lot of good your promises have done so far today," I grumble. I tug on his necklace, bringing his mouth to mine. "Fine. But only if you go first, tell me exactly where every scare actor is going to be, and don't make fun of how much I scream."

"I hear you scream plenty. Listening to you yell my name is one of my favorite hobbies."

"It better be, given one of your other hobbies is murder."

Hunter grins. "I love when you're feisty, baby. I'll point out everyone to you. I'll even show you the buttons you can press in the house that trigger certain special effects."

"Okay, now *that* sounds cooler than being chased by a

werewolf." I loop my arm through his and rest my head on his shoulder. "Fine. I'll let you terrorize me."

"See how much fun all of this is? Maybe next year I can get you to do all ten houses."

"We have very different definitions of fun."

Hunter walks us to a special entrance no one else is using. He flashes a golden badge and is welcomed inside with a wave from someone who looks very official.

"Feels like they should be rolling out a red carpet for you," I say.

"I don't know why. I'm not special."

"You're so special. So much so, you get free admission into Adventure Oasis whenever you want. I can't wait to see the Christmas lights go up."

I smile as we head through the park. Hunter points out the different scare zones and the stories behind them, and I notice there aren't any other guests around us. Every sidewalk is empty, and I frown.

"Where is everyone?"

"They're not letting anyone in for another twenty minutes. We get a head start." We turn down a small path that winds up to the haunted house where we met last year. It's a different theme this season, some apocalyptic television show the new backdrop, but the entrance is familiar. "Back to where it all began."

"I can't believe it's been a year. Thirteen months, really." I smile when Hunter unhooks the chain blocking the queue and lets me walk in front of him. "It's been fun, hasn't it?"

"Best year of my life," he says. "Come on. I'll give you the behind-the-scenes tour."

The lights are on when we step into the soundstage, and being able to see everything helps me relax. I find all the places the scare actors would hide if they were in their spots for the night. Hunter mentions the least desirable zone in the house to work, a small corridor that requires constant crouching and bumping your head while you wait to jump out and scare someone.

"How do you know when it's your turn?" I ask. "Is there a motion sensor that triggers the lights and sounds?"

"Nope. We do it with pedals." He points at a small pedal behind a corner, out of the guest's view. "It's called an AAD: actor activated device. We'll press that, then the sound associated with the spot begins to play."

"Really? Wow. Is it delayed? How long does it take before you have the timing memorized?"

"Only a few days, to be honest. You're doing it so many times an hour, eventually, you're on autopilot and don't think about it."

"Fascinating. Hey." I point at a fork in the path and smirk. "The infamous spot where I messed up. And, now that I'm seeing it with the lights on, I'm confused. Which means in the dark, it's even more difficult."

"They adjusted it this year. See the pillar they put up? It stops anyone from making a wrong turn."

"Darn. Guess there won't be any other haunted house meet cutes. That's a shame. It was so—am I allowed back here?" I ask when Hunter pulls me around the pillar he just mentioned.

"Given I'm kind of in charge of all of this, yeah. I'm saying you're allowed." He smiles and puts his hands over my eyes. "I have a surprise for you."

"You're going to make Halloween my favorite holiday with all these surprises." We come to a stop, and I take a deep breath. "Can I look now?"

"Close your eyes, then count to twenty," he says, his hands falling away from my face.

"Okay." I shift on my feet, following his directions.

When I get to twenty, I slowly open my eyes and find Hunter…

Kneeling on the ground with a velvet box in his hands.

There are candles around him. Dozens of flowers and white sheets hanging from the dark walls. I gasp and cover my mouth, my eyes welling with tears.

"Max," he says.

"What are you doing?" I whisper, looking down at him.

"When I clocked into work last year, I expected the usual night of drunk idiots and people getting in my face, trying to be funny. What I didn't account for was the beautiful girl who found her way backstage and grabbed my attention. I thought about you every minute after you left, and when you showed up again, I thought I was dreaming."

"I thought about you too." I step toward him, close enough to touch his cheek. "I was willing to push past my fears if it meant seeing you again."

"The second time I saw you, I was obsessed. I craved your body and hearing your voice. I craved your laugh and beautiful smile. I craved your mouth and your pussy, and I would do just about anything to see you again. And I did. You became a part of my life. My most favorite person in the world, which is why I'm finally asking you this."

Hunter opens the box, and I gasp at the ring that sits inside. The diamond sparkles and shimmers, exquisite in the candlelight. He reaches to his right, lifting a knife off the ground. Spinning it in his hold, he catches it by the handle and places the ring on the tip of the blade, extending it my way.

"Max Walters, I have loved you from the moment I first laid eyes on you. You're the most caring, wonderful person I've ever met, and it would be an honor to be by your side for the rest of my life. In sickness. In health. On the good days and on the bad ones too. You are the greatest gift I've ever been given, and I promise to continue loving you until the end of time." He smiles up at me, and a sob leaves my body. "Will you marry me?"

"Yes. Yes, *of course* I'll marry you." I reach for him, careful to avoid the knife. I throw my arms around his neck, my tears staining his shirt. "I love you so much, Hunter."

"Let me see your hand, angel." He carefully takes the ring off the blade and slides it on my finger, kissing my knuckles. "Perfect," he whispers.

"It's beautiful. I love it so much. I didn't—this was not on my bingo card for today." I laugh and wipe under my eyes. "You're sneaky."

"Everyone is at Janey's waiting to celebrate; Skyler, Leo. They'll all be there."

"You included everyone? They all know?"

"Of course they do. They're your favorite people in the world. I had to make sure I got their approval."

I hug him again, my shoulders shaking with a fresh wave of tears. "I really do love you so much, Hunter. This is—"

The lights in the haunted house shut off. I gasp and look around, my heart nearly falling out of my chest when Hunter pulls away from me, a Ghostface mask suddenly over his face. I scramble backward over the floor, trying to stand. He tips his head to the side, arms crossing over his chest, and I squeeze my thighs together.

I don't know what's going on, but I like it.

"Angel," he says, his voice low. "What are you doing on the floor?"

"I-I don't know." I stand on shaky legs. "Why are you wearing a mask?"

"I'm reminiscing." He holds up the knife, and I realize

it's real. "Do you feel like playing a game, my darling future wife?"

Hell.

I hold back a moan and bite my lip. I don't trust myself to speak, so I nod instead, my heart pounding in my chest.

"How about hide and seek? You hide, I seek. If you make it out of the house without me catching you, you win. If I find you, well…" Hunter trails off with a laugh. "My first time fucking you with that ring on your finger will be in a spot anyone could see us. Do you want the world to know you're the love of my life? Or my needy slut?"

Both, I almost yell, and I inch toward the path through the house.

"I'll play," I whisper, and I can tell he's smiling without even seeing his face.

"I'll count to five." He touches my cheek, his thumb grazing along my jaw. "Good luck, angel. You're going to need it."

Hunter leans against the wall and holds up his hand. The first finger folds down and I take off, sprinting away from him as fast as my legs will go. I hear his footsteps somewhere behind me, the easy, casual way he walks, and I take off into the dark, knowing no matter how this game turns out, I've already won.

ACKNOWLEDGMENTS

Well, this was fun! I'm not going to lie: it was kind of a breath of fresh air to write something less emotionally deep and more… unhinged would be a good word, I think?

Thank you to Hannah, my lovely editor and friend, for all your tireless work.

Thank you to my beta readers for your feedback. You all are my absolute favorites, and I'm always so grateful for you.

Thank you, Emily, for such a fun cover!!! I gave you an idea and you ran with it, and I am fully obsessed!

Lastly, thank you to all the content creators out there. I feel like I say this every single time, but y'all change lives with the videos and posts you create. Thank you for continually uplifting your favorite authors. I appreciate you immensely!

ABOUT THE AUTHOR

Chelsea is a flight attendant and romance author who writes fun, fresh, and flirty love stories with plenty of spice. When she's not making fictional characters banter for twenty chapters before they finally kiss or serving chicken or pasta on an airplane, you can find her trying to pet as many dogs as she can.

Stay up to date by signing up for her newsletter: https:// authorchelseacurto.myflodesk.com/newsletter

instagram.com/authorchelseacurto

tiktok.com/@chelseareadsandwrites

threads.com/@authorchelseacurto

amazon.com/author/chelseacurto

ALSO BY CHELSEA CURTO

D.C. Stars series

Face Off

Power Play

Slap Shot

Hat Trick

Love Through a Lens series

Camera Chemistry

Caught on Camera

Behind the Camera

Off Camera

Holiday Novellas

Dashing All The Way